Angel—
My pr[...]you
own journey [...]
He Knows the plans He has for you, plans to
prosper you and not to harm you. Plans
for a hope and a future - Jeremiah 29:11
Keep Your eyes fixed on Jesus -
Love -
Catherine Mae Clifford

MW01231384

My JOURNEY HOME

CATHERINE MAE CLIFFORD

outskirtspress
DENVER, COLORADO

Good News Translation® (Today's English Version, Second Edition) Copyright © 1992 American Bible Society. All rights reserved.

Scripture quotations marked (NLT) are taken from the Holy Bible, New Living Translation, copyright © 1996, 2004, 2007 by Tyndale House Foundation. Used by permission of Tyndale House Publishers, Inc., Carol Stream, Illinois 60188. All rights reserved.

All scripture quotations, unless otherwise indicated, are taken from the Holy Bible, New International Version NIV®. Copyright ©1973, 1978, 1984, 2011 by Biblica, Inc.™ Used by permission of Zondervan. All rights reserved worldwide. www.zondervan.com The "NIV" and "New International Version" are trademarks registered in the United States Patent and Trademark Office by Biblica, Inc.™

"Scripture quotations taken from the New American Standard Bible®, Copyright © 1960, 1962, 1963, 1968, 1971, 1972, 1973, 1975, 1977, 1995 by The Lockman Foundation Used by permission." (www.Lockman.org)

This is a work of fiction. The events and characters described herein are imaginary and are not intended to ref to specific places or living persons. The opinions expressed in this manuscript are solely the opinions of the author and do not represent the opinions or thoughts of the publisher. The author has represented and warrant full ownership and/or legal right to publish all the materials in this book.

My Journey Home
All Rights Reserved.
Copyright © 2014 Catherine Mae Clifford
v2.0

Cover Photo © 2014 JupiterImages Corporation. All rights reserved - used with permission.

This book may not be reproduced, transmitted, or stored in whole or in part by any means, including graphic, electronic, or mechanical without the express written consent of the publisher except in the case of brief quotations embodied in critical articles and reviews.

Outskirts Press, Inc.
http://www.outskirtspress.com

ISBN: 978-1-4787-2557-2

Outskirts Press and the "OP" logo are trademarks belonging to Outskirts Press, Inc.

PRINTED IN THE UNITED STATES OF AMERICA

God placed many incredible women along my journey. Their courage, faith, deep and abiding love, along with compassion for others is something to behold. Some continue to live through long sustained trials even after coming from hard and painful pasts. I've had the honor to observe God's hand of blessing on their lives as they exhibit tremendous faith and hope in Jesus. Each one has encouraged and prayed for me in my hardest life trials and testings. Together we have laughed, cried, mourned, rejoiced and stood in prayer through thick and thin. It would truly be a monumental task to mention each one by name. However, I've decided to give honor to one, sister and friend,

PEGI HODGES.

Pegi fights a courageous battle against ALS, Amyotrophic Lateral Sclerosis (Lou Gehrig's Disease). We are eyewitnesses to God's faithfulness and love as He carries her through this devastating malady. It is easy to see Jesus peace covering her while the world looks on in awe. She joyously and courageously displays true faith in the Lord Jesus Christ and His victory at the cross.

One day, Pegi and I rehearsed our future hope of seeing Jesus face-to-face. In that instant, we will receive a new, glorified body, and there will be no more tears, sorrow or suffering. Instead, we shall join with the angels singing and praising our Lord and Savior! As we continue our journey to heaven, we remember to keep focused on the Author and Finisher of our faith, Jesus! It is my prayer, dear reader, that I will shine the hope of Jesus to a lost and dying world around me, the way my dear friend has. No matter what you're going through, God is bigger and mightier! You're on the winning team, therefore, keep your eyes fixed on the Lord and above all, enjoy your journey!

*In honor of my friend, Pegi Hodges
I dedicate this book.
To her great fight against the wiles of the devil and
her victory already waiting in heaven
with the
Lord Jesus Christ!*

Acknowledgements

Words alone could not express my thanks to my husband, William Clifford and so many dear friends and mentors who helped me walk through this very trying time in my life. Your support, encouragement and love have truly been like the hands of the Lord extended.

Editor/friend, Shirley Singer, all I can say is thank you! I loved our times of brain storming, researching and laughter that flourished throughout the editing of this book. Your encouragement was priceless and your joy completely contagious. Each time I wondered if it would ever be finished, your gentle reminders of the original vision, stirred up the juices of creativity once again. Thank you my friend!

Thank you Wanda Lee, my new editor/helper/friend. Your prayers, kindness, gentleness and sweet touch of concern through my trials and while this book was being written are much appreciated. Your additions and sacrifice are truly a blessing. Again, thank you!

Jason Scott Henson, such a talented and gifted son of mine, thank you for designing the cover! You heard every word and far surpassed my expectations! Job well done! Thank you for always being a joy to my heart and delight to my soul. I'm proud of you for listening to the voices of wisdom and making your choices from the Word of God. Keep fighting the good fight of faith! Use your amazing talents to glorify the Lord! Thank you son!

To all the sweet ladies from the BBB and the Ladies Bible Study at Abundant Life Church, thank you! You are true friends and some of the best cheer-leaders and encouragers a gal could have! Your support and love echoed in my ears whenever I became discouraged through this trial and the project of My Journey Home! I love you dearly ladies!

I could not complete this project without thanking Paul and Jennifer Carlin and the Discovery Weekends team. Through your love, commitment, perseverance and example of the Lord's amazing tenacity revealed in your daily lives, I pushed through to the end! It is my delight to share in the joys of completing this book of healing, deliverance and facing issues of the heart. Truly, the Word of God is truth, whom the Son sets free is free indeed! (See John 8:36)

To my Lord, Jesus Christ, I am so grateful that you called and chose me as Your own! Thank you for Your love, mercy, grace, comfort, presence and especially for the price You paid for me. How I pray that all people would know how deep and wide, long and high is Your great love for Your children. Through this trying time and this project, You have proved Your faithfulness, provision and tender mercies every step of the way. Thank you for this thorn Lord, it had accomplished so much more than I could ever have imagined. In Your hands I place my heart, love, and a deep appreciation for everything You've done in and through my life. It's all YOU, JESUS—it's all about YOU! Praise His Name!

My home is a haven
and
my house a delight—

In dedication
to
Shirley Singer
delightful friend and editor
2012

Dearest Reader,

I'm so glad you decided to come with me on My Journey Home. My prayer is, as we walk this path together, you will find that my home and yours are similar. Home is an eternity spent with Jesus, free from any entrapping of this world. However, while we are here on earth, the Lord gently takes us through training in reigning. As we travel together, my prayer is that you will feel His love surround you and that you will find healing the same way Salome (Sal-a-ma) did. Come now, it's time to head home.

Dear friend, if you already know Jesus as Savior and Lord please take this time with me to pray. My heart's desire is that through the words on the pages of this book, God would gently lead you through the valleys and mountains so you can become the beautiful woman of God He has created and designed you to be.

Lord, give me clean hands and a pure heart before You. I give You full permission to dig through all areas of my heart and wash away anything that is not of You. Then, I can live a life filled with Your presence within me. Shine the light of Your truth as I read through the words of this book. Expose any and all lies I have embraced as truth and set me free. I pray this in the holy name of Jesus, my Lord! Amen.

Forget the former things,
do not dwell on the past.
See, I am doing a new thing!
Now it springs up;
do you not perceive it?
I am making a way in the desert
and streams in the wasteland.
Isaiah 43: 18-19

ALTHOUGH IT TOOK every bit of strength and resolve inside her, Salome determined nothing would stop her from taking the first steps homeward. Breathing deeply she mused, *It is the perfect day for a drive in the country*. However, in spite of the tranquil atmosphere, a battle raged inside her heart. She set her jaw, unwavering in her decision. This time she would not give into her own anxiety. Fear stopped Salome from reconciling with her dear friend and mentor far too often. This first part of her journey would be completed today! With tenacity blazing in her heart, she pressed her foot down a little harder on the gas pedal.

Clear, bright blue skies were spread out as far as the eye could see. The countryside atmosphere exuded peace as the expansive scenery stretched across the horizon. A soft breeze gently blew, causing the fields of long grass to sway in an elegant dance of nature. In the distance, a herd of Guernsey milk cows snacked on the lush, thick grass. Occasionally, a cow glanced up from their feast to notice the passing vehicle. A barbed wire fence, held in place by old cedar posts, added the final touch to the beautiful meadow. Gazing beyond the field, Salome could see an old, two-story red barn and beside it stood a plot of beautiful sunflowers. This fantastic scene could have popped out of the pages of a magazine.

Salome became conscious of how long it had been since she'd traveled to this side of the parish. She didn't live far from there, yet it seemed she had purposely left it behind. Slowing down, Salome rolled down her car's window to feel the crisp, clean air. Taking in a deep breath, she slowly exhaled. As she breathed out once again, she became aware of how tense she felt. All her muscles were tied up in knots from the anxiety.

Salome reached over and turned the radio louder. Just then, drums from the song, **Prepare Ye the Way**, by Michael W. Smith, leaped through the speakers. *How fitting*, Salome thought. *What an appropriate song this was for the circumstances. Lord, I know You're in this, thank You for preparing the way before me.*

Memories from days gone by began to flash through her mind. Good memories, so why had she kept running? "How did I ever get this far away from home?" she whispered. Traveling westward on the interstate in her Honda Civic, Salome's imagination played different scenarios of the reception she might receive when she faced Jade, her mentor and friend. *I miss her so much, and I miss belonging to a "family". A family, who loves, cares, encourages and embraces me, especially when I fail. God, please plant me in a family once again, and please change my husband's heart,* she prayed to herself.

Salome had prayed this many times during the last few years. She needed a body of believers, a family who cared for her especially now, with all the medical issues she faced. In past years, her physical maladies and the wounds of her heart were handled by herself and God alone. Beyond a shadow of a doubt, the only way she continued to stand was because God was carrying her. But in recent weeks, God made it plain to her that running was no longer an option. Over the past several months, her desperate need for connection and love began to override the fear controlling her.

Pondering the past, she wondered why she and her husband, Lewis, left their home church in the first place. From the time Salome and her family left their church, nothing made any sense. They attended other churches that were good, yet Salome never felt like she belonged. The atmosphere in those churches left her with a sense that she was only being tolerated and used, instead of becoming a loved member of the congregation.

While away from her home church, God placed Salome in a smaller church family through Prison Fellowship Ministries (PFM). However, this congregation could not take the place of her original church body. The PFM members held her up through some pretty hard times. She remembered one time in particular. She had panicked about a threat her ex-husband made. Calling her pastor, he assured her in a quiet, loving and calm voice, "All he can do is try, but he will not succeed. It will be okay, Salome. Trust God." Afterwards, her pastor prayed for her! Salome was filled with peace by the time she and her Pastor hung up. Sometimes all a person needs is a calm voice and a reassurance someone cares.

Salome stopped her musing and prayed, "Jesus, I need Your help. You died so I could be free. My becoming free is more important to me than giving in to this fear. Lord, it is my desire to be all You created me to be. I want to use every gift and talent to glorify You and help build up the body of Christ. In order to do that, the first person I must build up is me. Therefore, I place my heart in Your hands. Have Your way Lord, in the name of Jesus."

The "whys" of what happened were no longer important, all that mattered was taking these first steps back home. However, as much as she knew this was a God idea, Salome shuddered because of the fear of rejection that still remained in her heart. The question went through her mind once more, *Will they receive me or will I experience rejection yet again?*

"It is time to relax and just simply trust God!" she encouraged herself. "One step at a time," she whispered. "I can do this! *I can*, because I can do all things through Christ who strengthens me." Salome always felt empowered by Philippians 4:13.

Once again she inhaled, enjoying the freshness of the new season as she tried to fill her thirsty soul. Just then, Salome saw the sign: **Exit One Mile**.

"This is it. There is no turning back!" she said out loud. Seeing the exit up ahead, Salome began reducing her speed. Putting on her blinker light she veered right, *Almost there*, she thought. As she drove down the off-ramp, the traffic light turned red. Salome took a few more deep breaths and tried to relax.

What do I have to fear, but fear itself? Isn't that what everyone says? God's Word tells me differently. Second Timothy 1:7 NIV says, 'For God did not give us a spirit of timidity or fear, but a spirit of power, of love, and of self-discipline or sound mind, she thought to herself. The light changed just then and she turned left onto the main highway heading south toward her destination. *This could be a whole new beginning for me and my husband,* she thought.

Salome's and Lewis's children were grown with families of their own. Not all of his or her children were serving the Lord but, it remained a continual prayer in Salome's heart. *One day they will all know the Lord*, Salome thought, *God does keep His promises. He has heard all of my prayers and He will answer them.*

She glanced at the dashboard clock and saw that it was 1:00 o'clock. The afternoon was just beginning. As she turned her gaze upward, she saw beautiful, blue skies spread out in front of her as a memory came flooding in.

Mr. Allen, a man she formerly worked with, sang the same song each time he caught a glimpse of her. Salome tried to avoid him like a plague because anyone who gave her a compliment always made her very nervous. He would touch her shoulder; look deep into her eyes and sing, *"Blue eyes, baby's got blue eyes."* Afterwards, he would simply smile, wink and say, "I've never seen that shade of blue except in the sky! You have beautiful blue eyes, Salome!" She would lower her head. Yet, inside her heart, she would smile. Salome blushed at the memory as though he stood right in front of her. "What a crazy thought! Why would I think about that now?"

When she was younger, people often told her how beautiful she was. Her shoulder length, dark-blonde wavy hair framed her tanned face, which only made her striking blue eyes stand out more. She had a small frame and lovely figure, or so she was told. However, in her own eyes, Salome could never quite measure up.

A gust of air blew unexpectedly, causing leaves to cascade into a beautiful waltz. It was only September, but already the autumn leaves announced the change of season. *Maybe this will be a change of season for me as well*, Salome hoped.

"I'm almost there," she announced to herself. Excitement and apprehension built inside her stomach. Lowering her sunglasses, she obtained a clear view of the prestigious neighborhood up ahead. She could see majestic pine trees, stately oaks, and beautiful sycamore trees growing in the flowerbeds dividing the entrance and exit lanes of The Estates. As she approached the traffic light in front of the neighborhood, it turned red. She was glad she had to stop. Now she could sit and enjoy this lovely vista.

While she waited, Salome admired the lovely array of plants and flowers displayed in the colorful beds, along with a rustic, ivy-draped sign announcing the name, The Estates. She hoped this serene, cheerful scene bode well for her.

Inwardly urging the light to turn green, she was assailed with memories of a happier time. A time when Salome felt a part of the family she was on her way to visit, and hopefully, to make amends for her long absence. Her mind raced back to a time of years ago. How many years had passed since she'd been here, eleven or was it maybe twelve? Time does fly, she thought. She had been away much too long.

Salome placed her sunglasses back on the bridge of her nose and accelerated when the light changed to green. Slowly entering the subdivision, she could see that each beautiful manicured yard held its own unique display of nature. Freshly mowed lawns spreading out before her exhibited the pride held by the residents.

Reaching the first Stop Sign she whispered, "Ok, after the Stop Sign, how many houses is it? Oh, I can't remember!" Suddenly she saw their house, "There it is!"

The residence sat on the left side of the street, about seventy feet back from the road. She slowed down preparing to turn into the long driveway. Salome noticed nothing about the house or yard had changed after all this time.

Oh, the memories held within the walls of that house, Salome thought. Closing her eyes, Salome remembered a scene from a Christmas Eve of years gone by. What a shock she experienced as she walked into their house and saw Jade coming toward her with a gift in her hand. Every member of Jade's family welcomed her with arms of love. They held no expectations of Salome except one, just that she should be herself. How wonderful! Honestly, even now years later, she was still utterly confused about who she really was.

Tom and Jade's home was such a welcoming place, yet Salome wondered, "Will they really accept me after all this time?" Reflecting back, she remembered her own family's rejection. Somehow, she could never measure up in their eyes. No matter what she did, she always seemed to fail as far as they were concerned. Would Jade and Tom be the same way? Salome's stomach fluttered and her heart began to beat faster. Her heart held so many regrets. She yearned for those long-ago days and wished she had done things differently.

Half-way to the house, she suddenly stopped the car. I can't do this, she thought. Her heart was beating a mile-a-minute, her hands felt clammy, and sweat popped out on her forehead. *What if they don't want me? I thought the Lord was directing me here to make things right. Oh! What am I going to do,* she fretted?

All of a sudden the Lord spoke to Salome. *"Do not fear, child, I AM with you. You are allowing the evil one to usurp the plans I have for you. I have brought you here for a reason, and I've prepared the hearts of your friends. Peace, Salome."*

Dear Lord, thank You. I will trust You with this visit. Taking her foot off the brake, she proceeded down the driveway. Her heart was filled with hope.

Coasting to the end of the driveway, she spotted a large shed in the backyard that hadn't been there before. She stopped the car, turned it off, and took out the key. Then she breathed deeply, composing herself in her new-found peace.

Instead of shame, My people
will receive a double portion, and
instead of disgrace,
they will rejoice in their inheritance
and inherit a double portion in their land,
and everlasting joy will be theirs.
Isaiah 61:7 NIV

CHAPTER **2**

SALOME OPENED THE door, but before getting out, she sat still for a second. Even though she trusted the Lord, she still felt a little apprehensive. Taking authority over her thoughts, Salome got out of the car gently shutting the door. Gazing around, she soaked in the peaceful atmosphere.

Salome thoughts turned to her appearance. Dressed in pale blue slacks and an ivory shell with a matching cardigan, she knew she looked her best. However, she grimaced when she glanced at her shoes. Since the injury, she could no longer wear high heels, cute sandals or even small heels. Now she could only wear flats, but that was a small price to pay considering the outcome could have been much worse.

Tucking her purse under her arm and striding towards the veranda, Salome gave an impression of complete confidence, but things are not always as they seem. One glimpse into Salome's eyes, and anyone could see the despair lurking beneath their depths. It wouldn't take long to see that things were not as wonderful as she tried to portray.

The lovely veranda was filled to overflowing with beautiful, lush, potted plants and large hanging baskets of bright yellow and white flowers. Standing in the center of the veranda, sat a concrete fountain with an angel on top. In the angel's hands was a jar of water that trickled down into the basin below. As she approached the carport, she could hear the fountain's splashing water, and felt so much more at ease. Smiling, she thought, *All this needs is a hammock and it would be perfect!* Leisurely, she headed toward the gate.

Suddenly, she heard a racket in the green shed to her right located just off the carport. On the shed was a large, rustic cross hanging in the center above the double doors. The shed was surrounded by holly bushes filled with bright red berries. Just then, Tom emerged from the door under the cross.

Feeling awkward and fearful of his response, Salome smiled timidly and said, "Hey Tom, it's been a long time. How are ya?"

"Sal-o-me!" In his sing-song voice, Tom sang her name as he always had, sporting a smile that destroyed any fear Salome held. "You haven't changed a bit! Jade can't wait to see you. We danced a jig after we got your call! I'll let her know you're here." Strolling up to her, Tom stopped, looked deep into her eyes and gave her a slow tender hug. Then he placed a sweet kiss on her cheek as he softly touched her face and said, "It's great to see you. You have been dearly missed! Wanna come in?"

"No," Salome said, "I'd like to sit here on the veranda and wait if that's okay. Tom, this is so beautiful. You've created an Eden!"

Chuckling he said, "Jade is always cooking up another project for me! Guess she believes it will keep me out of trouble! Like **that** will do the trick!" Snickering, Tom walked inside the house.

Salome realized that her heart had really never left this place! The years since her departure had been dreadfully hard. So many catastrophic events occurred that only confirmed her fear of being completely alone in the world. Salome knew that God never left her or forsook her. Still, her heart was shattered and she needed to know somebody cared.

Pondering the past years, it was clear to see God was the only reason she survived the things she did. The betrayal of family and so-called friends left scars and wounds deep inside her heart, and quite honestly, she had no idea how to begin the healing process. How had she wandered so far away from home? Considering the answer to the question, it suddenly became crystal clear. It had been a slow process, step-by-step and, that would be the same way in which she would come home and move forward with God. Step-by-step!

"Salome!" Jade screamed with excitement, running toward her with a great big smile stretched across her face. Love for Salome poured out from Jade, a love that had never left Jade's heart. In a breathless voice Jade called her name again, "Sal-o-me." Her eyes filled with tears as they twinkled with delight! "It has been so long dear girl; I have anticipated this meeting since you called. You look more beautiful than ever!"

Salome's eyes overflowed with the tears she had held back for what seemed like decades. Turning toward Jade, Salome tears of joy continued trickling down her checks.

"It's been too long, Salome," Jade said, "I am glad you've come home!" Slowly, Jade wrapped her arms around the other woman and held her close. She knew in her heart the years away from home had been cruel to Salome. Jade wondered, *What in the world happened to her?* Reluctantly, she released her hold on Salome. "Please," said Jade, "let's sit and visit. We have so much to talk about. Would you like something to eat or drink?"

"No, thank you. I'm fine. I have a bottle of water," Salome replied.

Just as she finished speaking, Tom came outside carrying a fancy silver tray with two glasses of sweet, peach tea. Each glass was decorated with a sprig of mint placed on top of the drinks. A fresh batch of home-made chocolate chip cookies rested on a beautiful antique platter placed on the other side of the tray. On Tom's other arm, a dish towel lay draped across as though he was a butler. "Did someone say snack and drink? How about some tea and cookies? Looks like you could use a few pounds, Salome!" He hooted several times snickering as he set the tray down on a small wrought-iron patio table.

Salome looked at Tom and giggled. Picking up the glass of tea from the table, she coyly said, "Did you put your finger in the tea to sweeten it. Wow, you bake, too?"

"You remembered! Sweetness just runs off of me, Salome! I actually did bake these cookies. I took them out of the fridge, opened the package, and cut them up. Then, I stuck them on a pan, put them in the oven for 10 minutes, and ta da! Cookies made all by myself." Amusement shone in Tom's eyes at Salome's teasing. "I missed ya, Salome! Who else can I tease like this?" Tom had a gift for making a person laugh and feel at home.

Jade chuckled, "Well, my goodness! I better roll up the legs of my pants! It's getting deep out here. Crazy man! Don't you just love this guy!"

Smiling, Jade nudged Tom in the ribs. Anyone watching this scene knew how deeply Jade and Tom loved each other. With that, Tom winked at Salome and whistled as he sauntered into the house taking the tray with him.

Jade turned her attention back to Salome. "Salome, how many years has it been since you gave your heart to Jesus?" she asked.

One of the sweetest smiles Jade ever saw gradually spread across Salome's face. Fixing her eyes on the heavens, her blue eyes twinkling, Salome spoke about the Lord of Heaven and Earth. "It has been twenty-two years since Jesus came into my heart. I know, in God's eyes, all my sins are washed away and I am whole." Looking down at her clasped hands she sadly said, "Unfortunately, I cannot say the same thing for other people or for my own heart. Jade, I'm so confused about everything. I feel like I am only now realizing just how far I've wandered from people. It wasn't intentional. I love the Lord, but the people around me and events that happened left me completely drained with hollowness in my heart. Through it I wondered, where is God while all this chaos flows into my life? I never asked for this, did I?"

Jade knew Salome had no idea what a real family structure was. The family in which Salome grew up, and the family she married into, was far from the example of what God calls family. Jade remembered Salome sharing parts of the emotional and physical abuse she lived through before finding Jesus. If recollection served her right, she believed Salome was raped as a child and again as a young woman. Sadly, to Salome and those like her, abuse is normal "love". Real love is something completely fearful and unnatural. Kindness and compassion are things Salome ran from instead of toward.

Thoughtfully Jade answered, "Salome, the Bible tells us in John 16:33 NIV, *I have told you these things so that in ME you may have peace. In this world you will have trouble. But take heart, I have overcome the world.* It is only when we are hidden in Christ that we experience peace. He never promised crazy things would not happen to us. We cannot control people. Unfortunately, many of us have to learn that the hard way."

Quite obviously, Salome's fight with fear and rejection continued. A thought came to Jade, "Salome, when did your mama pass away? I heard about it after the fact, or I would have been there for you."

"I know Jade; it was a crazy time. It has now been three years," Salome said. She smiled, yet in her eyes, Jade saw tears of pain. "As mama lay dying she asked me to forgive her. Mama and Dad both said they didn't know how to love me." Salome lowered her head, trying to regain control, but a sob coming straight out of her heart broke past her lips. She looked Jade right in the eyes and asked, "Am I that hard to love, Jade?" With the lie finally brought to light, a moan from deep in Salome's soul broke forth. "Don't get me wrong, I've forgiven Mama," she continued with a sob. "I know she could not give me what she did not have. There was no love in her heart for me, Jade. I was nothing more than Mama's scapegoat, a pebble in her shoe. People in my life don't normally hang around. Given enough time, they leave or disown me." Under her breath, Salome whispered, 'Or drive me completely crazy!'"

Jade knew Salome referred to her marriage but first she had to help Salome deal with the issue of her Mama. After a moment, Jade responded, "Salome, don't allow your family's issues to define who you are. You are completely loveable, dear child. I believe the problem is, *you* believe you are unlovable. That's not the truth, Salome! God loves you and so do many other people. Why do you believe your mother behaved toward you the way she did?"

Salome answered, "It was all she knew to do, I guess. The similarity between us is uncanny. We could have been identical twins. Many of the gifts and talents I have came from Mama. The older I get the more I resemble her. The only difference is I have my dad's eyes. After Mama died, Dad filled me in on her past. I was shocked to realize she experienced some of the same behavior from her father I endured from her. Sadly, she seemed to resent anything I tried. My piano lessons, sewing, arts and crafts, speeches for 4-H, would send her through the roof. It was my grandfather who first involved me in piano lessons. He bought my first piano. The sewing machine and kitchen were off limits to me — that is, except when I had to clean it or set the table for dinner. Mama seemed to resent the fact I was alive.

In one of her railings, she told me, 'I didn't want another child. I lost a boy between you and your sister. He is the one I wanted. When you were born, you ruined my life.'

In a way, I guess I truly understand how she felt. You know, disappointed and overwhelmed. My youngest child was in sixth grade when Lewis and I got married. My kids are a joy to me, don't get me wrong! We shared great times together, and I raised them to pick up after themselves and to be independent. I encouraged my children to step out and be all they could be. When they were young, I began talking with them about 'when' they would go to college and 'what' they would do. It was a continual joy to help dream about their future.

When Lewis moved in, the days of being fully responsible for my children's lives were long gone. I was not prepared to deal with his children. Really, no one could have prepared me for how needy the kids were, but, I know that was not their fault. They had no stability. Their mom has many issues; among them, being mental illness and drug addiction. They walked through things children should never have to go through. However, I did not resent them. Instead, my heart went out to them! They were deeply hurt by all they were forced to endure. At times, I wanted to scream but I knew that was my issue, not theirs."

Jade, her mother's instinct showing through, spoke in anger, "Well, Salome, have you ever considered your Mama could have chosen to raise you opposite from the way her father treated her? She could have chosen to make sure you never felt fear or rejection like she did. How about the gifts within you? She could have helped you develop those gifts long before the Lord stirred them up. After all, isn't that what you chose to do with your own children and Lewis' children?"

As Salome contemplated Jade's comments for a moment, she realized that although true, it was not a path she wanted to pursue just now. That part of her past was finished, over and done with. Nothing could change the events that happened. She knew the consequences of reliving the past led to unforgivness, bitterness, and anger. Her mind could walk her down that road far too quickly if she entertained the thoughts. No, she had to release all thoughts of the past and move forward. The road of unforgivness and bitterness was the one her Mama and family chose to travel. She would not!

Suddenly, revelation dawned on Salome. In her heart, she was emphasizing that same journey of unforgivness and bitterness again, only now with different people. This time it was with her husband and his family.

During the past three years, Salome's heart grieved over the wasted years between her siblings and her mama. Deeper relationships and friendships should have been built with her birth family. Salome faced the fact that those relationships were finished. Close ties with her siblings would never be formed. Sadly, it seemed history was determined to repeat itself with Lewis and his family.

At the same time, she could rejoice because her dad developed a relationship with Jesus. Her relationship with her dad was slowly growing because, once trust is lost, it is hard to rebuild again. You cannot have trust without complete forgiveness.

Jade interrupted Salome's musing by asking, "How is Tanya? Does she have any children yet?"

The relationship with Salome and her step-daughter, Tanya, was wonderful. In Salome's heart, Tanya was no 'step' anything, she was her child. She came into Salome's life at the age of nine. There were many moments during Tanya's growing-up years that Salome wanted to scream. Yet, Tanya matured into a beautiful, responsible and joyful young woman with a family of her own.

Salome's smile traveled to her eyes at the mention of Tanya. Jade loved watching Salome's eyes because they were an open book to her heart!

"Yes, she has one sweet little boy. His name is Andy. He is just the cutest little guy on earth! As Tanya describes him, he has lots of personality and "tude"! One day I texted her after one of Andy's escapades and asked, 'Where do you think he got that personality and "tude"?' Tanya promptly replied, 'His dad!'

Jade and Salome both roared in laughter. Salome smiled and said, "I'm so proud of her, Jade." Salome pulled out her cell phone and showed Jade pictures of Andy, Tanya and her husband, John. "When I think about all she's been through, I am thankful God allowed me to be a part of her life. God rescued Tanya from a future doomed to sadness and drama. It's a testimony of His deep love for her. I'm praying she will begin to see that once again."

"I love my son-in-law, John. He is a blessing to our family. Even a tree could enjoy John's conversations. My dad loves to sit and listen to him tell story after story of his Navy days. Dad was in the Army in WWII. So, those two can sit all afternoon hemming and hawing over war stories. I am so blessed whenever I think about our children," Salome shared with a smile.

"Salome, what about Jacob? He's married now and expecting a little boy, right? I saw your post on the website," Jade stated.

"Yes, Jacob married Mary last March. As a matter of fact, they were married just three weeks after my back injury. Their baby is due in January, so maybe he'll be a New Year's baby!" Salome said with delight. "I cannot wait to meet my newest grandson! My hope is that I will be able to travel when he's born. All depends on what the doctor decides to do with my back. I'm proud of Jacob! He's done well for himself and now that he's married, I know greater things are in store for him. Mary is such a delight and patient as the day is long. She is a Proverbs 31 woman in progress for sure!" Salome answered.

"Addie and Doug are doing well from what I hear. Their little sweetie is a heartthrob! What's her name, Lizzy is it?" Jade asked.

Salome's eyes twinkled again as she spoke about her family. Her heart filled with pride and thanksgiving as she thought about how greatly God blessed her. "That's it! Lizzy is a bundle of joy, and she reminds me so much of her mom. Only Lizzy and Addie would say the things those two do! Whenever I'm around Lizzy, all I can do is chuckle! She is one-of-a-kind! Her dark hair, hazel eyes and china-doll complexion make her a beauty in her own right, but it's her character I especially love! She tells you just like she feels. No need to guess where you stand in her eyes. Addie asked her to do something the other day, and she hesitated, so Addie proceeded to explain the importance of obedience. She may only be three, but she understands quite well. Lizzy looked up at Addie and held her gaze. You could see her internal struggle! Suddenly, she set her jaw and replied, 'But I don't want to obey!' All I could do was walk out of the room before I burst into laughter. When I regained my composure, I walked back into the room and expressed my opinion. I said simply, 'If that is not a picture of the flesh!' Once Lizzy obeyed and started playing again, Addie and I looked at each other and gave into hysterics!"

Jade chucked and said, "Grandchildren are the best gift God gives us, my friend! I believe they are a reward for all the heartaches we had while our children were teenagers."

Salome replied, "You can say that again! I enjoyed my children, but I would not want to venture back to their teenage years. Those were some of the most heartbreaking periods in life. I heard someone once say, the reason God made teenage years is so a parent would be ready to let the cute little and cuddly child leave!"

Jade chuckled, then nodded her agreement. Salome's eyes scanned the yard from where she sat on the veranda. For the next few moments, Jade studied Salome. She still seemed sadden in spite of the wonderful joys she had just shared. Jade pursed her lips and decided she would ask the question that had been on her mind since Salome called. "Salome, how are you and Lewis doing?" Immediately, Jade noticed the change in Salome's countenance.

How do I tell her this? Salome thought. Just moments before, they laughed and enjoyed their time together, but this one question seemed to suck all the joy out of Salome's heart. Jade sat waiting patiently for the answer to her question.

Finally, Salome opened her mouth and spoke the truth. "If I were not a Christian, I would already be divorced. Life has been hard with Lewis, and once his son, Josh, became involved with drugs, life with Lewis became awful. There is no relationship between us. He goes his way, and I go mine. Jade, the man never speaks to me. How do you have a relationship with someone who never shares his heart? I have no idea what he is thinking. Many things have surfaced during the past few years. All I can say is this marriage has sucked the life out of me. How do I continue to live like this for the rest of my life, Jade? Is this what God wants? No one has to tell me what the Bible says, *I know* God hates divorce. *I know* marriage is a covenant between three people, husband, wife and God. A few years ago, I had biblical grounds to get a divorce. Yet, when I prayed about it, I felt God say 'Salome, trust Me.'

"I'm scheduled to have back surgery in December. My recovery period is supposed to be four to five months tops. So what in the world am I going to do? Jade, I could lose my business. If I do, how will I support myself? I can't count on Lewis to be thoughtful because he has no clue what being thoughtful really is. He never thinks ahead, Jade. His reasoning is all about the present and himself. He never thinks how a decision, today, will affect the future, tomorrow. I don't understand how he thinks. Honestly, my heart has shut down toward our marriage and Lewis. I don't know what I feel anymore."

Jade spoke gently, "Salome, I'm sorry! I had no idea it was this bad. If you don't mind my saying so, it sounds like you resent Lewis. Do you?"

Jade's statement is all Salome needed. "I do, Jade! I'm so angry with him! The easy way out is all he looks for. He cannot see past the nose on his face. I hate the way he threw the responsibilities of our kids and home in my lap. All he wanted to be was a friend to his son when Josh needed a father, not another friend. There is no fruit to be found in his life. He goes to church whenever he's off work, but just because he goes to church does not make him a Christian. Honestly, he falls asleep through sermons; therefore, even if he's in church he doesn't hear the Word being preached. He is clueless about how to have a relationship with anyone. There is not a friend anywhere in his life. Lewis is a closed book that refuses to open to anyone.

His mother is manipulative and controlling. She called me a couple of times to cuss me out."

Jade looked shocked and said, "NO!"

"Oh yes, she is fine as long as she has control and you don't step on her toes. If you do, watch out," Salome fumed.

Jade knew she had to allow Salome the freedom to get everything out in the open where they could handle it one-step-at-a-time. "What did you do when she called?"

"That is the easy part," Salome replied! "It had to be God, because I remained calm and said, 'This conversation ends now. Goodbye.' Then I hung up!"

"Very good, Salome, it sounds like God did lead you," Jade retorted. "What happened to prompt her call?"

"Lewis and I separated under a pastor's guidance. Actually, we've separated twice since we have been married, both times with a pastor's approval." Shaking her head, tears began to flow from Salome's beautiful eyes. The torrential tide of emotions began to burst loose.

Jade got up and walked toward Salome. After reaching her, Jade held Salome while she released all the pent-up tears of disappointments and hurts she'd endured over the years. Staring into Salome's eyes, Jade finally spoke, "Salome, listen to me, this is not the end. On the contrary, this is only the beginning. We will pray together and watch God do a miracle in your life and your marriage. He is the only One who can cause something dead to rise again. Do not give up hope. Believe every word the Lord spoke to you concerning your marriage. You know as well as I do, divorce or a marriage like the one you described, does not bring God glory! If God chose you to walk through this, Salome, it is only because He has given you the grace and mercy to do it. Watch, because we may just see a miracle happen right before our eyes. That miracle, my friend, is God raising your dead marriage to life!

You are in a battle, Salome, and this battle is God's! Your

victory is sure to be won. This is the time to stand and believe, no matter how things appear. You are not standing alone, Jesus is here with you. I will be here to help hold up your arms just like Aaron and Hur helped Moses hold his hands up in the battle against the Amalekites. Remember, when Moses was in that hard place, the Lord revealed Himself as the Lord My Banner! Salome, the banner over you is LOVE Himself! Believe it will all be fine in the end. (See Exodus 7:8-16 and Song of Songs 2:4)

Salome kept her eyes on Jade and knew everything she said was the truth. She had to believe, but she also had to be open and honest with Jade. Gathering her thoughts, Salome finally spoke, "That's not the only problem, Jade. I've had two cortisone shots and am scheduled for another one in three weeks. From all appearances, I will have surgery. Again, I may lose my business, and I have to step down from the women's prison ministry. Without those things in my life, who am I, Jade? I feel like I'm losing my identity as well."

Jade knew all about the type of surgery Salome would face. Jade had back surgery a few years earlier. She would not say it now, but four or five months is definitely an optimistic view. In all reality, it is more like nine months to a year. Once again, Jade's understanding of Scripture came through, "Salome, your identity should not be in your job or ministry. Your identity can only be in Jesus. Anything else is shaky ground. Since you are an eternal being, your identity can never be in something as temporary as an occupation or anything you do for the Lord. If you don't have your identity in Jesus, you will easily fall. Have you ever considered this could be the very thing God is trying to show you? It's not what you do or don't do that makes you special. Salome, you are special because you are one of God's chosen. The Father chose you to walk the straight and narrow path. It is your choice to either continue on the path He marked out for you or to veer from it. One thing is certain, when you stay on the path, He is there. Do you realize why, Salome? It's because Jesus loves you just because you **are His**. Until you understand that, you are on an unstable foundation."

In her heart, Salome knew Jade's words to be true. This was it, part of her journey homeward. The fear Salome faced before she came was gone, and she knew this must be walked out step-by-step. She can do this. She will do this!

Salome looked at Jade to express the sincere gratitude she felt for this mighty woman of God. "Thank you! Thank you for opening your heart, arms and home to me, Jade. You will never know how much this means to me. I love you."

Salome glanced up to see the sun slowly beginning to set and she knew she needed to leave soon. Shades of pinks, deep reds, mauves, dark blues, along with the last golden rays of the sun, marked the near ending of the day. Already, the night songs of insects and frogs were weaving their sweet melody into the air, welcoming in the darkness of night. Salome turned to see Jade staring at her. She blushed, smiled, and said, "I really do need to go. Can I come back and visit again? I promise I won't stay away as long next time. It's just, I was afraid you didn't want to see me."

Jade laughed and said, "You better come back, don't you wait years before you come again. I love you too, Salome. You are never far from my heart." Getting up, Jade held Salome tightly then gazed into her eyes, "Salome, you are going to be ok. Do you realize that?"

With warm healing tears trickling down her cheeks, Salome nodded her head in agreement. "It *is* going to be ok. I feel so much better after getting everything out in the open. Thank you, Jade. You will never know how much it means to have you on my side of the court."

As Salome turned to leave, Tom walked out. Pretending to be upset and offended he placed his hands on his hips and spouted out, "Where do you think you are going, my dear? You weren't going to leave without giving me a proper hug, were you?"

This wonderful man always made her laugh. What a dear person he was! "I would *never* do that," she replied!

Strolling toward her, Tom slowly framed her cheeks with his hands, looked deep into her eyes, and said, "Salome, you are loved! Doesn't matter what happens, you will still be loved!" Softly, Tom pulled her into a hug then released her as Jade walked over to him.

Salome stepped to her car. Opening the door, she turned and said, "Thank you, I love you both." After a few seconds she looked toward them again and said, "More than you will ever realize." With that, Salome closed the door and started the car. As she backed out of the driveway, she looked up and saw Tom and Jade waving to her.

Once she was out of sight, Tom sighed and said, "This time, she'll be back. I can feel it. She's tired of running, Jade. That girl is ready to face those things that are haunting her. Coming here today is just her first step. Not knowing how we would receive her was a big hurdle to overcome. "

Jade nodded her head in agreement, "I do believe you are right, Tom."

Tom gazed into Jade's eyes and spoke, "Jade, you are just as sweet and beautiful as when I first met you." Then he smiled his clever smile and said, "I know I'm right, because I'm always right!"

Jade turned to head back toward the house, and shaking her head, she exclaimed, "Crazy man! You **are** always right!"

He went on a little farther and bowed
with his face to the ground, praying,
"My Father! If it is possible,
let this cup of suffering
be taken away from me.
Yet I want your will to be done,
not mine."
Matthew 26:39 NIV

CHAPTER **3**

AS SALOME TURNED from their driveway, joy seemed to permeate every part of her being. A song of praise leaped forth from the recesses of her heart as her spirit rejoiced because Jade and Tom did not reject her. On the contrary, they opened their arms of love and embraced her. Just under her breath Salome whispered, "Thank you, Jesus! You did this! I can feel the presence of Your Spirit. Honestly, I do not understand all You are doing, but I will trust You."

Salome reviewed everything she and Jade spoke about and realized how much better she felt! It came as a complete shock that she harbored some of those things in her heart. It was actually a surprise to realize she not only resented Lewis but, also, the dysfunction he brought into her life. When Salome thought about how their relationship began, the bare truth stared her in the face.

Lewis and Salome had dated only three months. Anyone could be on good behavior for that limited time. Salome had to admit allowing him to talk her into such a quick wedding is not something she would recommend. When a couple decides to get married, they should wait at least a year. Within that year they can experience how each family celebrates holidays, how much they have in common, witness each other's habits and anything else that could cause a rift in a relationship. It is so much better to deal with issues before the marriage covenant is made. What a shame that hind-sight is twenty-twenty.

As Salome turned onto the main highway, the clear, open view of the setting sun spread across the sky. The scene almost appeared as an otherworldly painting. The view displayed in front of Salome was stunning. She pulled her car over to the side of the road and sat in awe, gazing at the handiwork of the Lord that lay before her. *God, you make Yourself known through Your beautiful creation and within special people like Tom and Jade,* Salome thought. *Thank you, Jesus! You do make everything beautiful in Your timing.*

As Salome sat in her car watching the lovely sky, her mind traveled back to her reunion with Tom and Jade. "All this time I believed lies. Instead of testing those lies, I embraced falsehood and allowed it to steal, kill and destroy within my life. Makes me wonder how many other lies I have accepted as truth."

Scriptures began to come to Salome's mind, John 10:10 NIV, *The thief comes only to steal, kill and destroy; I (Jesus) have come that you may have life and have it to the full.* John 8:44 NIV, *You belong to your father, the devil, and you want to carry out your father's desire. He was a murderer from the beginning, not holding to the truth, for there is no truth in him. When he lies, he speaks his native language, for he is a liar and the father of lies.*

"How many misunderstandings would have been avoided if I had only spoken my true feelings? When I allow fear to keep me from sharing my thoughts, I aid the enemy. That allows him to drive a wedge in my relationships," Salome whispered.

Salome waited while thoughts continued to come to her mind. *As Christians, we should realize part of Satan's DNA is being a liar. It's the only thing he and those who follow him can do. There is **no** truth in Satan. Whatever he speaks, I can be sure it is a lie. In the Garden of Eden, he tricked Eve by adding a small bit of truth with his lie. He has one motive, to steal, kill, and destroy the child of God!*

When I distance myself from the Body of Christ, I give Satan place. What is it my pastor used to say? Oh yes, "The banana who gets pulled from the bunch is the one that gets peeled!" *I have had my share of peeling.*

"Lord, through the time I have been separated from my home church, I have indeed experienced deep wounds in so many areas, especially in our marriage. All I have left to offer you is the mess my life is, right now. However, I know You! You will still make it beautiful in Your time. I will trust You. When I think of the time I could have been with my church family—Oh Lord, it just makes me sick. Forgive me for believing lies, Lord," Salome prayed. "Help me see that in spite of all of this, You will still use it for my good and Your glory, conforming me more into the image of Jesus." (See Romans 8:28-29)

The sun continued its process of finishing its trek for the day. The first stars flickered high in the eastern sky. Glancing at the stars, she realized how long it had been since she stopped and looked at the evening sky. The twinkling lights made their appearance just as the moon began its journey. The glorious moon seemed to rise right out of the ground. Then it appeared to rest on the tops of the trees. Finally it continued rising to its fullness, chasing away some of the deep darkness of night. Salome felt this was a clear sign from God that a new start was just around the corner. Peace then flooded Salome's heart.

Salome pulled onto the highway heading for home. For the first time in ages, she knew she was back on the path God had chosen for her. Hope stirred in her heart as she remembered that **nothing** is impossible with God.

Salome's mind turned to the next few months. According to her doctor, she had no choice but to face back surgery. The only way to walk through this operation is to place all the "what if's" in God's hands. His Word is clear! Matthew 6:25-34 NIV counsels us about worry. In Verses 33-34 NIV Jesus stated, *But seek first His kingdom and His righteousness and **all** these things will be given* *to you as well. Therefore do not worry about tomorrow, for tomorrow will worry about itself. Each day has enough trouble of its own.*

"It's time to plan! I need to save as much money as I can in the next few months to prepare for the recovery period to come. I will trust You Lord, with all the rest. I want to spend as much time with my children and grandchildren as I can. Who knows what will come after surgery? Walking, resting and trusting You is my part on this journey. All the issues in my life are now Yours. You say in Your Word, *Be still and know that I am God! I will be exalted in the nations; I will be exalted in the earth!* (See Psalm 46:10)

That is my second step of faith, to be still and **know** *You are God*! You will meet all my needs according to Your riches and glories in Christ. I believe You will work on our marriage. Give me a love in my heart for Lewis, Lord Jesus. Please strengthen him and give him the wisdom and revelation about You and Your Word. Show me what I need to do to change my heart. Lord, I choose to give all of this to You! Thank You for working it all out for my good and Your glory, conforming us both more into the image of Christ, in the name of Jesus!"

With that final prayer, Salome took a deep breath and released all the stress and worry that had plagued her. Today, she drew the line in the sand and with God's help she would walk this all the way through!

There are still many things she could not understand about herself. As her husband slowly began turning more toward the Lord, Salome found that she was growing angrier. She was becoming bitter and, at times, wanted to scream at him. Over and over she searched her heart, yet could not understand her own actions. She really believed she forgave him, but if she did, why all this anger and where did the bitterness come from?

Suddenly, a picture of a lady came to her mind that she remembered from years gone by. We prayed for her husband's salvation. That poor woman and her children walked through much heartache due to her husband's behavior. All of us stood in awe because of her faith and trust in the Lord. No matter what he did, she stood on God's word." She encouraged us by saying, "God is doing something awesome, I know it." No matter what she said, the situation only grew worse.

Many of us were concerned about the effect of his lifestyle on their children. One only had to look into their eyes and see the wounds. However, in spite of our questioning, the day came. Pastor gave an altar call for salvation and her husband ran down to the altar, fell on his knees, and wept over the sins he'd committed against God and his family.

Those of us who had been praying for his salvation rejoiced, cried, and relished in the apparent victory over the devil! One more soul for the kingdom of God! However, no one was prepared for what happened next.

Months later, the sweet lady who held onto faith that he would be saved, left him. I remember how deeply it cut my heart. Why would she throw away her marriage after all these years of standing and believing for his salvation? As quickly as the question reached Salome's mind, God gently spoke to her heart and gave her the answer.

"Salome, isn't this the place in which you find yourself? All those years on the front lines battling in prayer for Lewis and his family are finally over. A new battle has begun. This one your husband must fight alone. It's time he learns to depend on Me.

In the war for your husband and his family's soul, you have incurred many wounds and the wrath of the enemy. Being on the front lines left you with no time to heal however, I watched you every step of the way. Now is your time to rest in Me. I am the Great Physician, and I am ready to heal every wound. Trust me! My Word will act as a scalpel to open the infected areas of your heart. It will also be the balm that helps them to heal. You always told the Youth Offenders that the 'Sword of the Spirit is two-sided', it cuts and it heals.

Salome, this is your greatest battle. It's the battle for your complete healing. Pushing aside or shoving wounds deep in your heart is the way you have always handled disappointments and offenses. You have to allow Me access into every part of your heart. In the midst of healing, I will give you revelations that will help you and Lewis. Consider this your Gethsemane, Salome. It's your decision."

Salome had no desire to go through anymore with Lewis. She knew if she was honest with herself, she did not want the marriage to work. However, this up-coming surgery gave her no choice. There is only one option, walking this all the way through and giving God the glory day-by-day.

Salome considered what the next few months could bring, and she knew how amazing and powerful God is. To herself she whispered, "You are Jehovah Rapha, my healer and You can heal everything! What an amazing thing it would be for Your glory if I flew through the surgery and recovery faster than anyone else! Doctors, and everyone involved would have to give the glory to You! What a testimony of Father's mercy this would be! Yes, if You did it like that, it would be an amazing thing!" With that, Salome turned up the music and continued singing until she was almost at her house.

Nearing her final turn, Salome resolved in her heart to put aside all the "questions" about the future. In light of that, she realized the blessing God placed in front of her. She always did her best work planning, organizing and making lists. Within the next few months, many wonderful things were planned with her family which always filled Salome with excitement and joy! Determination overflowed within her spirit as she set her gaze forward to the coming vacations and holiday events with family and friends.

She put on her left blinker, making the turn to her home. Her heart embraced all the things for which she had to be thankful. Although both Lewis and Salome had to deal with the issues in their lives, God had truly blessed them. Pulling up in her driveway she stopped for a moment, studying their home. To her, their abode was truly beautiful! Surrounding it stood long tall pine trees giving the place the ambiance of a state park. The white Acadian home with black shutters and a bright, yellow door welcomed people from the street. An old, charming, stone-ground walk-way, escorted visitors to the long, covered porch stretched across the front of the house. Studying the bird bath, with the angel in the center and all the lovely flowers and bushes, along with the sweet gentle tinkling sounds of her wind-chimes, she could only sigh, knowing beyond any doubt she had more on her list to be thankful for than she had to be concerned or gripe about. God is truly gracious!

We wait in hope for the Lord;
He is our help and our shield.
In Him our hearts rejoice,
For we trust in His holy name!
Psalm 33:20-21 NIV

CHAPTER **4**

MULLING OVER THE last few months, Salome could see that God's hand had to be in the midst of all the circumstances within her life. The second week of March started out to be a day like any other day. However, while at work, Salome reached over to pick up something and suddenly felt a severe pain in her lower back. In spite of the pain, she managed to finish her job. Her drive home was torturous and when she arrived, she barely made it to bed. When Lewis came home Salome asked him to take her to the doctor. She had no idea life was about to take a drastic turn.

After doing an MRI, the doctor diagnosed her with L4 and L5 ruptured disc that were pinching her nerves. Through her recent prayers, she had been expecting God to move in the situation between her and Lewis. Never in her wildest dreams did she believe God would use this to heal her and Lewis' relationship.

In spite of the injury, God in His grace allowed Salome to enjoy a banner year with her family before the surgery. After the mishap, she'd had three cortisone injections in her back. Because of those injections, she and Lewis had been able to travel to Texas to celebrate Jacob and Mary's wedding.

John and Andy pulled up in the driveway the day after Salome and Lewis returned home from the wedding. John had been discharged from the Navy. So he, Tanya and Andy were moving back home. Andy was only four months old and a complete delight! His

MY JOURNEY HOME ❧

smile melted his Nana Salome's heart and filled her with joy.

When Salome got home from work she would find Andy sitting on the living room floor surrounded by toys. His face beamed every time Salome walked into the room. She couldn't help but pick him up, snuggle and play with the little blessing. The three months Tanya's family stayed with them held priceless memories!

In September, Salome, Mary, Tanya and Addie traveled to Houston for a weekend getaway. This time of bonding with her beautiful, precious girls was one she would always remember. Although the IKEA showroom and the Galleria were fantastic, what Salome loved most was watching the three girls bonding! Her prayer for them was simple. *Lord, let them develop a close relationship with each other, regardless of what happens to me.* It was something she longed for with her own siblings. The love and acceptance of family is part of a legacy she hoped to leave her children.

Salome and Lewis shared a week's vacation with Jacob and Mary that October. In the midst of the Smokey Mountains of Tennessee, sits a small, rustic log cabin in which she and Lewis vacationed twice a year. Trees and mountains surrounded the hideaway and a babbling brook merrily gurgled its way past the front yard. Resting and listening to the water as it splashed against the rocks and boulders on its way down the mountainside, was so delightful. An old, weathered wooden swing, festooned with colorful pillows, hung on the front porch, creating the perfect place to quietly sit and meditate on the goodness of God. It was just one more favorite memory over the past year.

Walking along rugged, dirt paths in the center of the thick forest laden with God's majestic display of the colors of autumn, Salome enjoyed watching Mary's eyes light up as she surveyed the panoramic vista stretched out before her. Each turn in the path revealed another fantastic view of the mountain's glory!

Our cameras could not begin to capture the breathtaking

scenery laid out before us. Yet, each of us tried furiously, clicking away as fast as we could. During their meandering in Cades Cove they saw two black bears. One bear lay sprawled across the branch of a tall tree fast asleep, oblivious to all the excitement he caused on the eleven mile loop. The second bear stood a little way off the side of the road, rooting for food. The harder that furry creature dug, the more he grunted, ignoring everything but his quest to find food. Standing within six yards of the bear Mary delighted, as her camera clicked away. Smiling, Salome thanked God for the many blessings.

Tomorrow is Thanksgiving Day, Salome thought. *While each day should be a day of thanksgiving for a Christian, it is very different for me this year.* "Lord, I have so much to be grateful for. Thank You." As she reminisced over the past year it became clear that God's hand had been in every activity.

Salome sang a song of praise as she prepared Thanksgiving Dinner. Her heart overflowed with gladness for her family. Gratefully, she realized if God took her home right then she could say she had lived a life filled with His goodness.

Daily, Salome prayed that God would make Himself known in a tangible way to all her children and grandchildren. Thinking of this today, she added a new prayer. "God, help me show how much I love, appreciate and how proud I am of each one of them." Tears filled her eyes as she thought about the joy and gift every person is to her. None of the children have had an easy way in life. In the end, I believe, they all will allow God to touch their hearts and make their lives beautiful. Smiling softly, she blessed the Lord again!

"There are still three of my children away from you, Lord, yet I know You! This battle is not over; they are all going to serve You! I feel it in my heart. I don't know what they may have to go through, but I won't stop praying for them."

With the cornbread dressing slowly cooking, the turkey shot

up with Cajun seasoning, the green beans and sweet potato casseroles baking, Salome headed toward the other side of the house. All the things she felt in her heart had to be written within her journal for safe keeping.

Not very long after she had given her heart to Jesus, Jade suggested she start daily journaling. Salome remembered like it happened yesterday. "Salome, in your own private journal, write out every negative, angry or hurtful thought that comes to mind. After you record it, stop and really inspect it, then see what God's Word says about those thoughts. You will be able to replace hurtful thoughts with the truth from the Word. Healing is a slow process Salome. However, you will heal if you do what God says. His Word tells you that you shall know the truth and the truth will set you free! (See John 8:32)."

Now, twenty-two years later, Salome still loved to record the hidden messages held within her heart. Messages God taught her through the blessings as well as the trials and testings of life. Salome wondered how she would have gotten through the tough places of facing and dealing with her past had it not been for her journal. Walking through heartbreak, disappointments and broken relationships would have been impossible if it were not for penning the secret thoughts hidden within the confines of her heart. It enabled her to look back and see God's hand even in turmoil.

Journaling had become like the air Salome breathed. It seemed as though each time she opened her journal, God's presence surrounded her like the wings of a mother hen encircles her chicks. There, under the shadow of His wings, Salome loved to hide, rest, listen to His heartbeat and draw life from His presence. As she laid bare her heart to God, all the issues of life were left at His feet. He would gently replace her heartache and fill her with peace and joy words can't describe.

Walking into her sun-brightened office filled with books, Bibles and pictures, she slowly gazed around and thanked God for the year of blessings. Reaching for the stereo, she pressed Play and a sweet, flowing piano melody began to filter through the air, creating an ambiance of peace. She could feel God whisper, *'Peace I leave with you, My peace I give to you, I do not give as the world gives. Do not let your heart be troubled and do not be afraid.'* Salome remembered the scripture from John 14:27, NIV. Peace would be her portion and joy her strength. With that fully planted in her heart, she continued slowly into the room.

Reminiscing, Salome thought about how the office came into being. She and Lewis had often thought how nice it would be to share an office. Putting their heads together, they came up with a plan. The ideal site for the new office was an existing screened-in porch and, since it was a fairly easy build, they did it themselves. *I am thrilled with the way the new porch and office worked out. I love it! It's everything I ever hoped for and even more of a blessing since we were able to do it together,* she thought.

Glancing around the charming room, Salome admired each lovely cross and picture that displayed some of her favorite scriptures. With great care, Salome had chosen the décor of her office. She wanted to create a sanctuary and, in this, she had succeeded. Their home was everything Salome dreamed a home could be. God truly smiled with favor on her and Lewis throughout the years. If only something could happen now with their relationship.

"Is there too much water under the bridge, Lord? In Your Word it says, 'Nothing is impossible with You'. In this scripture, the Holy Spirit is talking about Mary becoming pregnant with Jesus, even though she is a virgin. Truly, a miracle! (See Luke 1:37) Therefore, I have to believe miracles can happen in this relationship. We desperately need Your help, Jesus."

Sitting at her desk, she faced the open window. This is the place wherein Salome witnessed the joyfulness of God's creation and where she studied her Bible. Breathing deeply, a thought came to mind. *Just how long has it been since I had time to really search through the love letters in God's Word?* Salome whispered, "Way too long. Life had become so hectic this year that I did not have time to dig in the Word like I should. I miss that, Lord!"

She fixed her eyes on the oak tree that was on the left side of the office window. The night before, a gentle, sweet evening shower had left droplets of water on its leaves. A light breeze blew as the morning sun shone down on the tree. Raindrops seemed to dance on its leaves in sweet surrender as the wind gently flowed through the air.

Tiny little birds fluttered from branch to branch, playing a game of chase. Their sweet, chirping sounds filled Salome with a delightful giggle. To the right of the tree-filled backyard, she witnessed a brown, chubby bunny jumping and hopping around, carefree, shaking his long ears as he played about the yard. He seemed totally untroubled, enjoying himself in a private game of chase.

"He is the culprit feasting on our garden," Salome exclaimed. "Mr. Bunny, no wonder you're so fat, eating all the yellow squash!" Chuckling, she watched his antics as he skirted back and forth across the grassy lawn.

"Freedom, Lord, is that what freedom looks like?" Gradually, the sun broke through the forest of trees as a sunbeam shone right by the window. There, sitting in the grass with the sun shining on it, sat a dark grey dove. It seemed to stare right at Salome as it cooed its lovely, haunting bird-song.

Where is its mate, Salome mused? Wondering, she thought, *Did something happen to it?* She knew doves mated for life and if you see only one, the possibility is that something happened to its mate. Many times, if one dove dies, its mate grieves itself to death. Considering the lone dove Salome said, "This is a picture of true love." She solemnly considered the dove as another question came to mind. *If something goes wrong with my surgery and I die, is there anything I have left undone?*

The first thing that came to mind is her relationship with Lewis.

She knew that they were like two ships passing through the night. He had begun to work swing shifts, which made their time together even less. When Lewis is not working, he is so tired that he falls asleep the minute he sits down. Because of his lack of sleep his temper is short and there is little or no communication.

However, no matter how much she prayed, it seemed as though there was nothing she could do. They were moving farther and farther apart. Salome tried her best, yet it was nearly impossible to spend any time together. The only solution is to go on with life.

Since the date for surgery was almost upon her, she had prepared the best she could. All of her life she had moved in survival mode; she could do it again. Salome had everything planned down to the last moment before going to the hospital. She would do as many jobs as possible and save up as much money as she could. From her calculations, she would be able to save enough money to make three house payments. Their income tax return should take care of the rest. She was confident that everything would turn out all right. She thought, *A quick recovery is what will give God the most glory, right?* One thing she decided for sure, she would enjoy these weeks before surgery, and cast all her cares on God, because she knew He cared for her.(See 1 Peter 5:7)

On the list of things to do, Salome planned to take Lizzy and Andy to see some of the Christmas lights around Walker and Denham Springs. There is a house that all kids loved to see and it is in Tom and Jade's neighborhood. Every inch of the yard is filled with lights, elves and mechanical decorations. The extravaganza takes quite a bit of time to walk through, and each year a new mechanical decoration is added. A crèche is placed somewhere within every scene to remind people of the true reason for the season, Jesus' birth. As much as she could, Salome would experience the joy of Christmas with her children and grandchildren.

One of the things written on her to-do-list is to decorate their home with festive holiday cheer. Lewis loved the way Salome 'decked the halls' of their home because she has a flair for floral arrangements and decorating. The kitchen, living room, entryway and guest bathroom are all fully dressed for the celebration of our Savior's birth. A small nativity scene is placed in each bedroom as a reminder of the real reason for Christmas.

This year, however, the only decorations would be some of Lewis's favorites. She knew that with his work schedule and her recovery period, it would be nearly impossible for her to take everything down after the holidays. Therefore, she made the decision to only decorate the living room.

Salome knew that on the day after Thanksgiving, she and Lewis would spend their time pulling out all the decorations they would need. Lizzy and Andy loved all the twinkling lights from the Christmas tree and the many Nativity scenes spread out on the mantel, shelves and table in the entryway. Three year old Lizzy loved to rearrange the Christmas tree ornaments from the floor up as high as she could reach. The ornaments hung there were unbreakable. Each time Lizzy visited, her section of the tree had a whole new look. Salome would chuckle when she watched Lizzy step back to eye her newest creation, making sure everything was just right! What a delight!

Salome wondered what Lizzy would do this year! "Lizzy, you will have to share the tree with your new cousin, Andy," she chuckled! Andy was just a little over a month old last Christmas. Everyone who came to the house tenderly picked him up and rocked or cuddled that sweet little guy! "What a joy it is to have them living close by for Christmas! This year, Andy is sure to give Lizzy a run for her money," Salome laughed!

Now a year old, Andy is certainly a very curious little fellow. He wants to know how things work. He gravitates to anything using motor skills. You can see his little mind working as he tries to figure things out.

Turning back to her to-do-list, she marked through Christmas shopping; all Salome had left to do is wrap the gifts. It will be a light Christmas because of all the pain she was going through. But, hurting or not, she just had to bless those precious grandbabies!

December 14th is the day scheduled for surgery. It could not come soon enough for her! *Waiting is the worst part of the whole thing but there is so much to do I know the days will fly by,* she thought.

Also on her list was to clean her house from top to bottom. Addie and Tanya promised to help as much as they could while she recovered. If she could help it, they would not have to worry about trying to take care of her house as well as theirs.

From the looks of things, in just two days Salome would have the majority of the cleaning done. That only left having fun with the babies! With that thought in mind, pent-up anxiety was released and taking a deep breath she began to relax.

Praying she said, "Ok, Lord, my life is held in Your nail-scared hands. I will trust You to be the hands of the surgeon extended and believe for great results from the surgery. Friends and family are praying for a speedy recovery with a limited amount of pain. I would prefer to have no pain, Lord but. . .You're able….

Lord, I also trust You to take care of our family and my relationship with Lewis. Jesus, You **are** the Author and Finisher of my faith. That promise is recorded in Hebrews 12:1. Therefore, I know You wrote my story long before time existed. My prayer today is that Your will be done, Your kingdom come in our lives as it is in heaven. I'm looking to You, Lord! Thank You, in Jesus' name! Amen!"

Just then, the doorbell rang. Salome wondered who it could be. As she walked to the front door, she saw a Fed Ex truck backing down her long, gravel driveway. Opening the door, she saw a large box placed on the doorstep. Stooping down, Salome picked up the package. The return address read, Bertha Ducote. As she stared at the box, she said, "What in the world is this? I've not heard from Aunt Bertha in years. Didn't she die three months ago?"

I have loved you with an
everlasting love;
I have drawn you
with loving-kindness.
Jeremiah 31:3 NIV

AUNT BERTHA MOVED years ago. Salome could not remember the last time she spoke to her. As a child, whenever Salome stayed with her aunt, she went to church with the family. To this day, Salome still remembered that little church. It was built in the shape of a cross. Sunday school classes were held before service in rooms on either side of the main sanctuary. When it was time for worship to begin, the teachers would bring the children to their parents in the main building. After singing a few hymns, the congregation sat down as the preacher stepped up to the podium.

Dressed in a long, flowing, black robe and with a loud voice he would say, "Even before the world was formed, Jesus loved you. No matter what you have done, Jesus still loves you. You can never lose His love no matter how far away you may roam."

As Salome considered the memories, she realized all the words that preacher spoke years before, were still resonating within her heart. Sweet Aunt Bertha, so different from the rest of the family. Salome mused, *She'd been thinking about **me**!* With a smile slowly stretching out upon her face, she opened the package. Inside the box, nestled in a worn, purple velvet cloth, rested a huge, old, leather-bound journal. Delicately, Salome ran her hands over the journal and wondered who the author could be. The leather was soft and smooth, evidenced by the obvious use. Fearful of tearing it, she gently reached in and took the treasure out of the box. As she lifted it, a note fell to the floor. Placing the book back in the box, she picked up the note and read:

Dearest Salome,

It has been a very long time since we have seen each other, yet a day has not passed that you were not on my mind. I've prayed for you many times because I knew some of what you were going through. Salome, you are dearly loved, please, don't forget that!

Enclosed, you will find your great-grandmother's journal. This book has been handed down from generation to generation. Those of us who received the journal were blessed by the wisdom penned within its pages. You were named after this grandmother. She was the first to be born-again in our family, a trail blazer for all of us. Salome, she had to believe God in ways we will never be able to imagine. Inside this diary, you will find her insight into some amazing women of the Bible. Embrace her words as gold that has been tried by fire.

I know you have been through some pretty rough spots in your life. Most of your days existed without the knowledge of unconditional love. Nor did you understand how to love others in the manner God created us to love. This great-grandmother's legacy is one to be proud of and encouraged by. Dear niece, as you read though her writings, allow Jesus to heal your heart and take you on a journey homeward to His heart of love for you.

I know you are a born-again believer. I know your

desire is to please Jesus in everything you do. Yes, Salome, news does travel. I've been watching you from afar believing, praying for, and trusting God to heal you. Salome, He knows everything that happened to you. I am proud of you. You have always had a special place in my heart.

Later, begin praying about who will receive this journal when you go home to Jesus. Write her name down and keep the paper in a place where a family member will find it after you've gone.

Right now Salome, God wants you to have it! Always remember, He knows the plans He has for you, my love, plans to prosper you and not to harm you, to give you a hope and a future. (See Jeremiah 29:11)

His love and mine,

Aunt Bertha

Placing the letter aside, Salome gently picked up the journal again. She wondered how many other hands it had passed through. Had those women found the answers they searched for within the covers of the book? As Salome held the diary of her great grandmother, she wondered if it was the same person her maternal grandmother spoke about years ago. That grandmother lived many years before, yet, when Jesus entered her heart, her life was changed as she gave herself to the Lord.

Tenderly, Salome opened the first pages of the beautiful, worn journal. How many lives had her grandmother spoken to without realizing it? Suddenly, Salome recognized the opportunity that was before her. It was now her time to embrace her grandmother's wisdom.

With tender, loving care Salome held the journal tightly,

thanking God for choosing her. Sitting down, she carefully opened the book and began to read. It was a prayer.

Dear Lord,

How far I have fallen! Yet, seeing Jesus on that cross and hearing His words of life, I understood that even I could have a new life in Him. As I study, Lord, please help me to write everything down for other women to learn from the things You teach me. Thank You for giving me this chance, Lord Jesus! Please touch each one of my future daughters and granddaughters so they too, can experience a changed life through Your death, burial and resurrection. I love You, Lord. Thank You for saving me!

All my heart,

Salome

Closing the journal and holding it tightly to her bosom, Salome slowly understood what a precious gift she had just been given. Reading more of the journal would have to wait until after surgery. She had a lot to do before then. The months of recovery would give her ample time to dive into her grand-mother's writings again.

Praying, Salome said, "Lord, I cannot imagine the wisdom held in this chronicle. Please help me to see everything my grandmother learned about You so that I can live a life pleasing to You. Thank You for this priceless treasure in my hands. I'm not alone, am I? I never have been. The proof of that is evidenced by my aunt's letter and my grandmother's journal. I am truly grateful Lord, in Jesus' name."

Holding the book, a tear trickled down Salome's cheek. A light began to shine on all the darkness that seemed to engulf her. The message beginning to be engraved on her heart is simple. She had never been alone. God was with her. He had always been with her and He will continue to be with her, forever! Also, He deeply loved her no matter what had happened.

With that in mind, Salome reached for the phone and called Jade. "Jade, you will never guess what I just received in the mail!"

Jade chuckled at Salome's excitement and replied, "I cannot imagine what could have you so fired up? What is it Salome, don't keep me waiting!" Jade smiled as she recognized the favor of God on Salome's life. If only Salome could see it!

Salome could not contain her enthusiasm, "Aunt Bertha, who I have not seen or heard from in years, just sent me this package. Three months ago she passed away and she left it to *me*! It's an old journal that has been passed down from generation to generation. In her letter she stated that God told her to give this to *ME*!! Can you imagine?"

"Yes, Salome, I can!" Jade added. "You sell yourself so short, dear girl! I'm so excited for you. Just think of the wisdom you will learn and be able to pass down to those God places around you."

"Really, do you think that's true Jade? I cannot tell you how long it has been since I've been this expectant of great things that only God can do," Salome answered.

"My dearest friend, can't you see the effect you have had on others lives already? Salome, you're a walking testament of God's goodness and faithfulness. Everywhere you go, you exude His love, mercy and grace and I'm not the only one who has noticed, everyone has. Just a few days ago, I overheard a conversation where you were the subject," Jade responded.

Salome immediately reacted, "What were they saying about me, Jade?"

"Actually, their exact words were, 'All one has to do is look at Salome and know she has been in the presence of the Lord. Joy pours from her heart and if you ever watch her praise the Lord, her face glows.' Salome, people love you! Dear girl, begin to believe that God not only loves you, there are many people who love you as well. Forget all the lies of the enemy and take a step of faith and just believe," Jade countered. "One of the wonderful things God is going to teach you through this is the fact that HE loves you and so do many others as well. All of us have seen the change in you. It doesn't take long to understand that while God had you out of this flock, He continued to mold and make you and use you for His glory."

"Jade, do you really believe that?" Salome whispered almost afraid of the answer.

"Yes, Salome, I DO really believe that," Jade responded. "I've held you up in prayer asking God to reveal Himself to you and bring you to the place of understanding who you really are in the Lord. The devil knows that once you accept this, there will be nothing he can do to stop you from receiving everything Jesus died to give you."

"Jade, you and Aunt Bertha really do believe in me, don't you? God believes in me as well," Salome mused. "It's time for me to start believing that I can, and will be, all Father God dreamed for me to be and stop listening to the father of lies!"

Laughing, Jade retorted, "The enemy is on the run now Salome! Don't you stop, keep going forward! God is going to do a great work through this whole situation. Keep focused on Him and HE will keep you in perfect peace."

With tears in her eyes, Salome answered, "Thank you Jade. God knew I needed a cheerleader! I love you and thank God for you each day."

"I love you too Salome," Jade responded. "Enjoy your time with your family and *rest*. God has this whole thing in the palm of His hands and He knows exactly what He's doing. Remember Proverbs 3:5-6, trust in the Lord with all your heart, and lean not on your own understanding. In all your ways acknowledge Him and He will direct your steps."

Hanging up the phone, Salome sat down and reviewed the conversation with Jade. *She is such a wise mentor, Lord, thank you for placing her in my life. What would I do without her? She is a Titus two woman, the older lady teaching and cheerleading as needed, this younger woman.*

Trust in the Lord with all your heart
And lean not on your own understanding,
In all your ways acknowledge Him and
He will direct your paths.
Proverbs 3:5-6 NIV

CHAPTER **6**

STARING AT HER doctor, Salome listened as he spoke. "The recent MRI revealed severe damage to two discs on the L4 and L5 vertebra. Salome," her doctor ordered, "it will take at least a full year before your bones will be completely fused. You must be careful during this time, no bending, twisting or lifting anything over fifteen pounds. This is dangerous, those bones must have time to heal and fuse together. It is a process that cannot be hurried. Screws and pins will be set in the bones to hold everything in place, however; the same screws holding your vertebra will also compromise the spinal column. You must do as instructed and before you say anything, I do understand how hard this is. No housework, cooking or picking up grandbabies either, Salome! That is out of the question for a few months. Also, no driving until your x-rays show the area is beginning to heal, around two to three months."

"That's good, but God's gonna do something amazing. Doc, you'll see," Salome replied, more to convince herself than the doctor.

Giving her a strange look, the doctor countered, "Salome, I'll see you at the hospital tomorrow."

Walking out of his office Salome headed toward the elevators. She could not forget how serious he sounded. This visit to the clinic was the last thing to do before tomorrow's surgery.

Tomorrow everything I know as "normal life" will change,

Salome thought. All the things on her to do list were done. The small suitcase she planned to take to the hospital sat by the front door, ready for the early morning trip. It was quite a shock to realize she would be incapacitated for up to a year. Salome saw the doors to the elevator open. Stepping into it, she was relieved to find no other passengers and for that, she was grateful.

Trying to digest the information she'd just been given was more than she could handle. Her plans would not work out. *Yet, maybe the doctor is wrong,* she hoped. The only thing on her mind now was a desperate need to slip away. Since Lewis was due to be home earlier than usual, Salome knew she needed to find peace before facing him. She knew exactly where to go.

"One year," she sighed. "What will happen to my business?" Just then, the elevator doors opened and she stepped out onto the first floor.

Taking in her surroundings she saw the sun shining brightly on that December afternoon in spite of her ordeal. Several patients were waiting for the elevator as she walked off. A few people needed help to get in the elevator. Stopping, Salome smiled at a man on crutches and an elderly lady in a wheelchair. She asked, "Do you need help?"

The elderly lady smiled and said, "Oh, thank you." Once Salome helped her into the elevator, she placed her hand on one of the doors to hold them open until the man on crutches was safely inside. With a smile on her face, she said, "Have a great day." Regardless of what she was going through, she still wanted to help others in their distress.

Turning, she headed toward the double glass doors. As she stepped outside, she was caressed by the sweet smell that was carried on the wings of a gentle breeze. In that moment, Salome knew that she was right to head to the park. Praying she said, "Lord, You are with me! I know You are. Help me trust You to take care of me."

Tickfaw State Park was not far from her home. It was the one place she could go to be alone with her thoughts. Although her home was her sanctuary, at the park she would not have to deal with the phone ringing or people dropping by. Instead, she could take her time, digest the information, pray and then go home in peace over this whole situation.

Anyone who knew Salome understood this is how she handled most issues. She pulled apart from everyone, making space for her and the Lord, giving her time to mull over things in her mind. Then, she would be fine.

Entering the parking lot, she headed for her car. Reaching it, she got in, started it and eased into traffic heading to I-12 toward Tickfaw State Park. Leaving the clinic at 3:00 P.M. was perfect. The traffic was not that bad, therefore, she could make good time. Her mind seemed to swirl at all the new bits of information she'd been told. Driving in silence, she tried to consider the different scenarios that could happen. Before she realized it, she was out of the city and not far from the park.

Jade happened to call at just that moment. "Salome, you have been on my heart. Are you ok?"

"Jade, please, keep praying for me. The doctor just told me it would take about a year for me to recover. There is just no way," Salome answered.

"Salome," Jade asked, "where are you?"

"I'm headed down the interstate to Tickfaw State Park. I need time alone," Salome replied.

"Good," Jade responded, "you need time with the Lord. I'll keep praying. Call me if you need me, hon. I love you Salome, you will make it through this and you will find yourself moving closer to the Lord than you could ever imagined."

"Thanks Jade," Salome said with a choked voice. "God knows exactly what I need, when I need it! You are a jewel! I love you and will talk with you soon."

Hanging up, Salome continued heading west on the interstate. Suddenly, she noticed ducks flying forward in the same direction in which she was headed. As she watched, the ducks began to switch positions. The lead duck in the middle of the V formation slowed and fell back to the last place of the pattern. The last duck in line flew up front as the new lead. They were all rotating positions.

Salome recalled a sermon she heard years ago describing the V flight pattern ducks used to fly lengthy distances. Flying in this manner helps conserve their energy during their long migrations. Each duck trails behind the other in order to benefit from a reduction in the wind resistance. The lead duck had to be strong because he caught the full brunt of the wind's challenge. They deliberately tail each other and when the lead duck becomes weary they rotate and change places. Salome thought about this and wondered if God used the ducks to show her that this was her time to back up and let Lewis step up. A scripture came to mind from Isaiah 55:8-9 NIV. For *My thoughts are not your thoughts, neither are your ways My ways, declares the Lord. As the heavens are higher than the earth, so are My ways higher than your ways, and My thoughts than your thoughts.*

Salome noticed the Exit sign for the park just ahead. This would be her time to trust God in the midst of the situation and watch Him move. Yet, she also knew that she needed to make her way toward her own Gethsemane in order to embrace what the next few months could bring.

Salome turned off the main highway onto the little back roads going toward the park, and then remembered the other part of the sermon. Ducks also fly in formation because it allows the birds to communicate more easily. They also have good visual contact with each other so the flock stays together and minimizes the possibility of losing someone along the way. They trust that the oldest duck will lead them to their destination because he knows the way.

Salome immediately thought about Jade. The Lord truly

blessed her with the mentor/friend she had in Jade. The Bible tells us in Titus 2:3-5 NIV this very principle. *Likewise, teach the older women to be reverent in the way they live, not to be slanderers or addicted to much wine, but to teach what is good. Then they can train the younger women to love their husbands and children, to be self-controlled and pure, to be busy at home, to be kind, and to be subject to their husbands, so that no one will malign the word of God.* Yes, Jade fulfilled this scripture as she mentored many young women. Salome was thankful she was one of them.

The park entrance was just ahead. Pondering all her thoughts, Salome wondered what would happen when those ducks were tired, hungry or thirsty. Just then, she saw the park sign and turning to the left drove through the open gate to the park office. Lowering her window, she smiled at the attendant. Beaming, he asked, "Just one today? It certainly is a beautiful afternoon."

"Yes," Salome replied, "just one." Handing him a dollar bill, she mused, *I desperately need this time to grasp the severity of the situation. If I lose my business, what will I do?* She realized the attendant was talking to her. "I'm sorry, what did you say?"

He replied, "Have a great time."

Salome laughed and said "Thanks," as she put up her window.

Ironically, it was December 13th, the anniversary of D-Day. Tomorrow was her D-Day and there was nothing she could do to change it. According to the doctor's report, it was a miracle had she experienced such a wonderful year with her family. It had truly been a fantastic gift from God. He knows the beginning from the end and she could not lose her faith in God now. This is exactly why she was at the park, to be renewed in the Lord.

Driving into an empty parking space, Salome parked the car and sat a moment. Slowly she laid her hands and head on the steering wheel and took a deep breath then prayed. "Lord, I need help. This is worse than I thought it would be! Father, one year can destroy us financially. What do I do? Show me how to talk to Lewis about this."

The sign to the River Trial was just up ahead. As she considered which trail to walk, she realized there was not enough time to walk the long path to the boat dock through the forest. Therefore, she chose to walk the boardwalk over the swamp.

December is not always cold in Louisiana. Actually, it can be quite mild at times. January, February and March are the coldest months. Many people would not consider them cold at all. Salome thought back to several Christmas seasons when she remembered playing Frisbee or taking a long walk on Christmas Day in shorts.

Today the air was crisp and sixty-eight degrees. It was not very humid, which is a miracle in Louisiana. The sun shone brightly in a pretty, clear, blue sky. Salome inhaled deeply as a sweet-smelling fragrance drifted by. She began walking toward the trailhead that led over the swamp. It seemed strange that the only sound she heard was the gentle rustling of the few red and yellow leaves still hanging on some of the trees. Enjoying the peace, Salome made her way toward the river.

The swamp filled most of the park and hidden within it were treasures waiting to be discovered. Many people dread the swamp, but to Salome it is one of God's beautiful, live art exhibits. She could always count on the stillness of the murky water of the swamp as it nestled around cypress knees and ran circles around other tall, slender trees. She noticed a dragon fly as it fluttered from one cypress knee to the other, almost like a dance. An occasional alligator or two could sometimes be seen sunning itself on the banks of the river. Various other creatures, from muskrats to furry, brown rabbits, freely roam throughout the park, adding to the wondrous enchantment. All types of birds and water fowl make their home within the borders of the swamp and river such as large white cranes, graceful white egrets and blue herons all the way down to the tiny, brown sparrows. In the winter months ducks and Canadian geese stop by to refresh themselves. The swamp always held a mysterious atmosphere created by the ghostly, long, gray Spanish moss draping down many trees.

Salome smiled as she remembered tales of old. Her grandfather loved to share stories of swamp creatures and an old folk tale about the moss holding tightly to the trees for protection in a storm. Suddenly, Salome realized why the swamp gave her such peace. It is where she spent quiet times with her grandfather.

His life was such a beautiful picture of God's love for mankind. Maybe that is the reason she always headed to the swamp when she needed to find solitude with the Lord. The uniqueness of the swamp brings peace and calm to her otherwise wounded and anxiety-filled soul.

Like a cloud descending upon her, Salome suddenly felt embraced by the presence of the Lord. Tears filled her eyes, yet she held them back. She whispered to the Lord, "I am so confused. I really thought this would be a quick, maybe four to five month recovery, with no issues to deal with. I looked forward to having the down-time to spend catching up on reading and studying Your love letters. Now, what am I going to do with all this time off? My clients will not wait that long for my recovery before they are forced to find someone else to fill the position.

"This is Your will, Lord?" Tears of anger, frustration and doubt flowed down her cheeks. Looking up to heaven, she said, "I know, it comes down to one thing. Will I trust Your way and You will, or not?"

Continuing on her way, Salome abruptly realized that it could be a very long time before she would be able to come to this safe haven again. God's presence surrounded her, creating a sweet, peaceful release as she gazed up and took in a deep breath while wiping the tears from her eyes.

All of a sudden, the tranquil silence was broken by a very loud, boisterous noise. As she searched, turning every which way, trying to see who or what would dare disturb the sanctity of her peaceful solitude, they appeared. Ducks were loudly quacking out landing plans to one another.

Halting on the end of the boardwalk, Salome spotted the river silently winding its way around the swamp. She watched as each duck landed in a different spot on the water. Slowly and quietly she tip-toed ahead to the benches at the end of the boardwalk, then sat down. Salome gazed at the joy and exhilaration of the ducks as they splashed and dunked their heads into the water. What a loud, clamorous racket they made! Finally, the ducks settled down and calmly floated in the water.

Thinking back to the sermon, Salome recalled part of a teaching she'd missed earlier. After eight hours of flying, the fowl had to rest at least three hours before they could continue on their journey. As Salome sat on a bench at the end of the boardwalk she surveyed her surroundings. Here nestled in the middle of the thick cypress, oak and pine forest, with the swamp behind her and the river in front of her, she then understood. The "rest" she must endure is long overdue.

Lifting her head and raising her eyes skyward she said, *Lord, it is time for me to cast all my cares on You because I know You care for me. You promised me in Your Word that all this will work out for my good and for Your glory. You also told me to consider the birds of the air, they don't plant, harvest or store food in barns, yet, You feed them. I'm Your child, Lord, Your daughter, and since You take care of them, I know You will take care of me. I choose to trust and believe You, Lord Jesus.* (See Matthew 6:25-27, Romans 8:28 and 1Peter 5:7)

Surprisingly, a song Salome wrote a few years earlier came to mind. The chorus was created from words in scripture, listed in Psalm 27:13-14. At the time she was facing a situation in life that just did not seem fair or make any sense at all. Those words are what Salome held on to through that difficult period. Once again, she needed to hold them tightly.

I would have lost hope unless I had believed,

I'd see the goodness of the Lord.

Wait on the Lord and be of good courage,

and He will strengthen your heart.

Wait on the Lord!

As the words of the song played in her mind, she finally realized, the key word is **believed**. "This testing will prove exactly what my heart believes about You", she mumbled. Keeping her eyes on the beautiful blue sky, she understood the message God was giving her.

Softly, the Lord spoke into her spirit a simple question, *"Salome, what do you **really believe** about Me and what I will do for you?"*

For His anger lasts only a moment,
but His favor lasts a lifetime,
weeping endures for the night,
but behold joy comes in the morning.
(Psalm 30:5 NIV)

CHAPTER 7

THE DAY AFTER surgery, Salome woke up very sore, yet hopeful. The pain was not as bad as everyone said it would be. Last night, she had experienced a terrible reaction to both morphine and co-deine. In the stillness of that early morning, Salome wondered why anyone would purposely take the stuff. Yet, she knew many people who were addicted to pain-killers and she was determined she would not add another problem to an already serious situation. With the side effects she had experienced from both drugs, she was done with pain-killers.

The door to her room opened and Doctor Calvin walked in-side. "Surgery was successful, Salome". "Pain is expected, espe-cially with this type of back surgery. People are surprised at how many back muscles are required to do very small tasks. I have a prescription for medication while you are at home. Just take it slow, and I'll see you in two weeks."

Smiling, Salome said, "No more pain-killers, thank you! I've had my fill of those things. At the moment, I'm taking only muscle relaxers and I'm fine. Is there a non-narcotic pain-killer I could take when needed?"

"You're not on any pain meds now?" Doctor Calvin could not hide his surprise. "Most patients stay on them for at least three weeks."

Making a face, Salome said, "No, thank you! I've had enough.

My reactions to the drugs was horrible."

"All right, I'll give you a prescription for a mild non-narcotic pain-killer and another one that is stronger. Don't hesitate to take it if needed, Salome. Physical and occupational therapists are due to come in and show you the proper way to get up, walk and sit. Going home will depend on how well you do through those exercises. If all is well, after lunch you will be able to go home. Sound good?" Smiling broadly, Doctor Calvin opened the door to walk out of her room.

"Thanks," Salome said as he headed out.

The nurses came in bright and early to remove all the tubes and wires attached to her body. Salome remembered very little from the time the nurses and doctors had placed her on the gurney until sometime during the night, right before Addie left. Lizzy was sick and Salome remembered, very briefly, telling Addie to go home and take care of Lizzy. Honestly, Salome felt good about the surgery, although she had not attempted the feat of rising from the bed. That would be her next step.

Before surgery, Salome had exercised to strengthen her stomach, back, legs and side muscles. She hoped those exercises would help her recover more rapidly.

A few minutes later, the physical and occupational therapists walked into her room. Smiling at them, Salome stated, "I'm being double-teamed this morning!"

The physical therapist laughed and said, "Great, a patient with a sense of humor this early in the morning! How are you today, my dear? Ready for a waltz down the hall and back?"

Moving him aside, the occupational therapist stepped up and stated simply, "Do you think it might be a good idea to get her out of bed first?" Glancing at Salome, the OT shook his head, smiled and replied, "The PT always tries to put the cart before the horse, so to speak! OK, ready to try and roll over to the side of the bed? Let me put the bed down, and then we will start the process.

Where is your belt?"

Salome smiled and stated, "I didn't know my Doctor would send Mutt and Jeff to help me break out of here!" Laughing, Salome said, "The corset is on the chair."

"Ohhhh, a wise gal ok, we can handle that," The OT said with a laugh. "Now, slowly turn to this side of the bed."

Salome did as she was told and was surprised that the movement didn't feel all that bad. Maybe the pain meds did do something after all besides make her itch and throw up.

"Great job, now move your legs until they are almost hanging off the bed. Wonderful! Grasp the sidebars of the bed and carefully rise to a sitting position," the OT gently spoke. Watching every move Salome made, he smiled his approval as she accomplished each feat! "Wow, you are doing fantastic for your first time. I'm impressed," he chided. "Now I'm going to tell you something and I want you to take this very seriously. DO NOT MOVE!!! DO NOT leave that bed without your belt. This brace may be big and have the "look" of a corset but it will hold your spine in place. Let me see YOU put it on."

Salome smiled at him and slowly began the process of putting on the corset/belt. She looked up and said, "You sure are bossy this early in the morning. Gee, it's obvious you love your position of authority!"

The PT burst out laughing and simply stated, "She's got your number, Buddy, or should I say Bossy!"

Bossy smirked then spoke, "Don't worry, you're next!" Once he was satisfied with her ability to move correctly without causing damage, he headed for the door with one simple comment. "OK, no BLT for the next couple of months. Understand?"

Confused, Salome looked at him and asked, "What's bacon, lettuce and tomatoes have to do with this?"

"Not food," OT stated, "no **B**ending, **L**ifting or **T**wisting! BLT, get it?"

Laughing softly she shook her head! "You are crazy," she stated!

Mr. PT walked over and said, "Ok, now that you have your corset on, let's take a waltz up and down the hall. If you get light-headed, weak or dizzy, just let me know and we'll stop. First, let me pull the door open and tell the nurse something."

Salome stood slowly, making sure she had her balance, then began walking toward the opened doorway. Standing a few step from the bed, she waited for the PT to come back.

Walking into the room, the PT looked at her and said, "What are you doing? You *are* supposed to wait for me."

Salome smiled and stated, "You told me to stand up and get ready to walk, and I was just following your directions. You did not tell me to wait!"

The PT put out his arm as though he was her escort to a fancy ball and simply said, "Ok then, Sweet Pea, let's dance!"

Walking out of the room, Salome took her first step into the hall. Smiling, she suddenly felt the sweet presence of the Lord walking beside her. In that instance she was filled with peace and joy, understanding that He was indeed giving her the strength she needed.

The PT asked frequently if she was ok, cheering her on with each step she took.

Finally, Salome told him, "Goodness, I'm fine, how are you?" When they got to the end of the hall, she glanced at him once again and repeated, "I'm fine."

"Wanna waltz on down to the nurses' station," the thera-pist asked?

Salome said, "Sure, I love taking long walks in the hallway with big strong PT men!"

Laughing they continued their walk toward the nurses' station. Each nurse, one by one, stood at the station with their mouths hanging open. The first thing that came to Salome's mind was the stylish hospital gown with the wide open back the hospitals insisted people wear. Did the therapists forget to make sure it was closed? Turning, Salome tried to get a look at the back of her gown.

Her escort became upset and asked, "What are you doing? NO twisting, remember? Boy, we are gonna have to keep our eyes on you!"

"Is my gown open or something? Why are they all gawking at me with their mouths hanging open?" she questioned.

"Well, Sweet Pea, normally, patients can't walk this far after the type of back surgery you had. Actually, following each move, our patients usually do lots of moaning and groaning. The nurses are surprised at your attitude and your ability to walk. None of us are used to handling a spunky, sassy-pants gal the day after surgery. You must have been a very active person before this," he replied.

Excitement filled her heart! She could already see God's hand working on her behalf! "Actually, I prayed! God is the One helping me, so everyone will know there is a GOD in heaven who still answers prayer."

The PT gazed at her and said to all the nurses, "This girl gets to go home today!"

Cheers and shouts of joy went up in response! Salome smiled sweetly as she gazed to heaven and whispered a simple, "Thank You, Lord!"

For everything there is a season,
a time for every activity
under heaven.
Ecclesiastes 3:1NIV

CHAPTER **8**

GLANCING AT THE bedside clock, Salome could not believe it was only four A.M! Everything in her wanted to stay in bed, yet her body felt stiff from lying down. She opened her eyes and her heart filled with thanksgiving and prayer for all the Lord was doing.

Waiting in the silence of the early morning hours, she considered the events that had taken place since surgery. There is just no way around it. This jaunt of her journey would have to be walked out one step at a time. She thanked God for everything she could think of, her ability to walk, move, sit up, smile, see, hear and feel. Never before had she realized how much she took for granted.

Reflecting, she thought, *Has it already been three weeks since surgery?* Salome had been warned the recovery would be a slow and painful process yet, it wasn't pain that was keeping her awake. She was tired of lying in bed! Pondering back to previous days, she knew she was never one to sleep until noon, being way too hyper for that. This complete stand-still was a new thing and very hard to get used to.

By six A.M., Salome couldn't stand it any longer and decided to get up. She slowly turned to her left side, moved her legs toward the end of the bed and carefully scooted towards the edge. Pushing her legs over the side of the bed, she rolled to a sitting position. Weakness had been a problem since surgery; therefore, she sat still to stabilize. Cautiously, Salome stood up and made her way to the bathroom, taking her corset with her. She put it on and secured it in place. Standing quietly for a moment and donning her dark blue silk robe, she headed for the hall. Salome considered, *Who would ever think it would take so much effort just to get out of bed!*

Remembering how strong she had been before surgery left her feeling distressed. Never in Salome's life could she remember being so needy and reliant on others for even the simple things of life. Things like stepping in and out of the bathtub, picking something up that she had dropped, doing laundry, cooking, or cleaning her home. Bending, lifting or twisting was unattainable with the big corset in place. Standing for any period of time simply was not possible. A sitting position was no better. Lying down gave relief for only a short time before her body became stiff. It was the only time in Salome's life she remembered experiencing such helplessness. Depending on God is fine, but placing trust in people to help her is something she considered almost impossible. Whenever she depended on others, they would ultimately let her down. Trusting people was harder than she thought it would be.

Because a chill hung in the house, Salome turned up the thermostat as she walked toward the kitchen and dining room. She decided a cold front must have moved through during the night. Passing the hallway table, Salome picked up her Bible, notebook and journal, and then continued on to the kitchen. Already, she was dreaming of a big, hot, steaming cup of cappuccino. *At least I can still do that,* she thought!

Thoughts of her kitchen always brought joy and warmth to her heart. She and Lewis loved to entertain. This area was created to accommodate large gatherings of family and friends for all kinds of celebrations, of which there had been many.

Upon entering the room she stopped in the doorway, pressed the light switch and took in the scene before her. The large room contained both kitchen and dining areas. A beautiful tile-covered bar, with three lovely wrought iron high-backed stools divided the two areas. Salome designed the bar and was especially pleased with the way it complimented the two spaces.

Salome purposely chose the colors of nature for her home and she lavished this room in color. It was dressed in vibrant greens and yellows. The distressed furnishings were painted an antique black color. Pickled cabinets embraced the walls surrounding the kitchen area. The cabinets were hung with space between them and the ceiling to host an eclectic collection of antique glassware and figurines.

The dining room itself faced the backyard and was surrounded on three sides by large windows, giving one the impression of being in a four-season porch. Removing her favorite large black coffee mug from the cabinet, she measured and poured the cappuccino mix inside. Turning, she walked to the hot water dispenser and poured the hot liquid into the cup. Salome stirred the mixture until it was dissolved. Grabbing the Sweet Italian Cream container from the fridge, she poured it into her cup and slowly stirred it. With a big smile on her face, she breathed in the sweet aroma then took her first sip. "Yummy! Such a sweet treat on a brisk early morning," she whispered.

Walking toward the dining room with cappuccino in hand, Salome heard the voice of the Lord calling out to her. Enveloped in an aura of peace she sat down at the large dining room table and gazed outside but, at this time of day, all she could see was darkness. The dawning of the new day lay at hand, although the sun had not yet made its appearance.

Taking a sip of her cappuccino, she opened her Bible and begins reading. Early morning was her favorite time of all! Alone in the stillness just before the break of day, is where she approached God. At the crack of dawn everything is fresh and new and nothing seems impossible.

After twenty minutes or so she glanced up, suddenly struck

with the scene right outside the dining room windows. Everything appeared so much brighter. An outline of the forest and trees emerged before her, whereas just minutes ago everything remained hidden in complete darkness.

The house itself sat in the center of a clearing in a tree-filled acre-and-a-half lot. Toward the back of the property a full thick forest with a variety of trees stretched out. Encircling her home were tall pines, graceful sycamores, oaks and crepe myrtle trees. Salome loved their home and the yard surrounding it. The ambiance was quiet, peaceful and tranquil.

Squirrels, birds, ducks, rabbits, raccoons, dogs, cats and a possum or two, all lived within the confines of the property. The animals loved Salome's yard, filled with bird feeders, bird baths, gardens and a few scattered trails winding along the side of the house and woods. As her heart became lost in the blessings God poured on their little domain, all she could do was smile as tears of gratefulness trickled down her cheeks.

Spellbound, Salome kept her eyes focused on the horizon as the new day birthed before her. She watched the sun rise higher and higher in the sky and tangible details began to make their appearance. The forest and trees had been there the whole time, but in darkness, before daybreak, they stood aloof, hidden from view. Fusing the thoughts in her mind she understood that the time before the dawning of a new day, is exactly like the grey seasons in our life.

Psalm 30:5 NIV came to mind, *For His anger lasts only a moment, but His favor lasts a lifetime, weeping endures for the night, but behold joy comes in the morning.* Verse 11 and 12 NIV from that same Psalm says, *You turned my wailing into dancing, You removed my sackcloth and clothed me with joy, that my heart may sing to You and not be silent. O Lord my God, I will give You thanks forever.*

In that second, Salome knew God's plan for her was there, in what she deemed grey seasons. All she had to do was believe! These are seasons of unknown times in our lives, that time in life where we walk as though blind, when nothing seems clear.

When Salome walked through those places before, she wondered, *Did I miss God?* But in her heart, His words spoke in a sweet, gentle whisper, *"I am directing your steps. Just trust Me!"* (See Proverbs 20:24) Yet, trusting appears to be the hardest thing to do because **nothing** is clear. It requires blind confidence, belief and faith in God alone.

As Salome reminisced over all the things that had happened during the past few years, she could not make sense of any of it. Each time, she thought *Breakthrough surely is around the corner,* a bend in the road would appear and suddenly she would realize the path was longer than she imagined.

Once again, she plodded forward on a journey that seemed never-ending. Deep in her heart, she knew it was all part of a bigger perspective, God's perspective. After all, He is the Author and Finisher of our faith. (See Hebrews 12:2)

In one of the books in heaven, her story had already been written before the worlds began. She had to trust Him and walk in His ways. Then the story He had written for her life would play out here on earth.

A light rain began to fall and Salome could not resist the pull that came from deep within her heart. If she could step underneath His gentle rain, maybe the offences and sins in her life would be washed away. The Bible is clear; her sins were forgiven and washed away by the blood of Jesus but, in Salome's mind, she fought a continuing battle of guilt, shame condemnation and the ability to forgive herself. She would not be able to move forward until she let go the things of her past. *Lord, whatever your plan is, I may not understand it but I'm going to follow it.* She whispered.

Going out the back door to the porch, she walked to the screen door, opened it and stepped outside. Salome held her face up toward heaven and whispered, "Lord, wash the things holding me back all away and forgive me for doubting You. Even as the circumstances screamed *'You're going down,'* I know You, Jesus! How could I have doubt? Please forgive me and wash my sins away so I can move forward toward the destiny You've prepared for me. Above all, Jesus, help me to rely on You, no matter how the circumstances may appear."

Even though she was unaware of it, the greatest obstacles in her path were still pride and fear. Because she held onto the fear and allowed it to become bigger than God, pride took advantage and stepped in. *Sadly,* she thought, *if I search to the foundation of the walls I erect to protect myself, it always come down to pride.*

As she stepped back and considered the great love and tenderness the Lord had for her in the midst of her blunders, all she could do was rejoice in His greatness. Her smallness did not matter at all today. Breakthrough would come only by repenting and focusing on the Father and the Lord Jesus. Peace washed over Salome as she allowed Him to remove the hard parts of her heart and replace them with love and compassion. Choosing to embrace the fact that she is forgiven, changed, loved, covered and completely surrounded in His mercy and grace, is a decision only she could make.

Salome stood with arms outstretched, feet slightly apart and her face looking straight up to the sky. The falling rain gently soothed her in a fresh, cleansing stream. Each drop felt like God's kiss, and at that moment, she knew His love for her would endure for all eternity. His love, that perfect love, would cast out all fear.

As she continued basking in His presence, rain fell upon her face and continued in ripples down her cheeks to the ground. Turning, she slowly walked back inside the house. Hanging up her damp dark blue robe in the utility room, she picked up a silk, red-flowered robe hanging on the coat rack and headed back to the dining room to study the Word.

Today is the first day of the rest of my life, she whispered. *Muddling over the past years only reminded me of the story of Joseph.* (Genesis 37-50) She picked up her journal, turned it to a fresh page, and began to write.

Joseph went through many grey years in his life. As each day passed into another, his circumstances only seemed to get worse. Yet, his breakthrough finally came. In just one day, God raised Joseph from the prison to the palace. In Joseph's younger life he dreamed many dreams, most of which he did not understand. He never imagined that his dreams would come true, because his life was ripped apart when his jealous brothers sold him to passing gypsies.

Imagine how he felt when he was purchased as a slave in Potiphar's house. Finally gaining Potiphar's trust, he is then betrayed by Potiphar's wife. Joseph is thrown into prison for something he did not do however, when the timing of the Lord was right, God raised Joseph to his destiny!

Salome stopped writing for a moment and envisioned how Joseph must have felt. Putting her pen to paper, she began to write once again. *Joseph had to wonder if he had missed God. Would his nightmare ever end? How could he continue, one step at a time, in a path that seemed to lead to deeper agony and heartache? What happened to the dreams he had so many years before? These are the grey seasons in life, the time that exists between the dream or vision and its fulfillment. The grey season is a blind walk of faith while being shrouded in darkness.*

Salome needed to embrace her grey season and patiently walk through it. She had a decision to make. Would she choose to thank God and praise Jesus in the midst of it, or would she fight Him? The choice was hers alone. A scripture came to mind, Proverbs 3:5-6 NIV, Trust in the Lord with all your heart and lean not unto your own understanding. In all your ways acknowledge Him and He will direct your paths.

As Salome placed her pen on the table, she realized she had only one choice. She would pray for God's perspective through her grey season and praise Him, regardless. Closing her eyes, she imagined herself embracing God's plan to her heart, owning it, as Jesus owned the cup of Calvary's hill. Considering the cross, she realized how tiny her cup was compared to the horror Jesus walked through. Leaning on her own understanding would never do because His ways are not her ways and His thoughts not her thoughts. (See Isaiah 53:8-9) She also remembered Jeremiah 17:5-10 NLT, then wrote it down.

*⁵ This is what the LORD says: "**Cursed** are those who put their trust in mere humans, who rely on human strength and turn their hearts away from the LORD. ⁶ They are like stunted shrubs in the desert, with no hope for the future. They will live in the barren wilderness, in an uninhabited salty land.*

*⁷ "But **blessed** are those who trust in the LORD and have made the LORD their hope and confidence. ⁸ They are like trees planted along a riverbank, with roots that reach deep into the water. Such trees are not bothered by the heat or worried by long months of drought. Their leaves stay green, and they never stop producing fruit. ⁹ "The human heart is the most deceitful of all things, and desperately wicked. Who really knows how bad it is? ¹⁰ But I, the LORD, search all hearts and examine **secret motives**. I give all people their due rewards, according to what their actions deserve."*

Salome continued writing, *In times like this, the Lord allows a fire to burn away the chaff from His children. Anything that holds them bound will be destroyed by the blaze, yet the rewards are enormous. Once I get to the other side, freedom, courage, understanding and humility will be my portion. The Lord is the only One who knows the hearts of man, and if I lean on my own understanding the harvest listed in Jeremiah 17 is clear.*

As I trust in the Lord, He will lead me to the destiny He has planned for me. After all, Jesus is going before me preparing the way. If anything would cause me to fall, He is faithful to remove it as I diligently seek Him. (See Isaiah 57:14) As Salome thought about this new day, she realized it was the equivalent to those sometimes lonely grey seasons in her past.

I must become a watchman on the wall, observing, waiting, learning and eager for the dawning of the new day. Something good is coming and it is right around the corner. I can almost feel it, breathe it and see it. Psalm 126:1-6 NASB 1 When the LORD brought back the captive ones of Zion, we were like those who dream. 2 Then our mouth was filled with laughter and our tongue with joyful shouting; then they said among the nations, "The LORD has done great things for them." 3 The LORD has done great things for us; we are glad. 4 Restore our captivity, O LORD, as the streams in the South. 5 Those who sow in tears shall reap with joyful shouting. 6 He who goes to and fro weeping, carrying his bag of seed, shall indeed come again with a shout of joy, bringing his sheaves with him.

Salome stopped writing for a moment and began meditating on those verses. Suddenly, revelation soaked in! In grey seasons, we place one foot in front of the other and scatter the Word of God wherever we go. Our walk then becomes one of total blind faith.

Salome smiled to herself, thankful the Lord woke her when He did. Otherwise, she would have missed the dawning of a new day and the breakthrough she so longed for.

A thought struck her and she began writing again. *I wonder how many people miss this time with You, Lord? Every single person has this opportunity presented before them each day. How many rise, while it's still dark, to seek Your face in the quiet of a new day dawning? It is Your desire to spend time with Your children, to show them new revelations that only You can enlighten. Disappointments and discouragements can cause a heart to harden if they are not brought to You and left, lying at Your feet. In the quiet, hidden place within Your presence, we gain proper*

*perspective. People miss the privilege and joy of dropping every-
thing at Your feet, instead, they continue onward in the rat race
of life! If they could feel You surround them with goodness and
love, I know that they would welcome the time spent with You.
Understanding of Your great mercies would emerge like dew on
the grass at the dawn of a new day.*

Gazing out the window, Salome laid her pen down and allowed the Lord to permeate her in His love. She could finally
rest, knowing her heart and life were in His hands. A smile began
to spread on her face as she grasped the deep abiding love Jesus
held for her.

Embracing His love, she began to write again. *My heart is held
within strong hands, Jesus' hands that took nails that should have
been in my hands. Jesus' hands that hold me up when I am weak
and Jesus' hands that prepare the path ahead so I can walk and
not stumble.*

"Oh, Lord, they can't know what they are missing," she
whispered!

Salome continued to watch as the day dawned, and within its
dawning, hope began to birth deep within her heart. There, in the
quiet of the early morning hours, she laid her heart anew on His
altar of love. She turned all the hard areas over to Him. No more
survival mode! "I want to not only live life, but **feel life**, every bit
of it, she whispered. Picking up her pen she resumed writing.

*Hardened hearts cannot experience true joy, peace, or love.
Everything is filtered through the veil of those things that caused
hearts to be hardened. People with stony hearts cannot begin to
see through God's perspective because their spiritual eyes are
blurred. With His help, every veil covering my heart will be removed. I will face fear head-on, because I know that Perfect Love
and fear cannot reside in the same place. (See 1 John 4:18) They
are complete opposites.*

A new thought came to her as she continued to write. *Our*

physical heart has four chambers. If any of the chambers stop functioning, we die. So if our spiritual heart's chamber stays closed, our ability to function properly dies as well. The ability to love, laugh, feel, hurt, cry and grieve are gone until that part of our heart is freed. God must be allowed full access into all the parts of our heart in order for us to experience complete healing.

The scripture came to mind, *Love the Lord your God with all your heart, all your soul, all your mind.* (Matthew 22:37) *If I loved Him with **all** my heart, then I would give Him open access to every area.*

She remembered in Genesis 22, when God required Abraham to sacrifice his son, Isaac, on the altar. At that moment, Abraham proved to the Lord that God owned all of his heart.

Salome considered and realized something amazing. "What about us?" she thought. "God blesses us with vision, children, grandchildren, ministry, books, music, job, paycheck, home, walking, climbing, bending, lifting, health, land, clothing, food, cars, and so much more. Am I willing to give those things back to Him unhindered, letting them go completely if necessary? How about my broken and shattered dreams and the unforgivness and bitterness? Am I willing to trust Him with those, as well? The real question is evident. Do I really love God more than all of these? If so, my heart will let go. I will allow Him to have His way, especially in this, my grey season. Instead of the wall I erected, I will trust Him to be my protector!"

As Salome considered what God showed her, joy filled her as she began to understand that she could only go forward by letting everything go! Before she could face another day, she would have to place her future within the palms of His hands. With that revelation, she prayed,

"Father, please forgive me for closing any part of my heart to You. Forgive me for holding back anything I believed was mine. I have been bought with the price of Your blood on the cross.

Everything about me and my life belongs to You, my past, present and future. I know there are things in my heart that I am unaware of, but You know they are there. I hand over all the keys of my life to You. Open every area Lord, and make me Yours completely. Let every detail that You have planned for me come to pass. As the Author and Finisher of my faith, I will trust in You. I am ready to live whatever story You want to tell in my life. Lord, heal me and teach me how to help others who struggle as I have. As You close doors, help me to embrace Your will. As I turn to the next chapter of life, help my heart to welcome everything that comes with open arms. Prepare me and take any blinders or veils away from my eyes so I can see the truth You set before me. Open my ears to hear Your voice and my mind to understand Your revelations. Give me Your perspective, Lord, an aerial view. Thank You for new beginnings and for seeing things from a different point of view. Your perception, dear Lord, in Jesus', name, I pray."

She closed her journal as she finished praying. Holding the precious book to her bosom, Salome lowered her head and smiled. In that moment, she understood her battle was just beginning. However, in the midst of this battle, she knew that God would fill her with His peace.

Just then, God reminded Salome of the meaning of her name, peace and tranquility. Peace was the very thing being established in her life. In that moment she felt more love, peace, joy, mercy and grace than ever before.

A new page in her life was turning. Finally, she was ready to experience life in its fullest! The Lord gently whispered, *The devil comes to steal, kill and destroy,* **but I** *have come that you may have* **life and that life, more abundantly**. (John 10:10) *Now daughter, enjoy life no matter what it holds!*

Rejoicing in this new revelation, Salome laid her journal aside and started giggling. Trembling with excitement, she stood up from the table and grabbing her now empty cup, walked to the sink and rinsed it out. Singing and slowly dancing about, she glanced out of the windows and realized anew that God had allowed her to see the birthing of another new day. "Thank You Lord, for this privilege," she breathed.

Charm is deceptive and beauty is fleeting,
but a woman who fears the Lord is to be praised!
Give her the reward she has earned,
and let her works bring her praise
at the city gate.
Proverbs 31:30-31 NIV

CHAPTER 9

SALOME WAS AN outdoor person. She thrived in the open-air, delighting in long walks, hiking through woods and riding her bicycle. The inability to get around as she used to was hard. Where striving quickly had been a part of her life, she was now reduced to what she felt was a slow crawl. Now, hopping around was really hobbling in place. But, all in all, she was progressing well considering surgery had only been five weeks ago.

Heading for some fresh air, Salome walked into the yard outside and breathed deeply. "Already five weeks since surgery!" Gazing toward heaven, Salome said, "Thank You, Lord, only one more month of wearing this corset and prayerfully I'll be able to drive again!" The brilliantly clear, crystal-blue sky stretched before her with not a cloud to be seen. A gentle breeze blew, swaying the tall pine trees in a soothing dance. Ducks waddled across the yard creating their raucous, quacking sound as they headed for the pond next door. Salome chuckled as they passed by, ignoring the fact that she was even there. Tiny birds sang their delightful, individual bird songs, and the sweet smell of jasmine floated on the wings of the gentle wind. The squirrels, not to be outdone, played a game of chase around the trunk of one of the trees.

The scene before her appeared like a magical fairyland. Smiling, Salome relaxed as peace and calm floated down upon her like a fluffy cloud. *No matter how things appear, God is in control*, she reminded herself. Nature always seemed to serve as a silent reminder that God is here and He cares!

She continued toward two large pine trees and slowly lay down in the chaise lounge. There, in the otherworldly atmosphere, was the very place she needed to be. Resting, she basked in the knowledge that God has everything concerning her in the palms of His hands and He loves her. Jeremiah 29:11 NIV said, "I know the plans I have for you," declares the Lord. "Plans to prosper you and not to harm you, plans to give you a hope and a future."

As Salome lay there, the conversations of previous days began to roll through her mind. Many broken, young women had been seeking her for wisdom and advice from the Word of God. She remembered her own background and the struggle she had to accept God's truth and promises for herself. At that moment she began to apprehend exactly what they were up against.   Young women today are coming out of many tragic situations. Sad to say, they cannot grasp the joy of just being a woman, one adored by the Sovereign Father in Heaven. How can they, with no true example before them on earth?

Salome whispered, "With the role models Hollywood is parading before us today, what do we expect?" These precious young women are coming from broken homes, dysfunctional families; physical, mental and emotional abuse. They are treated like a piece of meat instead of the beautiful creature with the heart God has designed for each one. Hollywood's version of what women are supposed to be has influenced all of us.

Salome remembered shows like *Father Knows Best, Lassie* and *Leave it to Beaver* where women were treated like precious jewels, gifts from God to be protected, cherished and adored. "O Lord, how this world has deceived us!" Salome whispered.

Some of the pressures women carry today are working a full-time job while taking care of the home, raising their children and paying bills. Forget about being protected or cherished!

Heartbreaking as it is, they are trying to carry a weight on their shoulders they were never meant to bear. Then there is the pornography industry that has driven our society to embrace women only as creatures to be used for pleasure as though they did not possess souls that could be wounded and broken. In the minds of some men women are considered nothing more than chattel to do their bidding.

The deception is not only in women. Men have no idea how they are to behave toward a woman or how to be the head of their household. Many men grew up without fathers in their home and watched while Mom had to handle all the responsibility. Where are the "true role models" for men or women to follow?

It seems as though Hollywood, television commercials, all form of media and pornography teach men that women are nothing but bodies to be used for their enjoyment. At the same time, these influences teach women that their worth is solely in their appearance instead of their heart, a heart that should be loved and protected. The deception is disastrous in marriages and families.

Has someone changed the rules along the way, without our knowledge? Do people know what a healthy marriage and family look like anymore?

Out of the blue, Salome remembered the "Woman's Lib Movement" of the 70's. As outrageous as it now seemed to her, she remembered being caught up in the movement, even participating in some of their demonstrations. However, even at the time she did not believe in everything they espoused. Actually, as she thought back on it, she wasn't sure what it stood for.

Solemnly she thought, *It seems as young adults, we have a tendency to embrace an agenda because we agree with a couple of points, not necessarily the entirety of the thing. In this way, the enemy uses young adults to accomplish his ends. Funny, I remember seeing everything through tunnel vision, because it is only through life experiences one can learn to see the whole picture. I remember clearly choosing what I wanted to see, hear and know.*

Meditating on this, she decided to look up the history of the "¹Woman's Lib Movement" to see how it evolved. Reluctantly, she slowly got up, leaving the comfort of her lounge chair, and headed toward the house. Walking away from the soft breeze and the overwhelming beauty of the day was hard; nevertheless, she knew it was something she needed to do. Taking one last look at the incredible cloudless, crystal-blue sky she walked onto the screened porch.

The fat twenty-five pound tabby cat named Minx, met Salome at the door. Knowing what was to come, she braced herself for the onslaught that was sure to occur. Meowing loudly in her deep gravelly voice, the obnoxious beast looked up at Salome and began to weave herself in and around Salome's legs. Arching her back, and purring loudly, the cat rubbed her head on Salome's foot. Grinning broadly, Salome reached down to pet the cat. The obnoxious creature swiped at her hand and growled loudly as if to say, 'My bowl is empty, bring me more food!' Being joggled, Salome headed toward the office when Minx reached over with her claws extended and grabbed Salome's pant leg, being drug behind as Salome tried to walk forward. Holding onto a chair, Salome shook her leg, finally dislodging the huge fur ball. Straightening up without delay, Salome made it through the porch and into her office.

"Whew," she breathed heavily! Chuckling, she slipped into her desk chair, turned and pushed the start button of her computer. When it opened, she clicked the "e" for Internet Explorer then sat back and began to do research on the root of the Women's Lib Movement.

The more she read the more startled she became! The movement did not begin in the 70's. It actually started in Europe in the 1860's. It was called the "Women's Suffrage Movement". Virginia Woolf's book *A Room of One's Own*, began the *first wave* in the

---

1   Information found in the following website: http://en.wikipedia.org/wiki/Feminist_movement

18th through the early 20th centuries. As with everything the enemy does, it had many good points. A woman's right to vote and to run for office in spite of marital status, were good reasons for the movement. Still, in the midst of Woolf's book, she declared that women were simultaneously *victims* of themselves as well as *victims* of men.

Salome thought, *In many countries, women **are** victims; they have no rights at all. Their fathers, brothers or husbands can legally abuse or kill them for any reason if they so desire.*

It wasn't hard to recognize Satan's work woven into the fabric of the movement. Many of the leaders of the first wave in America were from strong, conservative Christian groups. They were responsible for the 19th Amendment to the United States Constitution granting women voting rights in 1919. Those women paid a very high price for the privilege to vote that we enjoy today. This is a good thing, but still, something did not feel right. Finally, Salome realized what it was. The word *victim*!

Years ago, she recounted calling herself a "victim". The Lord told her to look up the word in the old 1923 *Webster's Dictionary* that her father had given her. Pulling that book off the shelf, Salome opened it and turned to the 'v' section and began to search for the word. When she found it, the definition illuminated the full meaning of the word "victim". From that moment on, Salome never called herself "victim" again. Webster's definition: **_Victim_**, *A living being sacrificed to some deity, as in a satanic sacrifice. Or in the performance of a religious rite; a creature immolated, or made an offering of.*

That's it! Satan convinced these women they were indeed victims instead of ladies to be cherished. What we believe about ourselves will define who we become. It is a choice; we will be defined by either the lies of the devil or the truth in God's Word. A small group of people, if they can make enough noise, can persuade masses that their deceptions are truth. Satan will always take a little truth and mix it in with his lies. In this way, people embrace the deception and throw away truth before ever examining the source.

The *second wave* of the Feminist Movement came to fight social and cultural inequalities as further political inequalities. This wave began in the 1960's and lasted through the 1980's. The book, written by Betty Friedan, *The Feminine Mystique,* fueled this movement. In her book, she described the problem with no name, the **dissatisfaction** of educated, middle class wives and mothers *like herself* who, looking at their nice homes and families, wondered *guiltily* if that is all there is to life. The vague sense of **dissatisfaction** plaguing housewives became a staple topic for women's magazines in the 1950's. But Friedan, instead of **blaming** individual women for failing to adapt to women's "proper role", **blamed** the role itself and a society that created it.

As Salome read through the article, the words **dissatisfaction** and **blame** caught her attention. Those two words cause more discord than anything else. If dissatisfaction of anything takes root in our hearts, we as humans, tend to blame someone else instead of searching our own hearts.

There is nothing new under the sun. It started in the Garden of Eden and it is sin! Instead of having thankful hearts, we bite the bait of dissatisfaction; then behold, the blame game begins. However, that sin set up the atmosphere for the third wave of feminism to do its damage.

The *third wave* of feminism arises in response to the perceived failures of the second wave. It called for a new subjectivity in feminist voice, where they began to focus also on racial issues. This led to the involvement and rallying of young feminists who really did not understand what had been involved in the previous movements. In this wave, the movement focused on equal pay and opportunity in the work force.

Salome had been part of this third wave and remembered *only* the equal pay and opportunities in the work force. She still believed if a woman did the exact same job as a man, she should be paid the same amount of money. Also, if a woman chose to work, more power to her.

At this time in history, divorce became more common and many women now found themselves to be single parents, fighting to make ends meet. Salome whispered to herself, "I've been though divorce and I promise the grass is only greener on the other side of the fence because there is a sewer tank buried there. Divorce is never easy. Two people that God made one in marriage are torn apart. If they had children, another level of pain and suffering surely comes with it."

Through the third wave, the movement accomplished the protection from employment discrimination, inclusion in affirmative action, abortion law reform, greater representation in media, and equal access to school athletics, congressional passage of an equal rights movement and more.

Oh my, as she read through that list, ABORTION law reform blew her mind! She noticed it was conveniently placed right in the middle where people could just read over it. Reviewing the things she had read, it was easy to see Satan's plan. There are great things worth fighting for. Yet, clearly, Salome could see that the breaking down and final destruction of the family unit and abortion all began in the feminist movement.

Everything written was one-sided, their view only. Through one woman's influence, because she was dissatisfied with being a stay-at-home-mom, the whole family structure changed. Apparently, this woman forgot about the great honor that is hers to raise loved, stable, secure and self-confident children. Instead, she planted seeds of dissatisfaction in the hearts of many young women. Today we have a nation that is filled with broken women trying to hold down several roles they were never designed to fill. How sly of the devil! He came in, planted seeds of doubt and discouragement and before you knew it, those seeds began to grow, producing the fruit of destruction.

We now live with the fruit produced from those seeds. Broken homes, broken children, abortion of millions of babies, all of this happened because of selfishness, dissatisfaction, blaming others and being blinded by lies of the enemy.

Dissatisfaction is a heart issue—not someone else's fault. It comes from a wound deep in our hearts that we choose not to address. The very act of dissatisfaction exposes one thing, pride. The feminist movement brought about many great things but along with it came much destruction. Salome knew first hand, that if you give the enemy an inch he will be delighted to take the proverbial mile.

A verse in **Philippians 4:11-12 NLT** came to mind. *11 Not that I was ever in need, for I have learned how to be **content** with what-ever I have. 12 I know how to live on almost nothing or with every-thing. I have learned the secret of living in every situation, whether it is with a full stomach or empty, with plenty or little.*

*1 **Timothy 6:6 NIV** But godliness with **contentment** is great gain. For, we brought nothing into the world and we can take noth-ing out of it.*

Overwhelmed by the enemy's cunning ploy, a thought be-gan to take shape in Salome's mind. Apparently, the woman who was so dissatisfied never read about the woman mentioned in Proverbs 31. If she would have ever taken the time to read Proverbs 31, I believe she would have been challenged by the character of this woman.

The Proverbs 31 woman was a great wife, mother, friend, neighbor, minister and business owner. (Proverbs 31:10-15 NASB) *Who can find a virtuous and capable wife? She is more precious than rubies. 11 Her husband can trust her, and she will greatly en-rich his life. 12 She brings him good, not harm, all the days of her life. 13 She finds wool and flax and busily spins it. 14 She is like a merchant's ship, bringing her food from afar.* [15] *She gets up before dawn to prepare breakfast for her household and plan the day's work for her servant girls.* (Today we could call her "servant girls", the dishwasher, microwave, washer/dryer, vacuum and the like.)

Can you believe, she grows her own garden and has her own business? (Verses 16-19) 16 *She goes to inspect a field and buys it; with her earnings she plants a vineyard.* [17] *She is energetic and strong, a hard worker.* [18] *She makes sure her dealings are profitable; her lamp burns late into the night.* [19] *Her hands are busy spinning thread, her fingers twisting fiber.*

This woman has no time to think about dissatisfaction because her eyes are on others not on herself. (Verse 20) *She extends a helping hand to the poor and opens her arms to the needy.*

There is no time for self, because her thoughts are centered on her family. Yet, at the same time, she does take care of herself. She makes sure all her family's needs are met and uses the gifts inside her to create a beautiful space around them. (Verse 21-22) [21] *She has no fear of winter for her household, for everyone has warm clothes.* [22] *She makes her own bedspreads. She dresses in fine linen and purple gowns.*

Because of her actions and life-style, her husband is well-known and respected. She also has another business using the gifts God has given her. (Verses 23-24) [23] *Her husband is well known at the city gates, where he sits with the other civic leaders.* [24] *She makes belted linen garments and sashes to sell to the merchants.*

As Salome looked up the next verses, she was amazed by the things she found. Being clothed with strength and dignity is the opposite of being clothed with shame and disgrace. You cannot have strength and dignity when you are clothed with dissatisfaction and blaming others for the things in your life now. Strength and dignity cannot hang around when you continue to hold on to shame and disgrace. This lady carefully keeps watch on everything to make sure the enemy has no access into her family! She is not lazy or selfish. As a matter of fact, it appears she had developed a balance of taking care of herself so she can be strong for her family and others.

Mulling this over, Salome remembered something her grandmother used to say. *An idle mind is a playground for Satan, especially for women. Gossip, slander, boasting and speaking what you "feel" are all playgrounds for Satan to destroy another's character.* That Proverbs 31 lady is such a beautiful woman, content and filling her mind with thoughts like family, neighbors, friends, the poor, hurting and needy. I can see no dissatisfaction within her life. (Verse 25-27) *25 She is clothed with strength and dignity, and she laughs without fear of the future. 26 When she speaks, her words are wise, and she gives instructions with kindness. 27 She carefully watches everything in her household and suffers nothing from laziness.*

This woman's life is so filled with joy and peace that it influences all of those with whom she comes in contact, especially her husband and children. Because of this, they arise and called her blessed and praise her for all she does. From what I see, her virtues have rubbed off on her family and friends. *28 Her children stand and bless her. Her husband praises her: 29 "There are many virtuous and capable women in the world, but you surpass them all!"*

So many women use their "charm" in order to get what they want. There is no thought about how it may affect others. I simply call it for what it is, *manipulation* or *witchcraft*. These are described under rebellion, which is related to the sin of witchcraft. 1 Samuel 15:23 NIV says: *For rebellion is like the sin of divination, (witchcraft), and arrogance, (pride), like the evil of idolatry. Because you have rejected the Word of the Lord, he has rejected you as king."* (Samuel is speaking of Saul who was crowned king. He did things his way instead of obeying God. Simply put, it is rebellion.)

Salome wanted to understand the definition of manipulation so she looked it up. This is what she found: *to control or play upon by artful, unfair, or insidious means especially to one's own advantage.* Whenever we only give one side to any issue, we are trying to manipulate the subject for our purposes. Nevertheless, while walking in the "act of manipulation", we are completely blinded to the truth.

Gazing through magazines, we see the young and beautiful. Yet, beauty that is only skin deep is deceptive. Physical beauty does go away eventually with age, in spite of face lifts, nips and tucks. However, a beauty that flows from a thankful and grateful heart that is in love with Jesus will never die. That type of beauty and charm is a rare jewel. The Proverbs 31 lady does not have to ask for praise because **her actions** automatically bring her praise from the One who loves her most, Jesus! *30 Charm is deceptive, and beauty does not last; but a woman who fears the LORD will be greatly praised. 31 Reward her for all she has done. Let her deeds publicly declare her praise at the city gate!*

This is who God destined women to be! As Salome reflected on the Proverbs 31 Woman, she could only think of words like creative, compassionate, merciful, filled with grace, charming, beautiful, accomplished, wise, courageous, strong, confident and dignified. She obviously was filled with joy, wisdom, kindness and peace. Her heart was free from fear and completely balanced, because God teaches her the art of living a full, stable life.

Desire sprang up inside Salome. She desired to be a woman described in scripture, so she prayed. *Father, as I read through Proverbs 31:10-31, I realize how far I have strayed from that beautiful woman. Bring me back, Lord! Show me the way so I can be all You predestined me to be! Please forgive every selfish, prideful and dissatisfied place in my heart then fill me instead with the virtues listed within these scriptures. Let this start with me, Jesus! Start in my heart and change me! Show me how to become a woman who keeps her heart, mind, eyes and ears turned to You, my family and those around me. Remind me of Proverbs 4:23 NIV that says,*

Above all else guard your heart, for it is the wellspring of life. Help me to guard my heart, Lord, and pay attention to what goes through my mind. I love You, Lord, and my desire is to please You and hear when I stand before You, "Well done my good and faithful servant!" I pray these things in the name of Jesus, amen!

Pondering this famous woman with no name, Salome knew that a deep, abiding love for the Lord would be another virtue to be desired. A woman who runs to the Lord when things happen, could honestly say, "I might not have the answer, but I will trust Him."

Now, this was Salome's time of resting, waiting and learning. God holds her future in the palm of His hands. She would trust Him to bring it about.

Scores of countless, young hurting women came to Salome's mind and she could only imagine what they are going through. Women who walked through divorce, abuses of all types, rejection, childhood trauma, etc all longing for and having need of "spiritual mama's"; mama's that would be sensitive to the Spirit of God. They need women who are patient and gently "dogmatic" in prayer and who would love them. Just like the Proverbs 31 Woman, Salome wanted to open her arms to them, reaching out with a heart filled with love and joy.

But first, Salome must be willing to allow God to deal with her own heart. Smiling, she understood that if God brought her to this "spiritual place", revealing this, He knows it is her time! Time to give Him access into everything hidden within her heart! Excitement for the future filled her! Yes, finally, she was ready to face everything hidden in her heart!

Footnote: All information on the Women's Suffrage Movement can be found at the following website. http://en.wikipedia.org/wiki/Feminist_movement

*This is now bone of my bone
and flesh of my flesh;
She shall be called woman,
for she was taken out of man.
Genesis 2:23 NIV*

CHAPTER **10**

THE GENTLE SONG of wind chimes woke Salome out of a sound sleep. It had been days since her sleep seemed this sweet and deep. Although she would normally love to hear the soft tinkling of the chimes, today, she would rather have had a few extra hours of sleep.

Rolling over slowly, she glanced at the clock on her antique bedside table. *What does that read? Only 4:00 A.M,* she thought. With a soft moan, she turned back and cuddled beneath thick blankets and an even thicker beige quilt. Lewis lay next to her gently snoring indicating he was asleep. Salome's lower back felt like a semi-truck rolled over it during the night. Groaning, she tried repositioning her pillows, yet nothing seemed to work.

She laid there thinking, *Was it almost a year ago when my back first gave out?* Salome remembered as though it had happened yesterday. March of last year, two discs ruptured and began traveling down her spine, to finally sit on her sciatic nerves. They sent shooting pains down her left leg. After three unsuccessful attempts with cortisone shots to control pain, surgery was inevitable.

Salome remembered waking up at three A.M. on a frosty October morning, for no apparent reason. She lay there silently gazing at the ceiling, when all of a sudden a thick soft blanket of peace floated down upon her, covering her completely. Smiling in awe, she felt the voice of the Lord softly speak within her heart, saying, *Trust Me, I will never leave you nor forsake you. You will go through surgery and learn new lessons throughout your recovery. Later, you will realize that the things you will learn have been there, within your heart, all this time. You will walk all the way through this. Now, rest, wait on Me and glean all I have to show you. I will shower you with peace in the midst of your storm as a testimony of Who I Am!*

Five weeks into Salome's recovery a "blood bubble" appeared on her back and continued to grow until it was the size of her fist. The doctor placed a large, gauze bandage over the bubble to cause her body to absorb the fluid. She could not determine which hurt more, the pain from the tape covering the bandage or the incisions and bubble. Her skin was super sensitive to tape adhesive and tore when the bandage was changed. Seclusion became her lot in life, yet she knew that God had specifically chosen this time to do His most intense and greatest work in her life. The Lord stormed the hidden depths of her heart, probing fiercely into its darkest recesses, revealing areas of pain and torment she had carefully hidden away.

The physical pain seemed unbearable at times, nevertheless, dealing with the spiritual pain was harder. God was the only one who could take that pain away. These problems emanated from the deep recesses where they had been buried in order for her to survive. Without realizing it, Salome had lived in survival mode for most of her life. God would not only expose the wounds, He would show her truth and His truth would set her free. (See John 8:32)

It had now been six weeks since the operation. In recent days the pain seemed more intense than right after surgery and, the reaction to the pain killers the doctor prescribed was worse than the actual pain. Whenever Salome became a bit anxious, she reminded herself of that October morning a few months ago when God show her that His peace would be her portion through this time. Once again, peace would become a shield against the fear, anxiety, loneliness and depression that seemed determined to overtake her.

A chill hung in the air, indicating the passing of the latest cold front. Salome couldn't believe it was already January 28th, a month-and-a-half had come and gone. She had great expectations for the New Year. But unexpectedly, it seemed life came to a complete standstill.

Due to the physically, challenging demands of her business, Salome had to close it. Closing the business was not something she was ready to do. Finances decreased considerably due to this and she felt as though the rug had been pulled out from under her. Life came to a complete standstill. Idleness became her enemy. Salome was used to doing things her own way and in her own time. Now she had to learn to wait on God's time.

Being an active person she loved gardening, hiking, long walks in the woods, playing with her grandchildren and serving others in any way she could. This time of complete stillness and seclusion was almost unbearable. One of her favorite volunteer positions was as a Bible teacher in a state prison. Once a month she also served as worship leader/speaker within other prisons. Being a people person, the separation began to take a toll, both spiritually and mentally. If she were to give it any thought what so ever, desperation, discouragement and depression would try to settle in on her like thick, dark, clouds sucking the very life from her. It was in this state of mind that she plunged into the study of women in the Bible.

―⸫⸫⸫⸫―

Grabbing her journal and Bible, she spotted her great-grandmother's journal sitting on the shelf in the box in which it came. Picking it up as well, Salome headed out to the kitchen to study. Slowly, laying the old, worn book on the table, she decided to first write in her own journal. Opening it, she saw that the last entry in her book was about the Proverbs 31 Woman. As it began to simmer in her mind, she thought about Eve.

Eve had no mom or dad to get in the middle of her marriage, no one to whom she could be compared. She is the first of everything womanly. Therefore, one would assume, she would have it easy! Although, as I consider how it truly may have been, I can imagine God's presence was a completely natural event. If I had to compare it, I think it would be the equivalent to bringing home a newborn baby. The parents would have prepared the nursery and supplied all the needs that baby might have once it made its arrival. In the same way, God prepared a garden oasis that would supply everything they needed to not only survive, but to thrive!

Salome glanced over at her grandmother's chronicle. Suddenly her curiosity was more than she could stand. Picking it up, she opened it to the first recorded entry. As she stared at the first sentence, she sat astonished. Apparently, she had inherited her grandmother's very, vivid imagination. She read:

I've been thinking about Adam and Eve. Without a good role model to follow, becoming the woman God desires me to be is a bigger challenge than I ever dreamed. Therefore, I've decided to study various women in the Bible to glean wisdom from them. Eve is my first choice, I can almost imagine the scene in the Garden of Eden.

Salome stopped reading as her jaw lowered in total amazement! Lifting her head, she whispered, "God, Your timing is unbelievable. Thank You, Lord! What chance is there that my grandmother would feel the same way I do?" With excitement flowing through her, she picked up grandmother's journal and once again began to read.

To Adam and Eve, it was likely a natural and normal thing for God to walk and talk with them. Actually, I suppose talking to the animals in a mind-to-mind concept, might have been nothing out of the ordinary for them, either.

Salome thought for a moment and remembered that some of her favorite authors wrote novels whose characters were talking animals. Humans and animals conversed together throughout the whole book. Just, maybe, this was not as far from the truth as we human beings believe. Can we really understand the way life was in the beautiful safe haven of the Garden of Eden? Lowering her head, she continued reading.

*God displayed His deep love for mankind in that beautiful Eden scene. He prepared a place for the first couple which met all of their needs. Adam was birthed as God breathed the breath of life into him. Imagine, Almighty God stooping down while He blew His life-giving-breath into Adam's lungs. As I picture this, it helps me understand how personal God is to each of us. The only reason I am here is because He not only designed and created me, but also because He has a plan for me and loves me. Sometimes, it seems **that** is the hardest thing to believe. God, perfect and magnificent, cares for a creature as insignificant as I am.*

I can envision Adam as he named the animals, and wondering, "Where is someone for me? Each animal has a mate but, there is no one after my own kind to become a mate for me."

In God's time, He caused Adam to fall into a deep sleep. Little did he realize that God would create a beautiful, precious jewel designed just for him. When Adam awakened, God presented him with the most glorious sight he had ever seen. God created this wondrous creature from a rib in Adam's side, just for him. She was not made of his head, to rule over him, nor of his feet, to be trampled on by him. No, she was carved out of his side to be equal with him, under his arm to be protected by him and, near his heart to be his cherished beloved! God did an awesome and beautiful thing when He created Eve.

I can almost envision the Father's delight and joy. It is there, in the perfect atmosphere of love, that the first marriage appears in scripture. What a beautiful, romantic setting God created!

Father gave Adam the responsibility of protecting and guarding Eve's heart. "You may eat the fruit from all the trees in the garden. However, do not eat from the tree in the middle of the garden, for on the day that you do, you will surely die," God warned. (See Genesis 2:20-23)

Everything in the garden was spoken into existence by God's Word; however, Adam and Eve were created, fashioned by God's hands. He formed Adam from dirt and He created Eve from a rib in Adam's side. She was a priceless gift, a treasure to be cherished and a worthy partner to encourage and influence Adam. The first couple lived in the environment of innocence and love. They never experienced shame, guilt, condemnation, fear or disgrace; they rested encircled by perfect Love, God, Himself.

In that environment, how did such a tragedy happen? Maybe Adam and Eve began to take their perfect and idyllic life for granted? Is that how the "fall of man" occurred? We must remember there is an enemy that may be unseen; however, he must never be underestimated. I can imagine the devil, sly as he is, whispering her name. "E-v-v-v-e." Being drawn to the Tree of the Knowledge of Good and Evil, in the middle of the Garden of Eden, Eve gave into Satan's deception. The same voice that speaks only lies, that twists truth, the same voice that tempted Eve with the forbidden fruit, is the same voice that speaks to us today. He hasn't changed. Perhaps for Eve, a "talking serpent" could have been an everyday occurrence. The serpent baited her, the same way he baits us today. That fruit looked good and pleasing to the eye. Oh, God, how many times have I bitten into that same type of bait!

"You will not surely die," the serpent said to the woman. "God knows that when you eat it your eyes will be opened and you will become just like Him, knowing good and evil." It is simple. The sly snake had Eve believe that God was holding out His best from her. "I cringe over the many times I have believed the same thing!"

When Adam and Eve bit the fruit, their eyes were instantly opened! Innocence was no more and they realized their nakedness. It only took a moment for shame, guilt, condemnation and then an unnatural fear of God, to consume their once pure and love-filled hearts. Their whole world crashed in around them and in that one moment of time, they knew, without a doubt, they had done something horrible, something unforgiveable. In reality part of them did die. One wrong decision had cost them everything that was good, pure and true. Due to their disobedience and rebellion, they were cast out into the unknown world. Their way back into the Garden of Eden, the only home they knew, stood forever barred to them.

Salome stopped reading and thought for a moment. Eve's mistake was listening to the serpent. Adam did not lead Eve, nor protect her from the serpent's deception. Instead, he accepted the forbidden fruit and became partaker of her sin. They were now swimming in a murky river of emotions caused by the knowledge of good and evil. A river God never intended them to experience.

Allowing all of this to simmer in her mind, Salome began to glimpse the true mercy and grace of God. God led them out of the Garden of Eden for their own protection. With a heart filled with all those negative emotions, what would have happened if they had eaten from the tree of life? They would have been tormented for eternity!

Quietly Salome whispered, "Oh God, many times I feel I've eaten forbidden fruit, fruit that has caused horrible torment of mind. There truly is nothing new under the sun. We are our own worst enemy." Bowing her head, she began reading again.

As the Lord God came into the garden, fear gripped Adam and Eve and they fell headlong into its trap. I can almost see the confusion and horror as Eve looked at Adam and Adam looked at Eve then whispered, "Hide! He cannot see us, He'll know we disobeyed."

Sin caused them to try and hide from the very One who created and deeply loved them. The only One who could help them. Condemnation, fear, shame and guilt consumed them when God called out their names. Now, the first blame game begins. God asked a very simple question, "Have you eaten the fruit from the tree I commanded you not to eat?" They never gave Him a straight answer.

Adam said, "The woman You gave me—she is the one who gave me the fruit from the tree and I ate it."

The Lord God said to the woman, "What have you done?"

Eve answered, "The serpent deceived me and I ate." (See Genesis 3, Fall of Man)

The whole scene is surreal and staggering and played out in many lives still today. No one takes responsibility for their actions. It's easier to blame someone else than to look in the mirror and accept that the person gazing back at you, is the one to blame. We are all responsible for our own decisions and actions. It's not mom or dad, friend or foe, it is me!

Salome stared at the words her grandmother wrote and saw the wisdom there. How many times did she blame Lewis, her mom and dad, whoever, instead of taking on the responsibility for her own actions? True, she had lived a life of abuse, however, the decisions she made from that point onward were hers alone.

Lowering her head, she continued reading. *God's love for Adam and Eve was great, therefore, because the Tree of Life is in the garden, He removed them from the perfection He had created for them. Sin came into being and He had to turn them out for their own protection. How it must have grieved the Almighty's heart to evict His very own children from the garden and His presence.*

This is the first example of tough love. In His mercy, He did not send them out naked. Jehovah killed the first blood sacrifice to cover their shame and nakedness with clothes from animal skins. Father God had their best interest at heart and loved them with an

CATHERINE MAE CLIFFORD

extravagant love.

How they must have craved and hungered, for the relationship they once knew with their Creator. To once again walk and talk with God, knowing that it could never be, must surely have created a profound longing and deep void within their hearts.

*Did Eve ask herself, "What have I done?" I wonder if she understood that she allowed the devil to talk her into becoming **dissatisfied** with the life God gave her. She sold their souls for a piece of fruit. And not only her and Adam's, but the souls of all generations to come. When we sin, we affect the people around us and even future generations. Once blaming became a habit, pride became a slave necklace that the enemy placed tightly around their necks, choking out their very lives. There was no going back to redo it.*

Meditating on their temptation, it is easy to see that the only thing the devil did was speak. That sly serpent didn't have to do anything else. Lord, help me to not listen to the words the devil whispers in my ears—keep me listening for Your still small voice.

Imagine, their life became a series of dissatisfactions, disappointments, pointing fingers and heartaches. Did they become bitter and resent each other? Did sin destroy their love for one another? Adam, the most intelligent and gifted man God ever created and Eve the loveliest woman both doomed because they listened to words, lies!

Adam and Eve bore sons, the first of many children. Cain followed by his brother Abel. The older, jealous of the younger, killed his brother. The first couple opened the door for every kind of sin imaginable and witnessed first-hand that sin not only continues but multiplies.

Salome raised her head and marveled at her grandmother's understanding of scripture. Grandmother saw the scene from a point of view Salome had never thought of. Lowering her head, she continued to read.

The wisdom Eve learned from her failure is wisdom all

104

women need to embrace and accept. Scripture says, **For this reason, a man shall leave his father and mother and be united to his wife, and they will become one flesh.** (Genesis 2:24 NIV) How heartbreaking it had to be when Eve's first two sons were torn from her life. Abel was murdered by Cain because of jealousy and Cain was marked and rejected from the company of all he had known and loved.

In time God blessed Eve with a third son, whom they named Seth. Countless numbers of children would be born to Adam and Eve and eventually, all of them would one day leave home. This is a natural part of the leaving process that begins from the minute the umbilical cord is cut at birth.

The older our children become, the more we witness this "leaving process" in action. As a child begins to crawl, they become more independent and through the stages of walking, running, feeding themselves and onward, the departure continues. We must understand that our children are only on loan to us. They really are the Father's and the more independent they become, the less they need us. As they mature they discover their own way and, hopefully, their need of Abba.

As a mother, I have to trust God with my children and understand He loves them more than I ever could. He knows the plans He has for them, plans to prosper them and not to harm them, to give them a hope and a future. (See Jeremiah 29:11) My job as a mother is to love, train and constantly point them to the Lord. I must let them grow and go into His hands. It is only through the leaving that they learn to walk with the Lord on their own.

It is not our children we are to cleave to, it is our husbands. We are joined to our husband as his suitable helper no matter what happens. Our husbands are our other half so if we cleave to anything else, we will miss the blessing God has created in marriage. As women we need to understand that we cannot receive the "love" we look for from our children nor our husbands. Nor *can we place pressure on them to "make" us happy and fulfilled. The only One who can fulfill that part of our heart is God.*

Salome stopped and examined her own heart. "Lord, is this what I have done? Did I cleave to my children instead of my husband?" As though a bright light came and lit up her heart, she realized it was indeed true. God was true to His word, He was revealing exactly what was in her heart and Salome began to glimpse how deceived she had been.

And we know that all things work together
for good to those who love God
to those who are called according
to His purpose.
For those He foreknew,
He also predestined,
to be conformed to the
image of His Son that He might be
the firstborn of many brethren.
Romans 8:28-29 NIV

CHAPTER **11**

PEERING FROM THE journal, Salome imagined Eve considering the future and what would happen to the daughters of man, her daughters. That one decision made in the garden would fall back on her. She wondered at the wisdom of her grandmother and was touched deep inside her heart that God chose her to receive this very valuable gift. Tears glistened from Salome's eyes as she considered the magnitude of what she learned. She looked up and cried out in her spirit, "How far we have turned from the ways of our Creator!"

Salome continued to read the prayer her grandmother wrote, one she was sure that Eve could have prayed. *"Lord, my daughters will not be close to the image You created them to be. The only one to blame is me. You gave women the gift of influence. Everything we say and do influences those around us either negatively or positively. As we live and move, we represent You and Your character to our husbands, children, friends, co-workers, church family and neighbors. Oh God, help my daughters! Return them to the original form You created them to be. My sin destroyed so much more than I ever dreamed. Father, please restore them."*

A deep abiding love took root inside of Salome's heart for her great-grandmother that day. As she closed the journal and held it closely to her bosom, appreciation of the gift she held within her hands filled her once again. Slowly, sweet tears of joy began to trickle down her cheeks as she thanked God for the heartbreaking life her grandmother must have lived and that she had the foresight to put it down in a journal for generations to share. Opening the journal again, she continued to read:

God, thank You for taking the devastating circumstances that we create then turning them around to fulfill Your plan. This is not the end, it is only the beginning! Eve did not know that You had a plan to bring Your children back into fellowship with You. That plan was sending Jesus, giving Him a body to offer as a sacrifice for the sins of all mankind on the cross of Calvary.

The horror Jesus went through from the time of His arrest in the Garden of Gethsemane through the journey to the cross, brought back everything Adam and Eve had lost in that garden. Women don't have to walk as daughters of Eve any longer. On the contrary, we can walk as daughters of the Most High God. Through the shed blood of Jesus, the price is paid, in full! Oh God, thank You for giving me another chance at life through the blood of Jesus! I, and prayerfully all my daughters and granddaughters in generations to come, will be changed because of that faithful time in history when Jesus lived, died and then rose again!

All my love is Yours, Lord!!

Salome closed the journal and thanked God for His saving grace through belief in Jesus and the painful road to the cross. Her mind tried to wrap around the immensity of God's love. No matter what tragedy or failure she lived through, one fact remained. GOD LOVED HER! As she considered her grandmother's prayer all those years before she was even thought of, God had placed it on the heart of this grandmother to pray for her grandchildren even though she would never know them.

Salome lowered her head and prayed, "Lord, thank You for this dear grandmother. You chose me to be part of her legacy before the worlds were ever formed. Like her, I'm praying for all my daughters and sons, granddaughters and grandsons to a thousand generations from now! Lord, draw them from the womb to You. Protect them from the evil one's schemes and place people, filled with Your wisdom, in their path to help guide them to Your side. Thank You, Lord, for loving us more than we will ever understand! This is a wonderful day—I will rejoice! I pray all these things, Lord, in Jesus' name!

Thoughtfully, Salome considered the many failures in her own life. Like Eve, she had listened to other voices instead of God's gentle, quiet voice. However, from the time of Eve, through grandmother's life and still today, God's redeeming love for His children is able to take horrid situations and turn them around. No matter how many times we fall and make wrong choices, God is still able to make all things beautiful in His time! (See Ecclesiastes 3: 11)

Hope stirred in Salome as she considered her present circumstances. Smiling, she thought, *These are nothing in comparison to God!* One thing she decided, each day she would make God bigger than any of her circumstances. However, she knew God did not want her to bury feelings of depression or hopelessness! On the contrary, He wanted her to run to Him and pour her heart out before Him. It is the only way to lay them at His feet! The only thing He wants us to hold inside ourselves is the truth that we are His and that He loves us more than we can ever imagine!

Softly, Salome whispered, "Healing is coming in more ways than I have dreamed and I will believe! You have never let me down, and in the middle of this pain; You have filled me with peace that passes understanding, outrageous love and an overflow of Your joy. Thank You, Lord!"

God gently reminded Salome about her relationship with her husband and the trouble within their marriage. Meditating on the message about Eve she began to embrace the many lessons she could learn from the first woman's mistakes. Whispering she said, "Just as You told me before, Lord; it is as simple as this! Who will I believe? There is nothing new under the sun and Satan's tactics have not changed."

With these truths in place, Salome had to make some changes. It was no longer an option to live life by the way things appeared in her marriage. Her choice was to fully *believe* God and trust God. Contentment is just three letters away from discontentment. Once a person cracks the door of discontent, we can be sure the devil will push it wide open.

Disappointment simply means missed appointments. As she meditated about that definition, God revealed that when our own desires fail, it is most likely because they were never part of God's plan for our life. He had something better planned.

Salome determined to embrace whatever God wanted for her and let her own desires die. She whispered, "I know that God orders my steps, therefore, wherever I am in life, if I keep to the path God has set before me, every appointment He's ordained will come about."

As she allowed the story of Eve to continue simmering in her heart, Salome found her frustrations with Lewis and pointing the finger at him caused her to forget about the part she played in their marriage. Reflecting, she could not deny that she, herself, played a major role in getting to where they were in their relationship now. She and Lewis would both have to rely on God to teach them how to be in tune with and supportive of each other.

A sudden thought floated across Salome's mind. The opposite of frustration is satisfaction. In order to turn away from the ploy of the devil, Salome had to begin to choose to be satisfied in every area of her life. Turning, she began to research the word satisfaction. Finding words that described satisfaction, she whispered, "Ouch!" Approval, pleasure, happiness, fulfillment, contentment and agreement all described a person who embraces and is satisfied with whatever is happening within his or her life.

From all this evidence, she should be the one repenting, not Lewis. God would not hold her responsible for Lewis, but He would hold her responsible for herself. With that in mind, she prayed: *Lord, please forgive me! All this time I thought I was complaining about Lewis, but without realizing it, You're the One I was really complaining about. My heart has been filled with discontent, disappointment, unhappiness, frustrations and complaining. I have sinned against You because I listened to the voice of the enemy, instead of embracing Your will for me. Lord, change my heart, I pray in Jesus' name.*

Peace began to flood Salome after she prayed. She remembered the scripture in Jeremiah 17: 9-10 NIV: *The heart is deceitful above all things and beyond cure. Who can understand it? I the Lord search the heart and examine the mind, to reward a man according to his conduct according to what his deeds deserve.*

Salome thanked God that He knew the things in her heart and that He was still working on her. He would not give up. There is also a reward to obedience for His Word and more than anything she did desire to be obedient to Him. It was time for change and that change would start with her. She had to take a step of faith and begin to simply believe God!

For ever since the world was created,
people have seen the earth and sky.
Through everything God made,
they can clearly see his invisible qualities
his eternal power and divine nature.
So they have no excuse for not knowing God.
Romans 1:20 NLT

CHAPTER **12**

IT HAD BEEN two months since surgery and Salome wondered if she was beginning to lose her mind. Since Lewis had been working nights, it gave her the opportunity to pray and try to make sense of the things she'd been living through. The sun had already set and, as she gazed outside, she spotted a little twinkle of light here and there within the darkness of the woods, "Lightening bugs," she said with a smile.

Laying her purse and keys down on the island in the kitchen, she opened the back door and stepped out onto the screen porch. Minx ran up to her with a faint meow and began rubbing Salome's legs, purring while she glided back and forth. Since one could never tell what Minx would do, Salome approached the sly kitty with caution. The sassy animal definitely had her own personality. Slowly, Salome bent down and rubbed her neck. Immediately the cat began purring while she rolled her fat body around on the porch floor. Smiling, Salome cooed, "You crazy fat kitty, when you behave you are so sweet."

Just then, Lucy, a striped grey and off-white, stray cat, which had adopted Salome as her owner, came sashaying around the beige, wicker loveseat. Salome was convinced that this feline was mentally challenged. The kitty had an almost comical look in her eyes. When she walked away, she'd raise her tail which would automatically form the shape of a question mark. This short-haired tabby sported a very strange meow, but mostly, Lu just wanted to be a part of a family. Her antics made her owner laugh with glee. That cat could run like lightening and loved dashing straight up the long, tall pine trees. She would hang there for a moment, then come down and walk away, almost as if to say, "Whew, I needed that!"

Salome was a sucker for the down-and-out, so she mercifully had taken Lucy in. However, Queen Minx was not very happy about the addition to the family. She basically just put up with Lucy. As Salome gently petted the felines, they purred almost in harmony. Bracing herself on the iron patio table, Salome slowly stood and headed toward the screen door.

Stepping outside, she focused on the woods. Tiny, twinkling lights appeared throughout the forest in a dance of sweet delight. Salome smiled as she watched their flicker of light sparkling throughout the woods. Just then, she turned her gaze heavenward. Caught up in the brilliance of a beautiful array of stars, a single tear began to slowly trickle down her cheek. The dazzling display of lights sparkling in the night sky only reminded her how great God is.

As tears of love continued to trickle down her cheeks, she whispered, "Lord, I desperately need You! What am I doing wrong? My greatest struggle seems to be with myself and the thoughts in my own mind. I'm trying to love Lewis, Jesus, yet it seems no matter how hard I try, I continue to fail."

As she continued to stare at the multitude of tiny pinholes in the velvet curtain of the night sky, she was reminded that God knew each star by name. Creation itself declares that there is a God. Through the stunning display of the stars, Salome felt Him close beside her. Standing there, staring into the brilliance of the firmament, she breathed softly and deeply and gradually let out a long, cleansing breath.

The corners of her mouth curved up in a smile as she whispered,

"God IS in control and He knows all about our issues. What He wants from me is to trust Him and simply come to His throne of grace unafraid, to receive mercy in my times of need." (See Hebrews 4:16) "He IS working this for my good and His glory. I have to believe and keep my eyes on Him. I cannot do this, Lord, You have to do it through me," she concluded.

Both Lewis and Salome grew up in dysfunctional family units. Neither had an idea of what a normal family relationship was all about. Salome continued, "Honestly, Lord, Lewis believes everything is fine. I know I've been running but I truly believe that he is running harder and faster than I am, yet, he doesn't even know it. What in the world is he running from, Lord? How can I help him if he won't talk to me? Lord, will we ever connect?" Frustrated tears dribbled from her eyes. As they continued down her checks, she wondered, "What can I do, Lord?"

"Father, I want to have a close loving relationship with Lewis. However, I cannot do that alone, he has to want this, too. Truthfully, I feel like a total failure, Jesus. The thoughts that run through my mind are disturbing. I need Your help. I cannot continue in this relationship much longer."

Salome walked to a chair that was sitting toward the back of the red-tiled patio located right off their screened-in-porch. She sat down carefully and began sorting through the wild thoughts drifting through her mind during the last weeks. Her head hurt from lack of sleep and she wasn't sure if it was the pain from surgery or the pain in her heart that was keeping her awake. The swelling and horrific pain from her back almost seemed like a piece of cake compared to the emotional pain that seemed bent on destroying her.

Walking out of the porch, Lucy slowly padded over toward Salome but stopped when she spotted a bug. Stealthily, the feline hid behind a flower pot, whipping her tail back and forth; as she braced herself on three legs ready to pounce on the little creature.

In one jump, she landed on top of it. However, instead of just killing the small insect, Lucy began tormenting it, although to Lucy it was just a game. Salome shivered, as compassion flowed through her for the little critter. Picking up Lucy, she placed her on the porch. She could no longer watch the horrid ordeal the bug was going through. Walking toward the little insect, her heart broke as the little injured thing tried to crawl to safety.

With tears now pouring down her face, she recognized she felt just like that bug. Something had been tormenting her mind so badly that she felt as though she was a prisoner, trapped in a cage, being tortured by her captor. Standing, she ambled back to the chair, sat down and silently prayed while lowering her head. *Lord, why is this so hard? Honestly, when I'm away from Lewis, I deeply desire to do the right thing but, as soon as he walks in the door, all my good intentions fall away. Resentment, along with a profound anger I don't believe I have ever felt before, rises out of the deepest part of my heart and I am powerless to stop it. Jesus, please help me!"*

Lifting a tear-stained face that was etched in pain, Salome again raised her head to gaze at the glittering stars. As she watched the vastness of the twinkling lights and an occasional shooting star, she realized how tiny she was in the scheme of life. In that moment, she embraced just how big God really is. *You will see me through to the end. I trust You, Lord, but this anger seems much bigger than I am. Please show me why I am like this. What has triggered this seemingly, deep-seated, anger? This is really not my heart, Lord. I want our marriage and our relationship to honor you. When a man and woman marry, they are supposed to be a "snapshot" of You to the world, yet Lewis and I seem light years away from that picture.*

Crying unashamedly in the stillness of the night, Salome prayed. "Lord, although I am married to a Christian man, our marriage is far from the example the Bible presents. At times, I've wondered if Lewis and I speak the same language. Since surgery, feelings of disappointment, depression, discouragement, hopelessness, loneliness and fear have continued to wage an unseen war in my soul. Everything that once brought me joy and a sense of identity is now gone. I honestly don't know who I am anymore, Lord."

Sitting quietly, as tears continued to pour from her heart, Salome suddenly heard the sounds around her. Closing her eyes, she allowed the orchestra of night resonance to calm her anguished heart. Crickets chanted their evening songs like a grand, invisible symphony. A big bullfrog croaked out a love-call for his future mate while several owls continued exclaiming the sound of "who, who, who". Suddenly, she felt the kiss of a breeze as it floated by and heard the tinkling of wind chimes ringing out a melody.

In this quiet place, the Lord softly spoke to her heart, *Salome, your identity is not in your job, your ministry or what you do or who you know. Your identity is hidden in Me. You are and will always be My child, chosen to be My beloved. Your name is written on the palms of my hands. I will never leave you. In the middle of what seems like the valley of the shadow of death, embrace this time with Me while I do a deep work within your heart and within your marriage. Now, have faith and **believe** that I AM! Trust Me! Do not look at circumstances! Remain faithful. Let Me deal with Lewis. Your task is to be still and **know** that I'm God and that you are resting under the shadow of My wing! I Am fighting all your battles, now rest!*

"Lord, I know these things in my head but, it seems that they keep missing my heart. I understand that in order to create one person out of two, both people must die." Gazing at the stars once again, she acknowledged that this was something she had to walk through. God is only just beginning! He promised He would make everything beautiful in *His time* and it will be done *HIS way*. (See Ecclesiastes 3:11)

Drinking in the beauty and sounds of God's wonderful creation, she knew, even in the darkest of night, God makes Himself known. Softly she sighed, "God, You will accomplish what is needed in our relationship. I must continue to trust You."

She and Lewis met through a series of events that only God could have devised. Several times before they were married, the Lord confirmed His will to her, *"This is the one I chose for you."* So why am I kicking against the pricks?

With that thought in mind, Salome confessed all the words the enemy had been speaking to her. The devil's message has not changed in thousands of years! Words like, *If God really loved you, **why** would He give you someone like this? God's holding out on you. If this is God's best, oh my, what a loser you are. You deserve this. Look how many times you have failed. After all, how do you know you really heard God? You could have missed Him and here you are. Your life is over, this is all there is! You are hopeless, a failure. Just look at your marriage. How dare you try to minister for God!*

The word hammered at her mind day after day yet today was the worst it had been. *Your life is hopeless so just drive off that bridge. Then, it will all be over. It's that simple. You will be singing with angels and finished with all this heartache in one second. DO it, come on, DO IT! Your mother was right; you are a mess waiting to happen. You will never amount to anything. You can't even kill yourself!"* As Salome finished confessing the lies, cleansing tears poured from the deep recesses of her heart.

Tenderly, the Lord asked her a question. *Salome, if this is all there is for the rest of your life, would you still love and serve Me? Would I be enough?*

Solemnly considering the Lord's questions, Salome began to ask **herself** a few questions. "Who am I serving anyway and why? If God never asked me to do anything else for Him, would I be satisfied? What is my life all about? One day I will leave this planet and live in His presence for eternity. Therefore, why do I allow this short life to affect my happiness and ability to praise Him?" His simple question became like a magnifying glass, clearing her perspective.

As she meditated on the questions, she felt Him say, *I Am the foundation on which **you** must build the rest of your life, Salome. Am I enough? Is it enough that you are Mine?*

Once again, Salome gazed up at the stars in the sky. Several fireflies gently floated by, one landing on her arm. Smiling at it, she studied the little insect as a thought began to build in her mind. This tiny bug was just enjoying life shining his light wherever he goes. It shines brightest when the night is at its darkest. The little creature had no idea it was being used by God. Could this be all God wanted from her? Simply to enjoy life and shine His light to all who came in contact with her?

Turning her face toward the dazzling night sky, she studied the stars while lightening bugs continued to float by. Then, at that very moment, a full moon appeared right on top of the trees as though it was sitting there, resting. It bathed the darkness of night with its luminous, eerie glow. Quietly she said, "Even darkness is light to You." (See Psalm 139)

As her mind continued to ponder the questions God asked her, she slowly got up. "I trust, You Lord! I have no idea what You are doing. Honestly, it feels like chaos. However, *I will* trust You."

Heading to the screen door, Salome opened it, stopped, and then turned to get one last peek into the majestic night. Hope began to swell within her spirit. She and Lewis would be all right, God would see to that. With a new spring in her step, she turned and headed toward her bedroom. This night, she just knew she would rest in peace.

If anyone is in Christ,
he is a new creation!
The old has gone,
the new has come!
2 Corinthians 5:17 NIV

CHAPTER **13**

THE FOLLOWING EVENING Salome and Lewis got into a terrible argument before he left for work. "It seems like I can never get ahead," fumed Salome. "I take one step forward and twenty backward! Lord, is this how it is supposed to be? I've had enough! I cannot believe You would want me to stay in something like this." With her last words, she heard the front door slam shut. *That went well*, she thought! "I cannot do this, it is just too hard! God, help me. Where is the line indicating things have gone too far?"

Breathing heavily, Salome walked into their master bedroom and slowly sat on the bed. The silence seemed deafening. *Oh, how I wish I could see from Your perspective, God! What am I supposed to do? I want out of this, Father. The way I see things, this marriage is driving me farther from you instead of to You.* Finally, Salome began to calm down from the rush of emotions that always seemed to happen whenever she tried to talk with Lewis.

A memory of a sweet, elderly lady appeared before her mind's eye. Salome remembered the conversation like it was yesterday. Mrs. Helen mentored and loved so many wounded women. As Salome's mind continued to reminisce, Mrs. Helen had shared a story that had helped many troubled wives.

"Remember that we are to be helpmates to our husbands. Ask him to do something once. If he doesn't do it then, remind him no more than two other times. If it still remains undone, take it to the

Lord and let Him handle your husband. Anything more than that is nagging." Chuckling, Mrs. Helen relayed a story wherein her formula worked a miracle for her.

"I asked my husband, very sweetly, to fix our porch swing. After a week, he had not even looked at the thing. Very calmly, I went to him, gave him a hug and inquired, 'Honey, please remember to fix our swing. I would love to sit and snuggle with you while we swing the night away.' One week after that, I fixed him a wonderful dinner and as we were eating, I requested once more, 'Can you find time to fix the porch swing for me, please?' Then, I took my request to the Lord.

Well, around three a.m. one morning, I woke up to a shrill banging. Bang, Bang, Bang! A chill began to travel up my spine and fear began to engulf me. Slowly, I reached over to wake my husband and found he was not in bed. My heart skipped a beat and I won't tell you the crazy things I was envisioning that could have happened to my dear honey-man. Horrid images began to play through my mind as I slowly picked up the baseball bat that was on the side of the bed and began to make my way across the bedroom. Listening, I continued to hear the BANG, BANG, BANG! Cautiously opening the door, I began to head for the front room with the bat poised over my shoulder, ready to swing. I thought, "Where is my husband?" Closing my eyes, I whispered a quiet plea to the Lord and prepared myself for the worst. As I turned the corner, I saw a light on. *Burglars don't use lights, I thought.* Confused, I lowered the bat and gradually headed forward.

Well, low and behold, there stood my husband, hammer in hand, fixing the porch swing. I opened the screened door and asked, 'Honey, what on earth are you doing at this time of night?' Giggling, Mrs. Helen gazed into Salome's eyes and said, "I will always remember his reply."

"I quote, 'The Lord would not let me sleep until I fixed the silly porch swing.'

With a twinkle in her eye and chuckle in her tone, she stated, 'Your husband may not listen to you, but I promise you this, it will not be easy to put the Lord off. Trust in Jesus, He does a far better job than any amount of fighting, strife and squawking ever could!"

As Salome considered the wise advice shared by her sweet counselor/friend, a smile began to form. *All marriages must go through these crazy situations,* Salome though. "Lord, forgive me, please. I forgive Lewis. He is Your problem, not mine! I just wish I could learn these things about ten miles away from him," chuckling, Salome was glad God had a sense of humor.

I've heard that insanity is simply repeating the same thing over and over, expecting a different result. Shaking her head, Salome said, "Well, that's it, no wonder I'm so outdone with all of this. I've been living in insanity for eighteen years, doing the same thing over and over!"

As her eyes slowly swept across her bedroom, the peacefulness and beauty of it was a testimony of God's blending. Softly God began ministering to her spirit! He had shown her how to blend old things with new. Her dresser and mirror, night stands and chest-of-drawers were all antiques from her grandfather's bedroom. The headboard was designed and created by she and Lewis. She took an old, enclosed computer cabinet and made a media-cabinet out of it. One year for Christmas, Lewis had given her a beautiful replica of an antique, standing jewelry box. Scanning the room again, she realized how each piece held a special meaning for her. Everyone was amazed at how well the antique and new pieces worked together.

Placed on Salome's dresser was a vase that held an arrangement of delicate, ivory feathers fanned behind sweet smelling, dried lavender flowers. Right beside it was the cake top from their wedding cake. It was a constant reminder that God desired them to love each other sacrificially. Above the chest-of-drawers hung a painting of Salome, her youngest son and daughter and Lewis's son and daughter. The painting was created from a picture taken while they walked a trail in Cades Cove, Tennessee two weeks after she and Lewis were married.

As she continued to drink in the warmth of their room, she realized the high hopes she had at the beginning of their marriage. At that time, they encouraged each other; however, she now understood that their primary focus had been making their blended family work. Salome realized they really hadn't built a relationship. Studying the picture she wondered, what happened? The children were grown and had families of their own. Salome found herself asking, 'Lewis, who are you? Where is the man I married?' As she stood there, she wondered if they had any idea what marriage was really all about. Salome allowed the memories to simmer in her heart and thought, *Lord what happen to us, how do I fix this?*

Salome knew all relationships would be tested. That is why the marriage vows say, '*Through sickness and health, for richer or poorer, in good times and bad times, until death do us part.*' Once again, she remembered the definition of insanity; I've been doing the same thing over and over and it hasn't worked. *Lord, I'm waiting on You. Show me what to do, Jesus!*

She decided to get her Bible and read before heading off to bed. Sleep had seemed like a fleeting friend for the last few nights and Salome was very tired. Going into the office, she picked up her Bible and walked back to the bedroom. Pulling back the bed covers, she slowly got in and settled down to read.

Since surgery, she could not sit up to read so she rolled to her side, opened her Bible and thumbed to the Book of Galatians, chapter four.

But when the set time had fully come, God sent his Son, born of a woman, born under the *law, to redeem those under the law, that we might receive adoption to sonship. Because you are His sons, God sent the Spirit of His Son into our hearts, the Spirit who calls out, "Abba, Father." So **you are no longer a slave,** but **God's** *child; and since you are His child, God has made you also an heir.* Galatians 4:4-7NIV

Verse 22- 31 NIV, *For it is written that Abraham had two sons, one by the slave woman and the other by the free woman. His son by the slave woman was born according to the flesh, but His son by the free woman was born as the result of a **divine promise**. These things are being taken figuratively: The women represent two covenants. One covenant is from Mount Sinai and bears children who are to be **slaves**: This is **Hagar**. Now Hagar stands for Mount Sinai in Arabia and corresponds to the present city of Jerusalem, because **she is in slavery with her children**. But the Jerusalem that is above is **free,** and she is our mother. For it is written: "Be glad, barren woman, you who never bore a child; shout for joy and cry aloud, you who were never in labor; because more are the children of the desolate woman than of her who has a husband." Now **you,** brothers and sisters, like Isaac, **are children of promise**. At that time the son born according to the flesh **persecuted** the son born by the power of the Spirit. It is the same now. But what does Scripture say? "**Get rid of the slave woman and her son**, for the slave woman's son will **never** share in the inheritance with **the free woman's** son." Therefore, brothers and sisters, **we are not children of the slave woman, but of the free woman.***

Galatians 5:1, 5-9NIV *It is for freedom that Christ has set us free. **Stand firm**, then, and **do not** let yourselves be burdened again by a yoke of slavery. (vs5) For through the Spirit we eagerly await by faith the righteousness for which we hope. For in Christ Jesus neither circumcision nor uncircumcision has any value. The only thing that counts is faith expressing itself through love. You were running a good race. **Who** cut in on you to keep you from obeying the truth? That kind of **persuasion** does not come from the one who calls you. "A little yeast works through the whole batch of dough."*

Suddenly Salome felt like she could not hold her eyes open one more second. Laying her Bible aside, she reached up and turned off the bed-side lamp then began to sink into a deep sleep. The last picture in her mind was that of a slave woman and a free woman.

—⟨⟨⟨⟨⟨ ⟩⟩⟩⟩⟩—

What is that sound? Is that the roar of the ocean? Salome could feel a salty, wet, violent wind blowing on her face peppering her with sand thrown by the blustery wind. Slowly, she opened her eyes and saw the gigantic monster of a violent, angry ocean. Waves were tumbling toward the shore with a force that caused them to crash viciously on the damp, gray sand. The sea reminded her of a huge fist as each wave hit the shore seemingly determined to crush her. Stunned and confused, she closed her eyes to the horrible site. Opening them again, she saw that the scene had not changed.

Fear began to engulf her as she strained to focus on her surroundings. Various shades of deep, dark-gray clouds covered the sky. They were so *low* it felt that if she stood and stretched far enough, she could reach out and touch them. A hurricane had to be approaching. Registering the sights in her mind she wondered, *What in the world am I doing on this beach?*

Bit by bit, Salome rose to a sitting position and began to take in the lay of the land. *Where am I and how did I get here?* The beach was completely empty and, from the looks of things, it seemed as though she was on a small island. As she continued to survey the area, she saw nothing, nothing but coastline and an angry ocean. The darkness of the menacing sky created an environment of alarm and panic. Just then the thought occurred to her, *I will face the brunt of this storm completely alone. Where is everyone?*

Glancing down, she wondered if she had washed up on shore. Her clothes were tattered and matted to her skin while clumps of seaweed, sand and salt were plastered on her legs, arms, body and face. As she studied her bare feet, she melted into total confusion. Testing her legs for strength, she slowly raised herself up until she finally stood upright. Lightning began to flash in the distance and the din of thunder roared across the sky. The wind blew her tattered clothing tightly against her skin. Brushing her wildly blowing hair off of her face, she shielded her eyes with her other hand, trying to get her bearings.

The storm blew so strongly it was hard to stay on her feet. She peered out toward the ocean watching the waves get bigger and bigger. *What in the world am I going to do?* She called out to God, "Lord, what's happening?"

As she continued to look around, in the far distance she noticed the outline of someone heading in her direction. Surrounding this person was a beautiful, brilliant, fiery light. Calm and peace seemed to exude from the form while he continued walking toward her. The ominous storm could not cross the barrier surrounding him and it appeared as though there was a shield, or protective wall, around him fending off the horrid storm. As she watched with unbroken concentration, realization opened like the dawning of a new morning. Softly, she whispered, *It's Him!*

With renewed energy, she rushed toward Jesus. Squinting, Salome swore that a smile began to appear on His face. He suddenly picked up His pace and stayed the course in her direction. Keeping her eyes on the approaching figure she began to feel hope and peace. She was not alone! With each step He took, the intensity of the storm gave place to the brilliant light surrounding Him. The storm had no power over Him, He was in complete control!

Quite astonishingly she realized her condition and, as she did, she slowed down her approach and finally came to a complete halt. Salome surveyed her state and suddenly heard voices behind her. Turning around, she spotted two women moving forward in her direction. One of the women had a bitter disposition. The other one wore a look of total and complete confidence. As they came near, she realized the difference between them.

One was dressed in tattered clothing; her hair was a disheveled mess and she desperately needed a good shower. No bath would do for this poor soul. It would take a downpour to wash away the dirt and grime clinging to her. The woman's face was flushed and covered with rage and resentment. Salome cringed as she looked at her. Lowering her gaze to the woman's feet, she saw a very large ball-and-chain attached to her ankle. Salome knew in an instant that the woman was a slave.

While considering the ball-and-chain, Salome took a step forward, and then tripped. Straining to see what she stumbled over, she was horrified to see that the same type of ball-and-chain was now attached to her own leg. As Salome glared at the thing, she heard the slave woman hiss, "See, she's my daughter, not yours! She wears the same clothing and has the same slave chain I have."

Gradually, the other woman came into view. Staring, Salome was stunned at the difference between what she considered to be the slave woman, and this woman who she knew was the freed woman. She had no ball and chain. This woman was clothed in a beautiful white flowing dress complete with complementing sandals on her feet and a stunning, jeweled crown upon her head. She seemed to float above the sand. The violent storm had no effect on her. Her demeanor gave the impression that she had been tried by fire and had come out shining like pure gold. Filled with joy, peace and love, this woman simply looked over at the other one and said, "We shall see!"

Four other women appeared behind the woman in white. Two of her four companions stood just behind her with an air of complete assurance. Softly the freed woman stated, "These are my two sisters, Wisdom and Understanding. Coming up behind them are Mercy and Grace. All of them follow me wherever I go."

Gazing intently at the women Salome failed to notice that the storm had stopped and the atmosphere was suddenly calm. Salome was now held within the eye of the storm. Everything was crystal clear to her. As she stared at the slave woman, she saw that she had followers, as well. They were clearly marked, Accusation and Condemnation. Other bald, disfigured, elf-like creatures had names like, Jealous, Guilt, Control, Self-Pity and Fear, just to name a few of those lined up behind her. They truly were a sinister group and as Salome stared at them, a shudder went through her body.

Behind Salome Jesus softly cleared His throat. As she turned, she saw Him standing next to her. It was there, in the eye of the hurricane, Salome could finally hear His voice. They stood face-to-face as His nearness broke the spell, then He addressed her. "Salome, do you see them?"

"The women and their companions, yes Lord, I do see them," she assured.

"Daughter, tell me what it is that you see," He coaxed.

"One woman, obviously a slave with the ball-and-chain attached to her leg, looks as if she has chosen all manner of evil to be her friends. They will surely help her slide into a trap the enemy has set for her. The creatures that follow her whisper wicked, vile lies, reminding her of the condition of her heart. They blame the wicked, destructive things in her life on others instead of helping her accept responsibility for her own actions. She is jealous, bitter, angry, hateful, and filled with resentment and self-pity. Her desire is to bring as many people as she can, into the cage of fear in which she, finds herself in. Each creature has placed a veil over her face which is blinding her to the facts that she alone is responsible for her reaction to the things that happened within her life. "

"Very good Salome," He softly spoke. "What about the other?"

"Lord, the one without the ball-and-chain is free, confident, knows who she is and has no fear. There is an aura of peace, joy and contentment about her and her companions. She is serene and there's something else, but I can't put my finger on it," Salome stated.

The Lord said, "That is correct. The thing you cannot put your finger on, is the fact that she and her companions know their identity and their authority in Me! None of this is about her or them personally. It's about Me and what I did at the cross. They walk in victory because they understand that although they may be in a battle, the war is already won!"

"Salome, the thing Satan does not want you to **know** and **believe,** is WHO you really are. He knows that when you finally accept and embrace that truth, his traps can no longer deceive you," Jesus said with a smile.

"Daughter, you have behaved as though you are the slave woman's child, when I have already bought you with the price of My blood. My child, you are no slave because I set you free! Don't you remember the proclamations of who you are written in My love letters to you?

You, Salome, are a child of the Most High God. You have been born again; you're a new creature in ME! The Father sees you as pure and holy. Not by what you do, Salome, but because of what I have already done! He sees you through My blood. You have the mind of Christ, a sound mind. You are the head, not the tail, above, not beneath. You are seated with Me in heavenly places. You are a joint-heir to My throne. You are My beloved bride, the apple of My eye. You are the light of the world, the salt of the earth. I have translated you from darkness into My marvelous light. Your prayers avail great victories. You are blessed coming in and going out. Sin has no dominion over you, because you're rooted and grounded in Me and I have ordered each of your steps.

Salome, if I am for you, then who can be against you? What can man do to you? I rejoice over you with song. Even in the night seasons, Salome, I will never leave you nor forsake you. I am your friend that sticks closer than a brother. I send laborers to whisper words of encouragement to your heart to remind you that NOTHING can separate you from My love! You are anointed, chosen, appointed and a mouth-piece I will use for My glory. It is your choice to believe the lies of that sly serpent and his companions or, to BELIEVE that I have broken the chain around your leg so You can be a daughter of the FREED woman. Now, My Princess, which do you choose?"

It seemed at that second the earth stood still, waiting for her response. Suddenly she heard a tremendous roar and the sound of horses' hoofs coming from behind the women. Joining behind the freed woman, she saw thousands of chariots-of-fire, along with legions of giant angels. Multitudes of saints, riding on horses, followed them. As far as her eye could see, there were horses and their riders. When each one came to a halt, the rider would dismount and wait. Lining up, the crowd gazed at Salome, smiled, then focused all their attention on Jesus. In unity, they bowed their knees before the King of kings and Lord of lords and cried, "Holy, Holy, Holy is the Lord God Almighty!"

Smiling, Jesus tenderly spoke, "Daughter, open your eyes and see. There are more for you than there are against you. Now, it is YOUR time to accept who you really are!"

—◦⫷⫸◦—

With a start, Salome woke up and realized it had all been a dream. Glancing at her clock, she saw that it was 3:33 A.M. Whispering, "It all seemed so real! That's it! Satan does not want me to accept and embrace WHO I really am! Thank you, Lord! I will believe. I will proclaim who I am to myself every day. When testing comes, I will also remember that there are many more for me than against me! My time has only just begun!"

*By faith Sarah herself also received strength
to conceive seed and she bore a child
when she was past the age,
because she judged Him
faithful who had promised!
Hebrews 11:11 (NKJV)*

CHAPTER **14**

THE NEXT MORNING Salome woke with a renewed hope and feeling of victory. Once she made her cappuccino, she headed for her office through the porch. A day without humidity was a mild miracle in the state of Louisiana! Salome felt like she could walk on water at that moment, however, she knew testing would come.

Glancing toward the tree-lined yard, Salome commented, "What an absolutely beautiful day!" Smiling, she stopped and whispered, "The birds are singing their morning praise songs, squirrels are cutting up, as usual, while the cats run in and out of the porch. Oh look, Lord, our neighborhood ducks," Salome laughed, as they quacked out a loud noise of glee! Gazing up toward heaven, Salome softly spoke, "Thanks for this blessed day!"

Opening the office door, she walked toward her desk and spotted her grandmother's journal. Softly rubbing her hand across the book, she decided to read it. Salome tenderly picked up the old, worn journal and carefully turned to the page marked by a faded, red-ribbon bookmark. The title read, *Woman of Faith.*

Recalling the past few entries in the prized journal, Salome began to realize the cost grandmother paid to become a Christian. From all indications her family threw her out after she became a Christian. The people in the church she attended were fearful of her so they only let her get just so close. Unfortunately, it was their fear that did not allow them to embrace grandmother as she desperately needed. Making a mental note, she chided herself to make sure to embrace every person God placed in her path with His love instead of her fears.

For a time, her grandmother's life was a blind walk of faith, believing God loved her. She became the trailblazer, with no mentor to show her how to become a Christian woman. However, through her journal, she left a map for women who came after her. "Lord, You helped her grow from being a slave woman to a free woman through the struggles she endured and the victories she ultimately won."

Just yesterday, Salome found a footnote in the journal that read:

The women's lives listed here come from God's Word. These are the women to imitate. As I learn the lessons each life teaches, help me to become a demonstrator of their faith walk with You. I choose to be an example of Your love to others who live and work around me no matter what their background may be. I trust You, Lord! May my life become a testimony of what You will do when a person sells out to Kingdom living. I am a new creation in Christ!

"Although my grandmother lived years ago, the wisdom held within the pages of her journal is fresh and still speaks today. It is only when our faith is tested that we learn You are indeed faithful," Salome whispered. Lowering her head she began reading again;

Mentioned in God's Word is the story of a faithful woman's life that was truly challenging. Not only is her story found in the Old Testament, she is the first woman listed in the Hall of Faith in Hebrews 11. She also appeared in one of Peter's letters as an example for all women to imitate. Reading her story made me realize the difficult experiences she had as a woman, wife and finally a mother. In my estimation, she could not have survived if she did not trust God and understand that HE was enough, especially when our life- story doesn't turn out the way we imagined.

I wonder what I would have done if my husband announced, "God has said for us to leave our country, home, family, friends and security to go to a place God will show us." (See Genesis 12: 1-3) However, that is exactly what Abraham did. I can imagine Sarah's heart. Being young in the Lord, I am finding first hand, that God doesn't necessarily ask us to do things that make sense. God's ways are not our ways, nor His thoughts our thoughts, we must take steps of faith and simply trust Him! (See Isaiah 55:8-9) Certainly, Sarah had to run to the Lord with her fears. I can imagine the questions running through her head, where are we going, what are we planning to do there, who will we stay with, when do we go, how do we make a living? Those are some of the questions I would ask. However, Sarah had to trust that Abraham heard from God. Even if he didn't, she had to trust that God would take care of them, regardless.

Ur of the Chaldeans was filled with idols of every kind. God's desire was to remove Abraham and Sarah from such a place and bring them into a promised land that flowed with milk and honey. A place where they could develop a deep relationship with the Lord by simply putting all their trust and hope in HIM!

Sarah had a choice to make. She could either operate in meekness or give into fear and defiance. Responding in meekness simply means placing our hope and trust in God Almighty, and bowing our knee to His will, whatever it may look like. Meekness creates an environment of unity and promotes peace and love. It is a blind walk of faith that says, 'God is still God no matter what circumstances we find ourselves in.' Simple understanding of meekness is strength under control, a strength that cannot be shaken because it comes from reliance in the only One who is in control of all. In essence, meekness allows God to break our will so we can embrace His will for our lives.

If we don't respond in meekness, we may find that we are striving with God. He is not the author of fear, confusion, division and strife. When our knees won't bow, we will find ourselves reacting in spirits of pride, rebellion and defiance.

Strife never comes alone. He brings with him anger, judgment, bitterness, hate and lies. A house divided will never stand. Sarah and Abraham would end up fighting against one another and the more they'd fight, the bigger the wedge would become that would eventually drive them apart.

Meekness creates an atmosphere of peace. As we conform to God's way and turn situations over to Him, our circumstances will turn around. I remember hearing stories told of an older, God-fearing woman. She shared much wisdom about meekness, truths we still pass along to our daughters even today. She declared:

"We are either running into Jehovah's arms or running away from them. Jehovah gives us that choice. Therefore, always bow your knees in meekness and turn toward Him! He'll meet you right there and show you what to do. While you are walking toward Him, He will fill you with His joy and peace and wrap you up in His blanket of love! Unfortunately, many of us tend to be very spirited, prideful, strong-willed and opinionated. It takes time to learn the beautiful art of walking in meekness and love. Once a woman can embrace that wisdom, its beauty begins to flow through her life like waters in a brook.

Take one day at a time, one victory at a time and, before you know it, you will find that meekness has become your best friend. Remember, meekness does not mean silence. Obey whatever Jehovah tells you and always share your heart with respect to your husband. Keep your eyes fixed on Jehovah, bow your knee and pray for your husband. When you act in meekness, your eyes are placed on Jehovah, not your husband. It takes all the pressure off him and places your hope on the only One who can do something."

Such wisdom! Trusting God is the legacy Sarah left behind for her future daughters. She resided in a world that considered women cursed by God if they were barren. How heart-breaking life had to be for Sarah. Barrenness became a trap the enemy used against her; sadly she fell, hook, line and sinker! I can imagine there were days when she felt overlooked and hopeless, as her faith was shaken to the core. However, we must remember, as long as we have breath, there is hope. God is not finished with us yet!!

A severe famine covered the land of Canaan so Abraham took his tribe in the direction of Egypt. Egypt was a picture of the world! Why do we always gravitate to the world in our famines of life? That is a mystery I will never understand.

With Egypt in view, I imagine Abraham pulling Sarah aside. I can see him gazing deep into her eyes, wondering if she would accept what he was about to tell her.

We all have areas in our lives where fear seems bigger than God and the Lord will bring about circumstances to force us to face those fears. Instead of placing our trust in God, we use human reason to make our plans. Each time we do this, we eventually create a mess.

Sarah, although old, was a very beautiful woman who could still turn heads. Abraham feared that the Egyptians would kill him in order to have Sarah for their own. Since she was, indeed, his half-sister, he told her to tell the Egyptians she was his sister, not his wife, just a little half-truth.

Whoever came up with the term, half-truth? It's either the truth or a lie, it cannot be both. When I think about the situation in which Sarah found herself, it makes me want to chuckle and applaud her. I don't think I could have handled that one with meekness! But, God gave her the strength to do it.

A dear friend told me, "God will never take you where His grace cannot keep you."

In difficult times, I remember her comment. I wonder if Sarah understood that, too. Eventually, Sarah ended up in the Pharaoh's household, living in the lap of luxury, while Abraham sweated in a dusty tent set up in the open landscape of the hot, desert sands. In the center of this trial, I am sure God filled her with peace. Peace is not the absence of conflict, but the presence of God. Sarah had to keep her eyes fixed on Jehovah, bow her knee in meekness and pray for her husband. Remember, meekness does not mean silence. Obey whatever Jehovah tells you and always share your heart.

As far as we know, Sarah did not share her heart. Maybe she acted out in a silent rebellion over her husband's demand. Honestly, I have to say that she is a better woman than I, because I would have had to share my thoughts with my husband. Pharaoh had a horrible reputation and was known for his brutality and violent treatment of women. However, I can picture God filling Sarah with peace in the midst of the storm.

In the meantime, Pharaoh gave Abraham sheep, oxen, donkeys and male and female servants in exchange for Sarah. Throughout that dreadful event, Abraham had no peace. Only from a distance, could he watch to see if he might possibly get a glimpse of Sarah.

The conviction of God must have lain heavy on Abraham. The Lord was displeased with this arrangement and one night struck Pharaoh and his house with great plagues. The following morning, Pharaoh called Abraham and said, "What have you done to me? Why did you lie and tell me she was your sister? She is your wife! What would have happened to us if I had taken her as my own? Now then, take your wife and go!" Pharaoh was so angry that he commanded an armed guard to escort Abraham and his entire tribe out of Egypt. What Abraham did in secret, God exposed publicly. Unfortunately, there are some who never learn!

———◦⫘⫘◦———

A few years later, God made His presence known to Abraham and promised him on two different occasions that his seed would be numerous; "I will make your descendants as the dust of the earth, so that if anyone can number the dust of the earth, then your descendants can also be numbered." (Genesis 13:16 NASB)

Later, God took him outside and said, "Now look toward the heavens and count the stars, if you are able to count them. So shall your descendants be." Then Abraham believed in the LORD; and He reckoned it to him as righteousness. (Genesis 15:1a-6 NASB) A covenant was made between God and Abraham for his descendants. Sarah's reproach would finally be wiped out when she gave birth to the promised child. Everyone would call her blessed!

Psalm 46:10 NIV says, **Be still and know that I am God. I will be exalted in the heavens; I will be exalted on earth.** *There is an understood word in this Psalm. The word is YOU—be still! Isn't it just like us? There is something about the "being still" part that we have a very difficult time accepting. I catch myself trying to reason how things will work out instead of casting my cares on Jesus, resting in His arms of love and embracing His timing for all things. Being human, it is easy to see how Sarah would begin to work out a solution for her barrenness.*

I can hear her now, "I have an idea, Abraham; go in to my maid, and maybe, through Hagar, I will obtain children".

We seem to be our own worst enemy. Through this decision, Abraham and Sarah created a disaster that still exists today. Abraham listened to Sarah and, doing what she suggested, went in to Hagar the Egyptian. Hagar conceived a child

Sarah's decision caused an enemy to Isaac's family line that continues to this day. How sorry I feel for Hagar. I can understand the bitterness she had for Sarah. Although the custom was very familiar to Hagar, I cannot believe it would be easy to have a child and hand it over to your Mistress to raise as her own.

Before long, Sarah's bitterness and anger got the best of her. Suddenly, Sarah reached her boiling point! Every emotion in her heart began to spew out. Anger, bitterness, manipulation, impatience, cruelty, jealousy and pouting were just some of the emotions that seemed to drown any sweetness or meekness Sarah might have had.

In her anger, she faced Abraham, blaming him for the situation. Bitterness and pride seemed to blind Sarah to the fact that it was "her solution" that was at the root of the entire situation.

Abraham, wanting to end the whole sordid thing said, "Hagar is your maid so do to her what seems right in your sight."

Steaming with bitterness and hate, Sarah treated Hagar harshly until Hagar finally ran away. Meekness and pride cannot reside together in a heart. How easily blinded we become when pride and bitterness move in. Did Sarah remember that it was through Eve's influence that Adam ate the apple? As I consider these truths, I am only now beginning to see there is no way to accomplish meekness unless we give Christ complete control of our lives.

⎯⎯◦𝕴𝕴𝕴𝕴〰⎯⎯

Hagar ran into the wilderness, hurt, angry and bitter. The letter written to the Hebrew church warns that a bitter root will spring up and defile many. (See Hebrews 12: 15) Meditating on the sad order of things, I think Sarah's bitterness was really directed at God for not fulfilling the promise in her timing, her way. As I mentioned, we are our own worst enemy.

What I love about this story is not mentioned very often. It is almost overwhelming to see the tenderness God had toward the slave woman, Hagar. It is the first place in the Bible where God's reveals Himself as El Roi, the God who sees. Wherever I am, God sees everything I'm going through. His name, El Roi, brings hope to all those who feel forgotten.

God saw the effect of Sarah's sin in Hagar's life. However, He did not condone Hagar's response to that sin. Jehovah gave her hope for a future then simply said, submit, be meek, and return because, I see all that was done to you. With that, He gave her a promise that He would greatly multiply her descendants, and then He gave her child a name, Ishmael. There in the desert, Hagar understood God is her God, too, and HE sees all.

◄◦◖◗◖◗◦►

Abraham was ninety-nine years old when God Almighty appeared to him again. Sarah was ninety! Once again, God promised Abraham that he and Sarah would have a son and call his name Isaac. Isaac would be the child of the promise between God and Abraham.

Later, three visitors came to Abraham and, as Sarah prepared a meal, she overheard them speaking to Abraham, "I will surely return to you at this time next year; and Sarah will have a son," the Visitor replied.

Sarah silently laughed and thought, 'After all, I am old and Abraham is old, shall I have the pleasure of bearing a child?'

At that the Visitor asked, "Why did Sarah laugh, saying, 'Will I bear a child when I am so old?' **Is anything too difficult for the Lord?"**

Yet, sure enough, a year later Sarah did have a son, Isaac, the promised child. Sarah's pregnancy did not happen when it seemed reasonable to man nor, did it happen in Sarah's timing. It did happen at just the **right time***. Through the waiting process, Sarah and Abraham grew in character and faith in God Almighty. Sarah learned much about herself and about the priceless gift God had given all women. It was not a gift to take for granted, influence is an endowment from God!*

Remember, when God's promises seem slow, we must beware. There is a place where my will and God's will collide. In that place, the enemy will plant seeds of human reasoning and bitterness. Satan will speak to us in lies and throw accusations against our spouse. His ultimate goal is to make us doubt God's love and His promise. Once we heed the sly devil's voice, the seeds he plants begin to grow and produce fruit of anger, bitterness, manipulation, impatience, jealousy, a temperamental spirit and hate, which ends in cruelty to others. From my perspective, Sarah not only failed, she also created a mess for all future generations because of her sin. However, God calls Sarah faithful. We seem to focus on our failures while God focuses on our finished character.

———❧———

Closing the journal, Salome meditated on the wisdom her grandmother gleaned from the events of Sarah's life. A thought began to form in her mind. God takes a Holy Spirit, blood-washed eraser and erases all our failures. Once we ask for forgiveness, God covers us with the blood of Jesus and we are a new creature in Him. From our inception into the Kingdom, until the seed of promise is birthed or fulfilled in our lives, God continually forgets. All God sees is Jesus's blood and our finished character!

Salome remembered her grandmother's words that were written in her journal. *When a child is born we love that child unconditionally. As their journey progresses, our child will walk through many failures and many victories. When she begins to stand as a woman, we rejoice in the person that child has grown to become. All the fights, strife, tantrums and rebellion of the teen years fade away. The memories we hold are the hugs, the butterfly-kisses, the joy and laughter and those sweet 'I love yous'. Our child's first steps, singing their first solo or going to their first art show all are etched within our memory. Pride from those mile stones of accomplishments is what we remember.*

Salome thought, "We are only a tiny shadow of who God really is. Why does His forgetfulness of our blunders surprise us?" Lamentations 3:21-26 NIV: ***Yet I still dare to hope when I remember this: The faithful love of the LORD never ends! His mercies never cease. Great is His faithfulness; His mercies begin afresh each morning. I say to myself, "The LORD is my inheritance; therefore, I will hope in Him!" The LORD is good to those who*** *depend on Him, to those who search for Him. So it is good to wait quietly for salvation from the LORD.*

Salome embraced the wisdom held within the heart of her grandmother. God, being the amazing Father He is, also sees His children in the same light! The scripture in Isaiah 43:25 NIV comes to mind; *I, even I, am He who blots out your transgressions for my own sake, and remembers your sins no more.*

Finally, Salome believed that God forgets, wipes **all our** sins away, and overlooks the blunders. "All our sins mean Lewis's sins as well!" Peace, forgiveness and cleansing began to slowly flood Salome's heart. God was not going to give up on their marriage. He was not finished yet. Both she and Lewis would make mistakes, but the choice to forgive and forget was entirely up to them. With God's help, she knew she could.

As she gazed out the window, it seemed as though a new freshness was not only in the air but, also beginning to build within all areas of her heart. Faith began to overtake any fear as she realized, once again, that God is and always has been the God of the impossible. At the cross, Jesus handed her the victory! Now is the time to stand confidently in who God created her to be! Something was changing. Suddenly, Salome felt beautiful! Smiling brightly and filled with assurance Salome whispered, *God sees me finished! I'm beginning to get a glimpse of that girl, too, and I love what I see! Thank you, Lord!*

Faith never knows where it
is being led.
But it loves
And knows the
One who is leading!

CHAPTER **15**

OPENING HER EYES to the morning sunshine peeking through the curtains, Salome basked in the revelations the Lord showed her the day before. Taking a deep breath, she rolled over and smiled as the cleansing stream of God's intimate love flowed over her once more. Stretching her hands above her head, she basked in the knowledge that she is loved, cherished and adored not only by God but also, by many women God was placing in her life. Before her eyes, God began transforming her life and heart into the woman He had seen in her all this time.

"This is an awesome day! The day You have made, Lord; I will rejoice and be glad in it," Salome whispered. "Thank you, Lord, for transforming me into a new creature! You have my best in mind even if it doesn't look like the best at the time. I'm placing all my hope and trust in You! You are not finished with any of us yet!" Getting up, Salome walked into the bathroom to dress. Once dressed, she headed to the kitchen as the phone rang. As she picked up the phone, Addie, her daughter, asked, "Hey Mom, how are you today?"

Salome answered, "I'm good! It's a beautiful day isn't it! Do you have everything you need for Lizzy since school will be starting soon?"

"Yes, I finally finished shopping for her," said Addie. "We got her school uniforms. The little rascal told me she would rather wear pink or purple; dark blue is not her color. This is going to be an interesting year with Miss Sunshine Kitty."

Addie and Salome both laughed, "We better pray for Lizzy's teacher! That lady is going to have her hands full," Salome chimed in.

Addie added, "Mom, Tanya and I would like to spend some sister time together before school starts. Would you be able to watch Andy and Lizzy for a little while? I need to get some school clothes of my own." Being a teacher, Addie would be in a classroom just down the hall from Lizzy.

"Sounds like fun, Addie." Salome glanced at her calendar and asked, "When are you guys planning to go?"

Addie conveyed, "We were thinking tomorrow, since Tanya, has the day off. She plans to come by my house first and pick Lizzy and me up, then head on to your house to drop off the kids. Would that fit your schedule? "

Salome opened the page of her calendar to that date and saw that her physical therapy appointment had been cancelled. She answered, "That sounds wonderful. It will give me some time with those two sweeties, especially before Lizzy starts school! I will truly miss that girl! Also, I haven't seen as much of Andy. He's so active and with this back issue, I can't chase him or pick him up. Oh my, wouldn't it be a joy if Max lived here? All the little cousins could be together and their Nana would be in heaven!" Jacob, Salome's son, and his wife Mary, had been blessed with Max in December of the previous year. Grandbabies are such a delight!

"Thanks Mom," Addie chuckled. "If you had all three, we would have to take you to the hospital once we came back! Andy climbs everywhere and I swear his short, tiny legs move faster than any of us. Lizzy will be the drama queen, playing the role of Princess Lizzy, Miss Sunshine Kitty or Rainbow Dash, not to mention her constant conversations to herself! Adding Max to the mix would definitely be awesome and interesting! Mercy! Thanks,

Mom. We'll see you around 9:30 tomorrow morning. Love you!" "Love you, too! Have a wonderful day." Salome acknowledged. After hanging up the phone, she smiled and thought, *What a treat to have both my little blessings tomorrow! They certainly fill a house with joy, laughter and just plain overflowing life!*

—◦Ⅲ◖♪◗Ⅲ◦—

"Lizzy, you are just too funny," Salome said. "Andy, you fill my heart with joy!" Slowly, Salome transferred a tiny, green reptile into Lizzy's hand. Holding the baby lizard tightly, Lizzy screeched with delight!

Andy, on the other hand, could have cared less about the green reptile. Running around the yard with the play lawnmower, he sported a smile and laughed with glee as he continued his laps around their large yard. Salome smiled and sighed, wishing she had just a tiny bit of his energy! As she continued to watch him run around she thought, *That boy has only one speed, fast!*

Out of the blue, Andy realized that Lizzy had a prisoner within her grasp. Plodding his way toward her, he suddenly stopped and stared at the tiny lizard. Not sure what to make of the four-legged thing, Andy continued to study the creature. Suddenly, the creepy crawly moved and Andy let out a scream!

Next thing you know, Lizzy screamed, then threw the chameleon in the air! Minx, the old fat cat, spotted the lizard and decided this was her time to play with the wretched thing if only she could catch it. Stalking out of the screened porch, she dropped into a crouch and prepared for the kill. Salome shooed the feline, trying to save the poor varmint from becoming a meal for the fat old kitty! Thankfully, Minx moved a bit slower than she used to, so the lizard got away.

Chuckling, Salome corralled Andy and Lizzy saying, "Time for lunch and a treat!" Thank the good Lord. It was pretty easy to divert their attention with food! A sandwich made of peanut butter and some of Nana's homemade fig jelly, along with a slice of sweet apple bread for desert, always enticed them. Tanya and Addie were due to come home any minute, therefore, Salome wanted to take all the time she could with her tiny angels.

Each grandchild was different in character. Lizzy, age four or Sunshine Kitty, as she called herself, was born an actress. Role playing seemed to come naturally to Lizzy. She is definitely a little drama queen!

Andy, on the other hand, is a doer and all boy. At two years old, he is already as smart as a whip and has an amazing understanding of electronic gadgets! He is known to send multiple texts to any number of people if he can get his hands on a cell phone. And if he wants to watch TV, he knows how to pull up his movies from the DVR, pick out the one he wants to see, and then proceed to sit back and watch it. He's our mini-lil-man!

Six-month old Max, Jacob and Mary's little one, is our deep thinker and an explorer. As you sit with Max, you can almost watch his little mind trying to comprehend things. Since he started crawling, he attempts to explore anything he can. He is a master at rearranging a room.

In our opinion, the grandchildren are the sweetest babies in the world and are so very diverse in their characters! I just wish I could spend more time with them. Lewis and I thank God that their parents allow the children to just be themselves and not try to make them fit into their mold!

Salome sank back for a moment and thought about her eighteen year old granddaughter, Marie. Such a beautiful and talented young lady, however she does not realize her great value to God and to us. Matthew, her brother and our thirteen year old grandson, is all about technology and games, such a smart and very handsome young man. Sadly, they live far away, as well. It is such a struggle to keep in touch when loved ones live far away. Suddenly, she realized just how much she missed the time when they were growing up. Yet, their distance away never stopped her deep love for them and the fact that they and their parents remained in her prayers and thoughts daily.

It did not take Andy long to gobble down his lunch. However; Lizzy chatted the whole time. That girl could talk the ear off of anyone willing to listen. Oh my, does she have serious opinions for a four year old!

Before Salome realized it, Andy had finished his lunch while Sunshine Kitty had barely taken a bite. He listened to Lizzy for a moment, and then decided he was not at all interested in hearing her commentary on lizards and all the little bugs in Nana's garden. Unexpectedly, Andy wiggled and slid off the chair to head outside! At just that moment, Tanya and Addie walked in the front door!

Tanya said, "Hey, Andy! Did you have a good time at Nana's?" Hearing her voice, Andy did an about-face, sporting his big sweet smile, and ran into his mama's waiting arms!

Lizzy, said, "Oh, hello Mommy and Aunt Tanya! We found a lizard in Nana's garden and I held it........ . . . ."

Addie gave her a gentle hug and listened to Lizzy's dramatic version of the story. Salome sat back and listened as the girls shared their shopping adventures, enjoying the sweet voices of her daughters and grandchildren. Smiling, she thanked the Lord for her beautiful family! No matter what happened to her physically, Salome remained swimming in the blessings from the Lord. Tanya and Addie cut themselves a slice of sweet apple bread. Tanya poured herself a glass of peach tea while Addie took a bottle of water from the fridge.

Tanya said, "Mom, I have to leave because John should be home soon, and unfortunately, dinner won't fix itself! Thanks for watching Andy. I think Addie and I needed some bonding time together away from the kiddos!"

Addie said, "Mom, thanks for watching Lizzy." Giving Salome a hug she smiled and said, "I really needed this day, thanks! Love you!"

Salome smiled and replied, "I love you, too. Andy, Lizzy, can I have a hug and kiss?" The two blessings ran toward Salome with arms open wide. She braced herself against the couch in order to keep her balance and, when they reached her, they covered Nana with kisses and hugs. Then they turned and raced to the front door. After the goodbyes were said, Addie shut the door. Salome took a deep breath and smiled as she basked in the peace and quiet of her home.

As Salome thought about the children's enthusiasm, she remembered the time right after she gave her life to the Lord. Softly she spoke, "Lord, I'm almost embarrassed as I think back to the beginning, twenty-two years ago when I was a baby in Christ. I had a lot of zeal but hardly any knowledge of You. Someone should have locked me up for a few years."

Shaking her head with laughter, Salome thought about her wild and crazy reasoning. Mercy was only a tiny seed at that time and seeds take time to grow. There definitely was no fruit of mercy in her heart and, quite honestly as she thought back, she remembered saying, "Anyone can buy a Bible at Wal-Mart. If someone doesn't want to know Jesus, it's their problem!"

Moaning, and embarrassed at that thought, she turned from the front door. Salome could feel the heat of embarrassment covering her face as she thought about those early days! Walking into the living room she headed for the couch. After the busy morning, she needed to rest. Lying down, she remembered something Lizzy shared.

"Nana, it's not fun being a kid. It is not fair that grownups have all the fun. They can have I-phones, drive a car, eat whatever they want. They don't have to take a nap." As Lizzy made the statement, she had a pout on her face and crossed her arms across her chest in deep, serious thought. The unfairness of it all seemed to overwhelm poor Lizzy. Growing up took too long as far as she was concerned.

Smiling, Salome replied, "You are right Lizzy but, when you grow up, you also have to go to work, pay the bills, clean the house, wash the clothes and the dishes, cook food and go grocery shopping. It's not all fun; there is lots of work, too."

Salome realized how life must appear from Lizzy's and Andy's five and two year old perspective. I guess it seems that everyone is always telling them what to do. They have to learn to trust that we have their best interest at heart. As children grow, we have to release some of the reins to allow them to learn things through experience. *Lord, You do those same things to your children. You also want us to trust and believe in You.* Salome pondered.

Just then Salome heard the quiet words of the Lord whispered into her heart. *Trust in the Lord with all your heart and lean not on your own understanding. In all your ways acknowledge ME and I will direct your steps. (See Proverbs 3:5-6) Remember Salome, you are a child of the freed woman. Remain free!*

Salome smiled at God's gentle reminder of her dream. She pondered the scripture in Isaiah 26:3-4 NLT: *You will keep in perfect peace all who trust in You, all whose thoughts are fixed on You! Trust in the LORD always, for the LORD GOD is the eternal Rock.*

Salome mused, *When the circumstances scream for us to take matters in our own hands, it is then that we must trust in the Lord. We must continue to trust Him, especially when we feel God is moving too slow.* Considering her growing up years, Salome knew that no one would believe she could be where she is today. That fact was sometimes hard for her to accept.

God is healing every area of my life, she thought. Suddenly, an inspiration occurred to her. If I could interview my great-grandmother, I'm sure she would be shocked to see how her life struggles still shine as an example today. I cannot imagine how many women she has influenced through the years, by sharing her thoughts and life-learned message.

Salome contemplated, *If she only knew! No matter what life threw at her, the lifestyle and writings she displayed, are still changing people today. Lord, there are many great people who turned their families around because they decided to submit, follow and obey You.*

Considering the progressive stages since she became a follower of Jesus, Salome realized our journey comes in levels. *It's almost like school,* she thought. *You must finish first grade to go to second and so on.* One thing for sure, Salome knew people could not just "know" about Jesus and be changed. In order to develop His nature and to become more like Him, one must draw closer to Him, deny themselves, pick up their own cross and follow in His footsteps daily. God expects changes in our character. He wants us to mature. Through testing and trials our temperament is changed and our love for Jesus deepens. A relationship with Him cannot come any other way. Even Jesus learned obedience through the things HE suffered. (See Hebrews 5:8) All through the New Testament we see that suffering is just a part of life. However, suffering is something none of us desire. We would much rather live out a fairy tale!

As Salome contemplated her own past and the lies on which her foundation had been built, she suddenly began to get a glimpse of why her faith had been so easily shaken.

What is it about humans, Lord? We believe and embrace that life is supposed to be a happily-ever-after romantic adventure. From childhood our play, stories and fantasies are about a princess and prince always ending up with a happily ever-after-ending.

Considering this, Salome remembered the imagination of her childhood days. "As a little girl, I dreamed of a magical, enchanted existence which included a most handsome prince, all dressed up in his princely attire. Of course, he rode a beautiful white horse with purple feathers attached to its head and velvety purple-roped reigns draped across its body. All the trimmings deemed necessary for royalty. My prince would show up in just the nick of time to rescue me from the horrid villain and his proverbial fire-breathing dragon.

As I played with my Barbie and Ken dolls, I could disappear from the dreary, ordinary days in which I lived and, for that period of time, I'd be transported into my own imaginary city. My parents, the king and queen of the country in which we lived, loved and cherished their little princess, me. Our enchanted castle was guarded with big, strong uniformed soldiers gloriously clad in purple and black, with gold-braid epaulettes on their shoulders. Anything that could jeopardize the joyous and sweet atmosphere enveloping the beautiful princess was eradicated by a very wide and deep moat surrounding the castle."

Continuing her musing, Salome remembered her aunt. Aunt Patrice was employed as a designer in a textile factory. Each time she came to visit, she brought along a bag of extra fabric. The material propelled me to envision myself becoming a great fashion designer. I designed clothing for my dolls and sewed them with my handy-dandy, pink children's sewing machine. I could see my name in lights, creator of fabulous wardrobes, with such fabrics consisting of smooth, soft silks to lush, thick fur coats made especially for Barbie and Ken. With the doll's perfect hair and bodies, everything came out beautifully! In my world of pretend, nothing was impossible. Each day's adventure always finished with a delightful ending of happily-ever-after.

Wild flowers grew in profusion around the fields of my "real life". As I skipped through the meadow filled with those beauties, I picked various varieties and dreamed of becoming a florist, a designer of stunning creations for weddings, parties and fancy homes.

Whether my dolls were heading off to school or going on a date, always with the most popular football star, life promised to be an amazing venture. I loved my world of pretend because it held much more promise than the real world ever seemed to.

In my little-girl world, I was popular, had perfect hair and was beautiful, with a flawless complexion and the ideal body. There, in my make-believe life I was filled with joy, love and peace. Everything was working on my side. My parents doted on me and smothered me with love. The people of the little kingdom respected me. Harsh words or abuse were never allowed. I fit there. It always promised to be a wonderful place, one that was very hard to leave.

So what happened to me? Life! It does not turn out like we dream it can in our little-girl worlds. In those times of imagination, I never thought about my prince turning into a troll or my moat filled with alligators and flesh-eating piranhas, let along the king and queen being anything less than perfect. However, I had to come to the stark realization that life is not a fairy tale. We live in a world with real issues and tragic circumstances. Testings and trials will come, it's a promise! However, they are there to mature us and build good character. The key is our response to them. Our response will determine what type of life we will live.

As I reminisced about my life's-journey, I believe my greatest regret is that I've been trying to find that imaginary place in which I can settle down and reside. How late in life for me to finally realize, it does not exist, at least not here on earth.

I remember the very moment this revelation came to me. Coming from a doctor's appointment, I thought for sure it would take me almost two hours to get home. My visit was at 3:30 p.m. However, I did not see him until 5:15. That put me leaving the clinic at 5:45 p.m. Taking a deep breath, I headed to my car, preparing to face horrible traffic. At that time of day in our city, the interstate becomes a parking lot. To put it mildly, it's a nightmare!

What a welcome surprise it was when God chose to have mercy on me! I was able to travel within the speed limit of sixty miles an hour almost all the way home. I smiled with delight as I caught sight of my speedometer and praised the God of heaven's armies. As I came to my exit, I turned right on the off-ramp and stopped, waiting for the line of traffic at the red light.

Sitting there, I suddenly had an epiphany! There is no perfect life on this side of heaven. Even the people whose life may appear perfect, isn't really. I witnessed first-hand that most of those outward shows are a farce. All sorts of heartbreaking issues take place behind closed doors. No one in this life is immune to trouble and tribulations. Each of us has some kind of burden to carry. We need to learn that it's ok to have them; we just can't let them control, discourage or destroy us.

While Salome pondered life's issues, she remembered a conversation with a friend she met while in pool therapy.

"God spoke to me this morning and asked me to embrace the physical suffering I'm going through. There is a reason for it and only God knows what it is. In the end, He will be true to His word and work this for my good and for His glory. However, in the painful present we must embrace the pain because through it, He is creating something beautiful within our hearts, even if we don't see it. This is where we learn our dependence on the cross of Jesus and our Heavenly Father."

Mulling over that thought in her heart, Salome remembered a study of the Cross. Jesus faced that agonizing time for us so we could walk free. Jesus took on Himself the punishment of the world's sins embracing it as His own. It's difficult to understand such love. However, the more trials and tribulations we do go through, the more God proves Himself to us personally. As we grow and mature spiritually, we fall in love with Who He really is. The whole while we are going through the trials and testings, He is wooing us to a closer bond with Himself.

At the beginning of my walk with God, everything seemed so easy but that was because I was a babe in Christ! Once I became a student of the Word, instead of only reading words, the levels in

Christ began. Each one was harder than the one before. However, each victory is so sweet!

With that thought in mind, Salome prayed, "I've walked a very long and hard path with many twisting and narrow turns. Yet each time, it only taught me more about You and gave me an opportunity to watch You move on my behalf. Lord, not only are You showing me who I am in You, but You are showing me that these trials and testings are here for a purpose. They are helping me become more like You and also acquainting me with Your suffering and the sorrow of those around me. In the midst of these testings, You are doing a deep work in Lewis and drawing us both closer to each other and to You! Oh, Lord thank You for this thorn embedded in my flesh—it has come to show me how desperately I love You and it's making me a better intercessor for others! Thank You, Lord!"

*By faith
Rahab the harlot
did not perish
along with those
who were disobedient,
after she welcomed
the spies in peace.
Hebrews 11:31 NIV*

CHAPTER **16**

REJOICE IN THE midst of the storm, keep your heart searching for Me. I'll turn your darkness to light, just wait and see! Over and over again, the melody of a song rambled through Salome's mind. Smiling, she thought, *I love when You wake me up singing, Lord!* Slowly, she opened her eyes and realized that Lewis was in the bathroom getting ready for work. *Rejoice in the midst of the storm, keep your heart searching for Me. I'll turn your darkness to light, just wait and see!* Again and again, the Lord continued to sing the song in her heart. The door to the bathroom opened and Salome said, "Good morning, Lewis. This is going to be a great day!"

Lewis leaned down, kissed her on the forehead and said, "Goodbye, I'm off to the funny farm."

Salome lay there for a time, realizing that even though her back was sore and stiff, there was still so much to be grateful for! *Thank you, Jesus, for our beautiful home, the wind chimes ringing their cheery song, birds singing their praise to the King and for so many things that would take me all day to mention! Nevertheless, thank You that my name is written in Your Lamb's Book of Life! This is a new day, and I will rejoice within it, searching for Your fingerprints and footprints throughout the day! I love you, Father, thank You for life, in Jesus's name!*

Rising, Salome headed toward the kitchen to feed the felines and prepare her morning cup of cappuccino. In her mind, she could already smell the delicious treat even before she made it to the kitchen. With great anticipation, she made sure the cats were fed and settled then began to mix up the luscious delicacy. As she poured the sweet cream into the cup and stirred, she then raised the cup to her nose and took in the pleasurable aroma.

Holding onto her cup, she turned and headed down the hall toward her bedroom. Walking down the hallway, Salome slowed to glance at the pictures of her family lovingly displayed on the wall. Taking a sip of her cappuccino, she studied each face and thought, *What a difference Jesus makes in a life! He has truly changed my life and restored many broken relationships.* As she continued to gaze upon the pictures of her parents, children and grandchildren, she suddenly began to grasp just how truly blessed she was! *God, You have never let me down! Your promises are yes and amen.*

Continuing to her office, Salome tenderly picked up the old, tattered and worn journal, holding it close to her heart. It had been through many generations of Salome's family before it found its home with her. Her grandmother loved Jesus and had much wisdom. Salome desperately desired to have some of that wisdom imparted into her heart.

She prayed, *Jesus, help me glean every bit of wisdom from the words written within the pages of this journal. As I read, open my eyes to see things I have never seen before. With Your Words, show me truth, in Jesus' name, I pray.*

Salome opened the journal to the bookmarked page. The pages seemed very fragile, just like life. She whispered, "To think, my grandmother penned the words on these pages years ago and today those very words are still making a difference in her family's life.

What a joy it would have been to know you, grandmother! I wonder what type of life you had. From everything I have read so far, life must not have been kind to you. Yet, your faith and trust in God stayed the course of your life journey. Grandmother seemed to have such a deep walk with Jesus. I desire to have that same type of relationship with You, Lord."

Salome stopped and wondered if her life would make a difference, not only in her family but, also in the people who walked within her circle. So many people have their eyes on everything but Jesus. In our world today, there are many gods. They loom above society in the form of debt, worry, the economy, sex, careers, the weights of this life, not to mention religious activities, false religions and cults. We must practice to keep our eyes where they belong—on a holy God Who created everything we can and cannot see. In the midst of trial and testing, we must keep our eyes focused on the Author and Finisher of our faith instead of the circumstances. Fact is also not necessarily truth! There is only one truth, the Bible! Remembering also, in times of testing, the Teacher is often silent.

With that in mind, Salome closed the journal, her finger marking her place. She turned and headed toward the music room, carrying the priceless journal. Walking into the room, she slowly sank down onto her chair and drank in the stillness of the room.

From ragged-painted walls, to beautiful creamy plaques placed strategically around the room, she had created an atmosphere of complete tranquility. Simple words like Love, Peace, Faith, Hope and Joy written on different garden tiles, reminded anyone entering that there was no other God except Jehovah! To the right of the door hung a large print of a beautiful tree-lined pathway, prompting Salome to remember that the Christian walk is a narrow path.

A Celtic cross hung on the wall to the left of the print. Salome made sure each room in her home had at least one cross as a reminder of the price paid for her freedom and salvation. She understood that these beautiful, ornate crosses are eye candy, pleasing to the sight but nothing like the real cross of Christ. In that period of history, the cross stood as a cursed thing. Romans crucified people all the time. They gloried in hanging people to die, driving nails in their hands and feet which held them to the cross. Roman soldiers lined the crosses up by the roadways so everyone could see the pitiful remains of those people who died in that atrocious manner.

History reminds us that the cross is not an easy thing to embrace. When Jesus said for us to deny ourselves, pick up our cross and carry it daily, He is referring to the old, rugged, wooden crosses from Roman days. *Oh Lord, we must get back to the realization that the cross is not a beautiful thing to be hung on walls or worn around one's neck. It means a harsh death, death to us,* she thought.

The atmosphere in the music room was filled with expectation. Salome's heart pounded with excitement to see what God would reveal today. *Thank You, Lord, You really are so gracious!* Lowering her head, she began to read her grandmother's journal.

God is placing sweet, godly women in my path to help me along my pilgrimage. My heart pounded inside my chest, with the feeling of filth and worthlessness from my past sins. However, today, a dear friend told me about a story of a brave woman in the Bible who believed God could turn a life around, in spite of her past.

How can a holy God want anything to do with me? From the tainted background I came from, I could only wonder, why Lord? It seems I move forward and begin to embrace Your promises then something happens and the flood of shame, guilt and condemnation come rolling back upon me again.

My friend and mentor is a wonderful story-teller and as she tells her tales it makes me feel like I'm sitting on the sidelines, watching the events taking place. Understanding and wisdom always flowed through her narrative so I thought I would share one special story here, in my journal. It is through this story, I embraced that the Blood of Jesus does indeed wash away every sin, as though it never happened. This woman's example, gave me the faith to take steps forward to grow up, to maturity in Christ!

━◦ɪɪɪɪ\ ᶂ \ɪɪɪɪ◦━

In her culture, prostitution is just part of "normal" life. She hated it, but it was the only way she had to support herself and her family. A little part of her died each time she entertained a client. The men who came to Jericho had to be some of the most evil, ruthless and horrible characters in the world. Each day the drunken, reviling and sexual perversion of the pagan culture hellbent on the pursuit of everything evil, stared her in the face. Could there be hope in the midst of such an existence?

This was Jericho! A part of the Amorite kingdom, a grotesquely violent and totally depraved culture bent on doing everything God condemned.

If Rahab's worth had been in her possessions, she could say she was a very wealthy woman. However, the cost for such prosperity came at a high price, her very soul. She hated what she had become no matter how accepted it was in that city.

The house/inn she owned was built inside the outer wall of the city, with a window looking out upon the countryside. From this window high in the wall, she could see a large part of the surrounding area. Her business was lucrative because she was a very lovely woman. Nevertheless, she despised every part of her life. Her existence was surrounded by the profane pursuit of carnal self-gratification. Rahab felt enslaved to the most diabolical kinds of passion, held in bondage to her own sin and a monstrous society destined to destroy itself.

People no longer saw her as a human being. On the contrary, she felt like a piece of meat, born for the sinful pleasure of man. Men treated her as though she had no heart and soul; she was nothing more than a body to be used for their enjoyment.

Her beauty became well-known throughout the city and the surrounding countryside. Male visitors to Jericho, looking for some entertainment, were always pointed in her direction. With large sultry black-brown eyes, framed by long fringed black lashes, it seemed to her customers that she could look into their very soul. Her long raven-black hair was thick and lustrous and hung down her back, brushing against her hips with each step she took. Rahab was gorgeous on the outside but broken, ugly and hurting on the inside. Her small frame and feisty spirit drew strong-willed men who seemed determined to dominate her.

From the beginning of this hateful life, she learned to play the game well. Since her family was poor, they needed financial help. In her culture, prostitution was the only way a woman could profit financially.

Listening to comments from some of the men who visited her, a common theme seemed to prevail. Because of that, hope began to grow within her heart, even though it seemed very farfetched! She'd been hearing about the God of Israel! Miracles, signs and wonders were performed against Egypt as the God of Israel demanded the release of His people. Their God destroyed Pharaoh, drowning him and his whole army in the depths of the Red Sea.

Tales rumbled through the area telling of the Hebrew nation's exodus from Egypt. Moses led his people to the Red Sea and since they could go no further, they camped there for the night. Fear gripped their hearts as they wondered what would become of them in the morning when Pharaoh caught up to them. The God of Israel held Pharaoh's army at bay with a pillar-of-fire. That night a strong wind blew and in the morning they saw that God divided the Red Sea. Moses led all the Israelites, over a million people, across to the other side on dry land. When Pharaoh followed them with his troops, the same God closed up the sea and all the Egyptians were destroyed, along with their chariots and horses. That is a God

Rahab wanted to know.

With everything in her, she genuinely wanted to believe. There were not many choices for women in her culture. *I am sick of this! Sick of my lifestyle and the world I live in. This is not a life; this is a slow, torturous, painful death. There has to be more! I know it deep inside. I know there has to be more! I cannot believe this is all I was born for. Yet, honestly, who would want me! Look what I have become. What would my future be?*

Rahab prayed to the God of Israel, *Help me out of this lifestyle, Jehovah. No one has to tell me I am a sinful woman; I know! Daily, I carry the shame of the life I have been forced to live. But I believe in You and I will trust You. Help me, please! Show me the way out of this life of being a slave to men and sin!*

━━◖〰◗━━

News spread through the city. The Israelites were camped across the Jordon River and fear began to grow like a thick, dark cloud within the city of Jericho. How do you stop a God who can split open the Red Sea? The Jordan River was a piece of cake for such a God. Everyone knows it is just a matter of time before the Israelites attacked.

Jericho's king sent soldiers to spread the word, "Be on high alert for any strangers. Ring the warning bell the minute anyone suspicious is spotted," the king ordered.

━━◖〰◗━━

Just about noon the next day, two men walked into Rahab's inn. "Do you have any place for us to lodge tonight?" they asked.

It was quite obvious these were the Israelite men the guards spoke about. Boldly, she asked, "Are you Israelites?"

Salmon and his fellow Israelite looked at each other then said, "Yes, we are."

"The king has ordered everyone to keep a look-out for you,"

she whispered. "Quickly, hide on the roof amongst the flax. When the soldiers come for you, I will tell them you have left and I don't know where you went."

It seemed strange to Rahab that these two men, Israelites, treated her with more respect than anyone ever had. *In their eyes, maybe they see me as what I am, a broken woman,* she thought. Lust did not reside in their hearts and it did not show in their faces. They spoke to her kindly, with honor and respect. The only thing that she saw in their eyes was dignity, something she had never experienced.

Suddenly, the soldiers banged on the door of Rahab's home. "Open the door!"

Rahab turned and gazed across the room, everything was in place and the door to the attic closed tight. Taking a deep breath, she turned and opened the door.

"We were told two strangers came into your home. Where are they? Are they the ones we are looking for?"

"Yes, the men came to me, but I did not know where they were from. They left the city just as darkness began to fall. Right after they left, the gate was shut. However, if you hurry, you may be able to capture them," Rahab said.

"Let's go," the soldiers said.

Rahab watched through her window on the wall as the soldiers left to pursue the spies. She saw the contingent of armed men speed down the road toward the Jordan. The gate was again shut tight as soon as they left the city.

From the time the Israelites were spotted across the Jordon River, fear and confusion became new residents within the city walls. As she stood outside of her door, watching the commotion, she realized a person could almost taste the fear permeating the air. Everyone knew the evidence was clear; The Lord God of Israel was going to destroy this city.

Rahab closed the door to her home and walked to the door

in the roof. She whispered to the men, "I know that the Lord has given you the city. The fear of you is in all of us and the people of the land around us as well. I have heard how the Lord dried up the water of the Red Sea for you when you came out of Egypt and what you did to the two kings of the Amorites who were on the other side of the Jordan. Our hearts melted with fear! There is no more courage here in Jericho because of the Lord your God. HE is GOD in heaven above and on the earth beneath.

I beg you now! Swear to me by the name of the Lord, since I have shown you kindness, that you will also show kindness to my father's house and my house. Please deliver us from death."

Salmon answered, "Our lives for yours if you don't tell of our business in the city and our whereabouts, then you will be protected. When the Lord gives us this land, we will treat you and your father's house kindly. Make sure all your family will be within your house. It is the only way they can be saved. Anyone who stays outside, will die, along with the rest of the city. We will not be responsible for the oath we swore unless you tie a scarlet thread and hang it from your window. Also, again, you must bring your father, mother, sisters and brothers here, **in** your house, with the scarlet thread tied in the window. Do you understand?" the men said.

"Yes, I understand and I will do all you have said. Thank you," she replied.

Rahab tied a rope through the window and let the men down. She knew they would keep their promise. They were not like the men of Jericho. They spoke truth from their hearts. "Go to the mountains and you will miss the soldiers. Stay there three days until they have returned to the city, and then go on your way," Rahab whispered. "I believe what you have told me and I believe in your God. I have prayed to the God of Israel for deliverance, and He will do it! I believe He will take my life and transform it." As soon as they were gone, Rahab took the scarlet thread and hung it out the window of her home on the city wall.

For the next three days, Rahab kept watch out the window and planned her next moves to protect her family. On the third day, when she spotted Jericho's soldiers returning to the city, she set her gaze high into the mountains. Then she saw them. The Israelite spies were heading back to their camp.

People in the city were watchful. No one had come into Rahab's inn for three days. In that time, she brought her whole family together, in her house, and shared the plan with them.

Prayer became a big part of Rahab's life. Whenever she prayed, she could feel the Lord God's presence and peace. Throughout the city fear and panic reigned, yet no one seemed sorry for the way they lived. Rahab noticed that fear only seemed to make people angry and defiant against God. They cried, "Our city's walls are large; we can run races on top of these walls. Nothing and no god can knock them down!"

For the next few weeks, there was no sign of the Israelites. Many began to wonder if they had moved on. The gate of the city remained shut. People had just begun to relax their vigil when word came that the entire Israelite army crossed the Jordan River on dry land. Once again, the dark, murky cloud of fear fell over the city.

All the people of Jericho knew the Israelite God could destroy them. If He could split the Red Sea, kill two strong Amorite armies and their kings and split the Jordon River, what could stop Him from knocking down the walls of Jericho?

Rahab had no idea what life could bring her once this was over, but she knew anything would be better than the way she lived. How could she survive living in such sin against a holy God? She knew her profession was an acceptable life in Jericho. It was the only way she knew to support herself and her family. As she closed her eyes, she wondered if she could ever forgive herself for giving in to that lifestyle.

Scanning her home full of family, she knew it was not going

to be easy for any of them. Everything they knew as normal was about to change. Rahab embraced the fact that this would be a new beginning, a fresh start. Jehovah God would lead them. She reminded her family what the Lord God had accomplished for Israel and assured them He would be there for them, as well. Suddenly, Rahab wondered what she had to give to such a holy and wonderful God.

She became overwhelmed by the whole situation and Satan took that moment to try and poison her mind. "What do you have to offer Him? You are nothing but a prostitute, a used-up one at that. Do you really believe you could live any other way?"

Considering her lifestyle, she realized how foul it truly was. She began to second-guess as to whether or not the Lord God would accept her. Then realization dawned on her that she was in a battle for her soul and the souls of her family!

"No," she cried, "I will not give place to doubt." Then she thought, *This is what she had prayed for, dreamed of and she would believe. God had heard her prayers and was answering them!*

Falling to her knees she bent her head in prayer. "Oh Lord, have mercy on my soul and the souls of my family. We are a sinful people living among sinful people. Show us the way to go from here, Lord God, and thank You for forgiving our sins and showing us a new way to live. Help us to walk in faith, not in fear, doubt or unbelief. We believe in You, Jehovah God and we will trust You."

For the next few days, the city remained in a complete uproar because of the shock at the behavior of the attacking Israelite army. Once a day for the past six days, Israel marched around the city, carrying the Ark of the Covenant, as the priests sounded trumpets made of ram's horns. The army would then return to camp.

The first few days that the horns blew, the people of Jericho stood on top of the walls shouting down at such carryings on. "Is this how you attack a city," one man shouted, "marching around in silence while your priests blow horns?" Then all the men of the city would laugh at the marching Israelites.

"What do you hope to do? Shake the walls down with your horns? That's not the way to defeat a city!" Again, all the men would jeer and fall down laughing.

Yet, on the fourth day, the blowing of those horns began to get on people's nerves. The silence of voices and the blasting of horns created an eerie suspense. As they looked and listened, the hair on the back of their necks stood up in a spine-chilling manner. Although it seemed impossible, the electrifying atmosphere alerted all Jericho that doom was fast approaching. Nothing could stop it!

Rahab's thoughts reverted back to the Red Sea crossing. She understood that God would not allow any man to get the glory for destroying the city. He gets all the glory. No army could defeat this city; but the God who could part the seas would. If He chose to use trumpets made of ram's horns, so be it. Didn't He use only a staff to split the Red Sea? God used the natural things to do magnificent feats!

Early in the morning, on the seventh day, the Israelite army began their march. "Something is different about today," Rahab said. "This may be the day! Prepare, family, to see the deliverance God will bring us. Make sure you stay within this house. To go outside means death!"

Returning to her window, Rahab checked the scarlet cord. It was still in place. She could feel it, taste it on her tongue and she knew! *The new beginning is waiting there at dawn!*

"One, two, three, four, five," Rahab and her family heard the count from the people outside. "They have been around the city five times and there they go again."

Marcus, Rahab's brother, could stand it no longer. "I have to go and see about my friends. What will happen to them? My heart is torn in two! I will be right back, Rahab."

Rahab stopped him just as he opened the door, "You know the promise. You will be lost if you are not within the walls of my home. Marcus, you will be lost! There's nothing you can do for your friends! You know if you are not in here with us, when the Israelites enter the city, you will die! Think about our mother and father. What will your death do to them? Forget these friends of yours and stay safe with us. Please Marcus, do not go out there."

"Rahab, I will be right back, I promise," Marcus replied with a reassuring smile. "I cannot stand this any longer. I have to see and besides, we don't know if they will even attack us today. They've been marching around us for seven days and still they have not made the first move to assault us. What makes today different?"

Just as Marcus began to close the door, Rahab heard someone say, "They have finished the sixth march around the city. Now they're going around again for the seventh time. How many more times will they do this and for what purpose?"

Rahab cried out, "Marcus, hurry!"

Rahab ran up to the door and leaned on it. Turning, she looked at her family, "This is your choice. If you are not inside this house when the city falls, you will die. Each of us is responsible for our own actions. Which do you choose? Will you go out, as Marcus did or will you stay here?"

Her father and mother looked at each other, and then to Rahab, "We are staying."

Her sisters and brothers stared in her direction and proclaimed, "There is no other place to be. This is where we belong. We also, choose to serve the God of creation, the God of the Israelites."

With that, Rahab ran to the window. The scarlet cord was still there. Lowering her head, she prayed once again to the only God who could save them. *Our lives are in Your hands, God. Have Your way and please give us your peace.*

All of a sudden, the horns gave a long blast and a shout went up so loud that it seemed to pierce their eardrums. Rapidly, the walls of the city began to shake as though the ground itself was giving way! The trembling came so swiftly it took their breath away and made it hard to stand upright. Yet, with all the shaking, the part of the wall in which Rahab's home rested, stayed in place.

Rahab could only stare out the window at the terror around them. The mighty walls of the city had fallen. Screams and cries of terror rose above the rumbling of the falling walls. Rahab and her family gathered in a huddle, holding each other as the younger ones cried out in fear. "Hold tight little ones, God is for us, He is here protecting us."

Suddenly they heard Israel's army's battle cries as they climbed over the rubble, destroying every human being and animal within the city. "Marcus is doomed!" Rahab cried. He chose to leave the safety-net God allowed us. With a broken heart, she knew that each person had to make his or her own choice to serve God or not. *Marcus is lost and there is nothing I can do.*

All of a sudden, Rahab heard someone calling her name! "Rahab," Salmon shouted! "You and everyone in the house may come out. I have prepared a place for you and your family on the fringes of our camp. This is where you will dwell. Your faith in Jehovah has saved you!"

Rahab and her family left the house, climbing over the rubble surrounding them. Astonished by the sight before her eyes, she dropped to her knees and gave thanks to the God of all! Her God! She prayed, *Lord, who am I that You considered me and my family? I have nothing to offer You except what is left of my life. So please, take it and use it for Your glory. Thank You for deliverance. Thank You for freedom. Show me the way to go and I will follow You. Thank you, Lord! You saved all who put their trust in You. You are not only a powerful and mighty God. You are also a gracious and forgiving God. I will serve you the rest of my life!*

As Salmon watched Rahab drop to her knees and pray, one

thing stood out to him. He had never seen such faith and devotion to Jehovah in all Israel! Salmon prayed, *Lord, this woman has lived through an evil culture and still, she has a humble heart of faith, courage and leadership that saved not only herself, but her family, as well. Bless her, Lord, more than she could ever imagine. Truly, I am witnessing a faith that has been tried through the fire.*

The Lord gave Rahab great favor in Salmon' eyes that day and in time, he took her to be his wife.

────⊙⦓〰〰⦔⊙────

Putting grandmother's journal aside for a moment, Salome was in awe as she thought of the wisdom and insight her grandmother gleaned, not just from the people in her life but also from her own relationship with the Lord. Rahab was a harlot after all, and look what God did for her!

Once again, she picked up the journal and continued soaking up the wisdom that seemed to exude from within the pages of that old book. Salome had an epiphany! *No matter how long ago the journal was written; it is all the Word of God and that makes it still relevant for life today.* Lowering her head, she continued reading.

God had plans for Rahab in spite of the circumstances of her life. In the past, she was a harlot and in the eyes of man, worthless. I am so glad God skips the obvious and looks at our hearts. He looks to the inward place that only He can see. When Rahab gave her life to God, I wonder if she realized she was no longer a slave to sin and the slave woman but she was now a child of the Most High God, a child of the freed woman!

We judge ourselves by man's ruler and do God a great disservice. Whenever God calls me to step out to do or say something, how many times do I reply, "Lord, I can't do this?"

What right does the clay have to tell the Potter "yes" or "no"? I must repent for believing the lie instead of trusting Him. God's Word says, "Jesus is living inside of me! The One who can move mountains, the One who has courage that can stand up to an enemy and declare, "It is finished!" That One lives in me and I can do all things through Him who gives me what I need in order to do His will.

As I heard the story of Jericho and imagined how it could have been for Rahab, I saw no difference between us. I was living my own type of Jericho when God delivered me. He saved me with the blood of His precious Son, Jesus. Yet, dare I say, "He's not enough?" Each time I say no, that is exactly what I am declaring. *Father, forgive me for doubt and unbelief in who You created me to be.*

Rahab had no idea of the plans God had for her life. Her first step was to simply **believe** Him! The next step, make the choice to **follow** His will! As she began putting her trust in God, He proceeded to change her life and eventually, the lives of her family. Rather than resist God, I saw her determination to commit herself to His care.

God chose her to be in the lineage of Jesus. I see her as a woman of faith, meekness, influence, courage and leadership. We would do well if we remember it is not a person's past that **defines** them. Rather, people are defined by the choices they make when they become aware of Who God is. It was Rahab's choices after submitting to God, which defined her character, not her past.

She is mentioned three times in the New Testament. Once in Mathew 1:5 NIV, *Salmon was the father of Boaz by Rahab.* Again in Hebrews 11:31 NIV, *By faith Rahab the harlot did not perish along with those who were disobedient, after she had welcomed the spies in peace.* Then in James 2:25 NIV, *In the same way, was not Rahab the harlot also justified by works when she received the messengers and sent them out by another way?*

Her faith, acknowledgement and trust in God defined Rahab and made her different than all the other people in Jericho. It is curious that a woman of ill-repute was the only resident of Jericho whose heart was not hardened to the living God. Instead, she opened not only her home, but also her heart to the spies and the God they served.

Rahab was willing to commit treason to help Jericho's enemy. That took courage. She was also a woman devoted to her family. In order to protect them, she struck the deal with the spies.

Rahab, a woman of valor! Her life demonstrates to me, I don't have to be perfect for God to use me in significant ways. God is free to use whomever He wills.

Rahab's story teaches me not to judge others and, most of all, to give myself a break. God uses ordinary people and ordinary things to accomplish His will on earth. He will use me right where I am if I give my heart completely to Him. All have sinned and fallen short of the glory of God. Rahab could have used many excuses yet, she chose to step out and believe.

Father, open my eyes to see from Your perspective. Lord, make me aware of all the things you have placed inside of me to use for Your kingdom. Fill me with Your confidence and love for others, Jesus, and show me the way You desire me to go. Thank You for Your mercy and grace, Lord. Thank You for Your longsuffering. I love You and I praise You for all the things You have done and are doing. I thank You, for making me a woman of faith, courage, wisdom and influence, in Jesus name.

◄◄◄◦❧◦►►►

As Salome finished reading the chapter, she could not believe how closely she could identify with not only Rahab but with her grandmother, as well. The more she read, the more curious she became about her grandmother and the life she must have lived. She remembered a passage in Ecclesiastes 1:9 NIV, *What has been will be again, what has been done will be done again; there is nothing new under the sun.*

"No," Salome whispered to herself, "there is truly nothing new under the sun! God is still God no matter what century we are in. He is still the lover of our souls and filled with mercy, love and grace for some of the most unlikely candidates around. I am so glad He chose me, so excited that God uses natural things and normal people to accomplish great acts of faith!"

Salome whispered softly, "Lord, here I am, the free child of the Most High God, daughter of the KING! I'm ready and waiting to move in a way that will show all the people I come in contact with that my God is an awesome God! Thank You for making me a new creation in You and for helping me grow up!" I remember the scripture in 1 Corinthians 13:11 NIV, *When I was a child, I talked like a child, I thought like a child, I reasoned like a child. When I became a man or woman, I put childish ways behind me.* In Luke 8:14, scripture warns us that the cares of this life, riches and pleasures can choke out the seed of God's Word so that they do not mature. Yes, indeed, it is time to grow up and begin to act like a true child of the God of all creation!!

Closing the journal, Salome could feel something inside her heart and soul that resembled an electric current beginning to build, similar to a mighty rushing river. "It is an excitement I cannot contain," she cried! As she sat waiting on Him, she knew just as Rahab did, something awesome is coming—and it will destroy any walls standing in her way! With that knowledge Salome got up, went to her keyboard, sat down and began to play and sing praises to the Name of the God of all gods and the King of all kings!

The only thing that walks back from the tomb
with the mourners and refuses to be buried
is the character of a man.
What a man is, survives him.
It can never be buried.
J.R. Miller

CHAPTER **17**

WHAT A NIGHT! Salome rolled over, glaring at the clock, "Only 7:00 A.M.," she moaned from the pain and soreness that seemed to travel throughout her body. Although the sun streamed in through the windows of her bedroom, the agony from her body caused despair and depression deep inside her heart. She closed her eyes for an instant remembering, *Jesus is here*. It is in that moment, she began to count her many blessings. "Thank you Lord, my hands don't hurt, I can breathe and it does not hurt. I can see Your majestic beauty because I am not blind. My ears hear morning birds singing their own individual bird song. No headaches so, my head is fine. Lord, my hair does not hurt and my teeth don't hurt. I am fine, blessed, my name is written down in Your Book of Life! There is a roof over my head, clothes on my back, food on my table, a car to drive, great friends and so much more! Every moment, I am not alone. You are here! Truly, I am blessed!"

Four months since surgery, yet the pain and discomfort still seemed unrelenting and, at times, harder than before. Salome had come to terms with the long, healing process and had even begun to embrace it as her own because she knew depression was there in the darkness, waiting for her to let her guard down. *God is in control and I will continue to trust Him no matter what happens,* she thought. *I'll trust in His Word that says, All things work together for good to them that love God and are called according to His purpose.* (See Romans 8:28)

A new development had occurred over the recent weeks. Salome could not believe she did not recognize the symptoms. Not only was her body fighting to heal from the surgery, but other symptoms had developed. Something was protruding from her back. The doctors argued that it might possibly be that the screws were too long for her small frame or maybe ever scar tissue. Whatever it was caused the sciatic nerve to send shooting pain down her left hip, leg and foot. The physicians believed something else might be causing some of the swelling, maybe a bone having grown too close to the nerve.

All Salome could do is laugh. *This is really becoming almost hilariously comical! I feel like Job! Did You and the devil have a discussion about me, Jesus? Seriously, I remember praying once after I read Job, 'I surely hope You and Satan never have that type of conversation about me!' Yet, here I am!*

Yesterday when the gastroenterologist came in he said plainly, "You have a flare-up of diverticulitis and there is the possibility your colon may need to be dilated again from the surgery you had five years ago."

The irritant on her left foot now had a name, a plantar wart. It appeared that Salome would have to get the thing frozen and cut out. There was no doubt left in her mind. Now she understood! Not only was the nerve impeding her ability to move, but the wart was playing a major role in the pain associated with her walking.

Rolling over, Salome began the process of getting out of bed. Lifting herself up to a sitting position, she perched on the edge of the bed. Murmuring to herself she stated, "This is worse than right after surgery. STOP! I capture that thought and command it to the obedience of Christ." Immediately she forced her mind toward Jesus. "Lord, help me remember!" In the last few days she could almost physically feel Him wrap His warm arms of love around her spirit. Her body throbbed with pain but her spirit soared on the wings of Love Himself. She never had encountered anything closely related to this before. *Lord, if this is the only way to become more familiar with You, then it is worth it all! My relationship with You is more important to me than anything,* she thought.

Finally she stood, and then headed for the kitchen to fix herself a hot cup of cappuccino. Walking slowly, some of the stiffness began to give way to become a deep, dull ache. As she peered from the dining room windows, Salome whispered, "It is a beautiful day. No matter what pain I experience, this is a day filled with possibilities. Stay focused on Jesus," she whispered to herself. Then loudly she said, "This is the day YOU have made. I will rejoice and be glad!"

Gazing out at the Lord's creation took her mind off the pain. "Feels like it's time to grow up. I remember the Word in 1 Corinthians 13:11 NIV, *When I was a child, I talked like a child, I reasoned like a child. When I became a man, I put childish ways behind me.* In the midst of it all, God used the situation to cause Salome to understand that her body was completely separate from who she really is.

Salome whispered to herself, "This body of death is slowly dying and one day, if Jesus tarries, it will be planted in the ground. Then I will receive a new, glorified body. Actually, I cannot wait! My identity is not tied up in anything earthly—my identity is heavenly and spiritual, hidden in Jesus! I am a daughter of the freed woman and my Heavenly Father." Musing over her thoughts, that fact sank deeper in her heart than she realized.

From the time Salome said the sinner's prayer, she had heard teachings about our bodies being described as a tent, an earth suit, a cocoon and more recently, her favorite yet, a shell. However, none of those describe the new revelation Father gave her.

Salome, the real person is held inside the shell. It is the person born of the Spirit of God. Look at an egg. The shell of the egg is not the chick. It only holds the chick until it is ready to hatch. It houses the fledgling through the time of transformation from a single cell to becoming the baby chicken. Once the metamorphosis is completed, it breaks through the shell and a new life begins.

God gently reminded her about an exchange with her grandfather. As a child she and Papa sat watching a chick in the process of breaking through its shell. Poor little thing had trouble cracking the surface. Then, Salome reached down to help the chick out.

Abruptly, Papa caught her hand and said, "Babe, you can't help the chick peck through. If you do, it will die. It must fight on its own so it can be strong enough to survive this life."

2 Corinthians 5:1 NLT says: *For we know that when this earthly tent we live in is taken down* (that is, when we die and leave this earthly body), *we will have a house in heaven, an eternal body made for us by God himself and not by human hands.* Understanding began to dawn on Salome like the dawning of a new morning!

Meditating on the scripture, Salome's heart longed to be clothed with the heavenly, eternal body prepared for her. Whispering softly she questioned, "Could it be that through this healing process, the new creature inside me has been preparing for birth?"

Before surgery, Salome had been forced into the roll as head of her household. Through this time of recovery, Lewis had no choice but to step up into the position God had created for him initially.

When a man allows his wife to lead, it is most often from a lack of association with Jesus. Any relationship will cost you. Our oneness with Christ requires death to self, so we can live for Him. In the middle of our trials, God proves His character and faithfulness along with His deep abiding love for us. Trials are here to test our character, challenging us to grow up in Christ.

Turning it over in her mind, Salome spoke out loud, "We decide if we will become bitter or better. It seems so much easier to embrace a wound, blaming others, than to open ourselves up to the Lord in meekness. It's difficult to allow Jesus to deal with our hearts. I don't know how many times I have embraced a wound and acted in pride instead of looking into my own heart issues. Then I can allow Jesus to show me the trigger so I can let it all go.

It is easy to buy into the lie that all good little Christians should just let things roll off our backs, suck it up, and then go on. Honestly, it doesn't roll, does it, Lord? It plants itself inside our hearts and later produces the fruit of bitterness. We ARE only human. When someone hurts us we bleed, both physically and emotionally. The key is to run to our Great Physician and allow Him to hold us through the pain, hurt or disappointment and then give it to Him. Just like Jesus did in the Garden of Gethsemane! His flesh did not want to go the way of the cross—He left us the example there as He prayed, 'Not my will but Thy will be done.' Lord, how blinded I have been! Please forgive me."

This is where we develop spiritual muscles and embrace everything Jesus died to give us. Freedom from sin, His armor, the Blood of Jesus, the Name of Jesus, the Word of our testimony and prayer are there for us to fight and win the battle raged by the devil. If we listen closely, the Holy Spirit fills us with wisdom and revelation about who God is and the victory already won at the Cross of Christ! As Salome thought about this it suddenly dawned on her that it was time for her to become the warrior Christ had called her to be.

Reflecting over the years of their marriage, Salome finally saw that Lewis' lack of leadership had indeed affected her and forced her into a roll God never intended for her. The situations were disappointing, discouraging, heart breaking and at times seemed hopeless. It was now evident that she had allowed a seed of deep-seated resentment and bitterness inside her heart. "Lord, you are showing me truth and that truth is setting me free. Thank You!"

Now, however, Salome was finally ready and in position to overcome the ploy of the devil through meekness, prayer and warfare against the spirits determined to destroy what God had put together. But before she could be prepared, she knew she needed to begin to take up the weapons of her warfare. Realization hit her, "Lord, when did I put my armor down and give up?"

Salome remembered the passage in the Bible in 2 Corinthians 10:3-5 GNT: *It is true that we live in the world, but we do not fight from worldly motives. The weapons we use in our fight are not the world's weapons but God's powerful weapons, which we use to destroy strongholds. We destroy false arguments; we pull down every proud obstacle that is raised against the knowledge of God; we take every thought captive and make it obey Christ.*

That's it, time to fight a Spiritual warfare for my marriage and family, Salome thought! "Lord, the devil's tactics surely are deceiving. We fight each other instead of fighting against the "real" enemy. The sly, crafty adversary causes us to walk in division and strife instead of joining in unity to defeat his working in our lives. Once he has accomplished that, all he has to do is sit back and watch! How easily we fall," she whispered. "Be careful if you think you stand lest you fall!" (See 1 Corinthians 10:12)

Taking a sip of her cappuccino, she smiled and began to pray for a battle plan. Scripture began to float across her heart, 1 Corinthians 2:5 GNT, *Your faith, does not rest on human wisdom but on God's power.* She realized the way to win this battle would not include human reasoning. It would be God ordained. Philippians 4:4-9 GNT ran through her heart: *May you always be joyful in your union with the Lord. I say it again: rejoice! Show a gentle attitude toward everyone. The Lord is coming soon. Don't worry about anything, but in all your prayers ask God for what you need, always asking Him with a thankful heart. And God's peace, which is far beyond human understanding, will keep your hearts and minds safe in union with Christ Jesus. In conclusion, my friends fill your minds with those things that are good and that deserve praise: things that are true, noble, right, pure, lovely, and honorable. Put into practice what you learned and received from me, both from my words and from my actions. And the God who gives us peace will be with you.*

Salome groaned over the past years as God opened her eyes to the tactics of the deceiver in their lives. "Unfortunately," she said, "I've listened to the lies of the devil instead of standing on these scriptures. Time to repent and prepare for war! Lord, help me place a guard over my mind and heart and mouth, to think on good things and remember to be thankful for everything, good and bad. You **are** working all things for my good and Your glory, to conform me more to the image of Christ!" (See Roman's 8:28-29)

Time to put on the full armor of God in order to stand against the wiles of the devil! Ephesians 6:10-18 GNT the full armor of God! *Finally, build up your strength in union with the Lord and by means of his mighty power. Put on all the armor that God gives you, so that you will be able to stand up against the Devil's evil tricks. For, **we are not fighting against human beings** but, against the wicked spiritual forces in the heavenly world, the rulers, authorities, and cosmic powers of this dark-age. So put on God's armor now! Then when the evil day comes, you will be able to resist the enemy's attacks; and after fighting to the end, you will still hold your ground. So stand ready, with truth as a belt tight around your waist, with righteousness as your breastplate, and as your shoes the readiness to announce the Good News of peace. At all times carry faith as a shield; for with it you will be able to put out all the burning arrows shot by the evil one. And accept salvation as a helmet, and the word of God as the sword which the Spirit gives you. Do all this in prayer, asking for God's help. **Pray on every occasion, as the Spirit leads. For this reason keep alert and never give up; pray always for all God's people.***

"Lord, the dream of the **freed woman** and **slave woman** comes to mind. Why do we so easily forget that our battle is not against people, but the spirits behind the people? Give me spiritual discernment to see the battle I'm fighting. Open my spiritual eyes to the forces behind them and reveal their weaknesses to me. Give me a battle plan, Jesus, that will defeat the enemy in our lives. Please fill me with the confidence of Who You are in me! Lord, I plead the Blood of Jesus over my whole family and all our possessions, in Jesus' name.

The Lord reminded Salome of a vision He'd given her years before. Only eight months old in the Lord, she was at a party when a man with a vile and vulgar attitude walked into the room. Her heart was broken when she witnessed his abusive behavior of the woman he had brought to the party. He treated her like a prostitute in front of everyone completely dehumanizing her. When Salome could stand it no longer, she walked out of the room. Laying her head against the wall trying to grasp what was happening to her heart she suddenly heard the soft voice of the Lord. "Salome, turn and look at the man."

Determined, she whispered, "No Lord, he makes me physically sick! I know what that kind of abuse feels like and I despise him."

Once again, the Lord gently spoke in a still small voice, "Look at him—you need to see him the way I see him."

Again, Salome said, "Lord, he deserves whatever he gets, he's horrible. I hate abuse of any kind."

With an authority no one could deny, the Lord spoke, **"Turn and look at him!"**

Turning slowly back into the room, she gazed toward the man and saw him through heaven's eyes. The Lord gently spoke, "Salome, this is where he will be if no one intercedes for him."

Before her, the man stood naked with flames surrounding him. A look of pure agony and complete torment had contorted his face. He was screaming out in terror as flames and something like bolts of lightning flashed through him. When she could not stand the horror any longer, she turned and hurried into the bathroom.

There, in the quiet of that room, Salome looked at herself in the mirror as tears trickled down her cheeks. Softly Jesus responded, "**That** is how I see him, Salome. Unless someone prays for him and dares to witness to him, hell **is** his destination. Child, are **you truly** willing to see people the way I see them?"

*Are not all angels
ministering spirits
sent to serve those
who will inherit salvation?
Hebrews 1:14 NIV*

CHAPTER **18**

CONVICTED BY THE scene from by-gone years Salome sighed and, bowing her head she prayed, "Oh Lord I am sorry, I forgot about that man. After the party, I did pray for him for a long time. Yet, honestly, I forgot about that lesson. How self centered I have become. I am not my own, I have been brought with the high price of Jesus' Blood. But for the grace of GOD, GO I! Father, I am willing!"

As soon as she spoke, a picture opened before her that was bigger than life itself. Her eyes widened and her mouth dropped open as she stared at the sight now laid before her. Had she lost her mind or was the scene before her real? It was the spirit world, more active and alive than the natural world.

Salome felt like she was watching and participating in a life size movie. Yet, somehow she knew it was more real than the natural world she could see. People stood silent, still, as they waited to be fitted with battle gear created especially for them. These people came from every nation, tribe and tongue of the earth. Ministering to and preparing the saints were, what Salome believed to be, angels. In the far distance she saw what appeared to be the enemy's camp. Somehow, she just knew that this army of the Lord was preparing to storm the adversary and recover family, friends and people who had been lost.

Two very large angels emerged from the crowd and headed

toward her. One angel's name was Faith and the other, Hope. They were as tall as the long, pine trees in her yard and fully dressed in battle armor that shone with a brilliance no words could ever describe. By some means, Salome knew that the brilliant shine was part of the Glory of the Lord because the angels were in His presence. The natural eye could not see the almost blinding light, it was only in the Spirit-realm one could witness His amazing glory! It reminded Salome of the story in the Bible when Moses came down from the mountain. He placed a veil over his face because it shone with the glory of the Lord because he had been in His presence. (See Exodus 34)

Continuing to stare at them, Salome realized they were carrying something. In their hands they held different sections of armor. Each section shone as brightly as the angels did. The angel named Faith stood in front of her as though he were sizing her up. Then Hope spoke, "Salome, you are almost ready to engage in battle again. We've saved your armor and polished it for you, while we waited for this time to arrive.

The first piece of armor to go on is the helmet of salvation." As Faith spoke, Hope placed the helmet on Salome's head. A spiritual mirror stood before Salome and she watched the change in her appearance when the helmet was in place. Hope said, "This helmet is here to protect your mind, Salome. Jesus paid the price for this section of armor with the crown of thorns pressed on His head. Never take it off. It is here to remind you that you have been bought with the price of the Blood of Jesus. Therefore, you can walk in freedom, knowing that you are welcomed into the Throne Room of God anytime. The veil that kept you out was torn in two when Jesus took His last breath over two thousand years ago. Walk in the knowledge that you truly are one of His chosen. His own beloved! You are not your own, You belong to Jesus!"

Faith held up the breast-plate of righteousness and slowly slipped it on and attached it in the back. "Salome, this part of your armor covers your heart. It is here to remind you to guard your heart. Keep watch over what you allow to influence your heart and mind. There are only eighteen inches between your mind and your heart and whatever enters the mind will eventually affect your heart. Remember, **your righteousness** is like filthy rags. If the devil can get your eyes on your own righteousness, he will take you down. However, Jesus' righteousness is covering you—you wear His robe of righteousness bought and paid for through the cross at Calvary. When the Father looks down and sees you, He sees you covered in the robe Jesus bought for you with His Blood. Keep it on at **all** times to defeat the onslaught of the devil. Also, remember that you have already been given a garment of praise to use against any spirit of heaviness. Be aware, that he continues to try and make you believe the lie of hopelessness. Salome, you should never be hopeless because the Lord of all HOPE is on your side.

Next is the belt created to hold everything in place. Hope said, "Salome, this is the belt of truth, you will know the truth and the truth will set you free. The only way to keep this belt in place is to study the Word of God and allow it to become a part of you. Read the Word, study the Word, practice using the Word because it is more than just your belt of truth. It is also the sword that hangs in the holster from your belt. It ministers to the deepest wounded soul and it defeats the lies of the enemy. This sword not only cuts, Salome, it also heals. The Word of God is alive and active, sharper than any double-edged sword. It cuts all the way through, to where soul and spirit meet, to where joints and marrow come together. It judges the desires and thoughts of the heart. There is nothing that can be hidden from God; everything in all creation is exposed and lies open before His eyes. And it is to Him that we must all give an account of ourselves. (See Hebrews 4:12-14) **Never** take this belt off! It will be comfort in the dark places and joy as His light shines, dispelling the darkness."

Holding a pair of shoes with six-inch-spikes sticking out from the bottom, Faith and Hope bent down and laced up the shoes of peace on Salome's feet. "Look at these shoes, Salome," Faith stated. "They will help you walk in peace through any trials. Instead of reacting in those situations, these shoes will help you act with wisdom from God that will bring peace in any environment. Remember, it is not the one who has the last word that "wins". Realize that the person who reacts is acting out in pride. Have nothing to do with foolish and stupid arguments because, as you know, they only produce quarrels. The Lord's servant must not argue, instead he must be kind to everyone, able to teach, not resentful. You must walk in peace." (See 2 Timothy 2:23-24) "Look closely at these shoes. When a warrior of the Lord walks in peace instead of strife, they are puncturing the enemy's head with those six-inch-spikes every step they take. Therefore, Salome, choose to walk in peace."

The angels stepped aside so Salome could see herself in the spiritual mirror. Spellbound, she stared at the shining vision in the mirror. Her clothes beneath the armor were just as brilliant white as the clothes the angels wore. Each piece of armor fit perfectly as though it was crafted especially for her. An aura surrounded her, almost like a protective shield. As she noticed the look in her eyes, a gasp slipped through her lips. Her eyes shone with a confidence of knowing who she was and WHO was on her side! This battle will be won. Tattooed across her forehead sat the words, "The Lord's!"

Just then, Faith, handed her a shield the size of a large door. "The more faith you develop in the Lord, the bigger your shield will become. This is your shield of faith! It is time for you to walk in faith, holding up your shield against the fiery darts of the enemy. There is a coating on the outside of this shield that quenches the fire from his darts. You must keep your shield in place and keep your eyes on Jesus, the author and finisher of your faith, not the battle at hand. Remember, for the joy set before JESUS, He endured the cross scorning the shame, then He sat down at the right hand of the Father in heaven and HE lives to do one thing, to intercede for His own, you are His own, Salome." (See Hebrews 12)

Hope said, "Jesus sat down because His work was finished, the battle won, when He died on the cross. When one of His chosen walks into a battle, Jesus stands up! Read about it in Acts 7, the account of when Stephen was stoned. When the disciple saw heaven open, Jesus was standing, participating in Stephen's victory of faith! No matter what happens, Salome, fight the good fight of faith, finish your course and keep the faith!" (See 1 Timothy 1:18)

When Salome first saw the shield, she wondered if she would be able to carry it. Picking it up though, she realized it was as light as a feather. Gazing up, she saw why it seemed so light. Salome's guardian angel, Love, stood behind her, helping her hold the shield in place. Astonished and overwhelmed by the power God gave her in the spirit, she looked at Love once more. Smiling, he turned and pointed behind him.

Slowly Salome turned and saw what Love was pointing to. She almost dropped the shield while she stared at the massive army of celestial beings standing behind her. A scripture came to mind, *One can loose a thousand, two can loose ten thousand angels!*

Love smiled once again and said, "Salome, we're waiting for you to pray and dispatch us into the battle. If you don't pray, all the authority and power that God has given you, sits there within you. All the while, we stand waiting for your commands. These angels' hands are tied until you say the word! They could not help you in your previous battles because you did not pray. Prayer is not just talking to the only One who can help you. Your prayer moves your angel army into battle and as you bring your petitions and supplications to the Lord we are loosed into action. When you bind the enemy, we take the battle cords and tie up the enemy and defeat your foe. Do not neglect warfare prayer, chosen one."

Overwhelmed by the numbers of beings waiting and ready

to take action, Salome stood humbled and convicted all at the same time. Digesting the information, she unexpectedly saw what appeared as a golden bubble, begin to completely surround her.

She then heard the voice of her beloved Savior and Lord, Jesus. "Salome, this is your next weapon; it's My Blood. When a goldsmith purifies precious metal, he brings the fire in the kiln to an intense heat. Dross begins to float to the top where he skims it out. Bending over, he then observes the gold to see if he can distinguish his reflection. He will continue to increase the temperature of the fire until he glimpses it. My Blood does that to my chosen ones. Therefore, when our Father looks down, He sees My reflection. Salome, you are one of My chosen warriors, dressed and ready for battle. However, don't fight just your own battle; help others fight theirs, as well. You've been trained, Salome, now teach others how to stand in confidence and battle position. Also, remember to use My Name! You would be amazed how fast demons flee when they hear the Name of Jesus!

There is one more weapon; it is the words of your testimony. Watch the words that come out of your mouth. Remember, your words have the power of life or death. Whatever you speak out of your mouth is being brought to life.

When I created the universe, I used words. I spoke things into existence. You do the same thing. Therefore, be careful what you say. Daughter, turn and see your army once more. Understand that they are fully armed, ready to move, prepared and trained to destroy the enemy that comes against your family, friends, neighbors, health, ministry, business and finances. I have given you all you need to destroy every works of the enemy in your life and the lives that surround you. Therefore, it is now up to you! Are you ready Salome?"

Without further a due, Salome raised her sword and began to pray in the Spirit. Suddenly a multitude of angels began running toward the enemy's camp. As she continued to pray, she saw fiery bombs flying overhead heading for the enemy. Shouting out "In JESUS name," Salome began to hear the cry from the foe.

A loud, hideous cry came from the adversary's camp. Turning, Salome could hear the enemy preparing his own troops for battle. They were loud, boisterous, obnoxious, and hideous. They stood in ranks. However, they were easily threatened when one of God's chosen stood up with his own army and face them.

Hope spoke softly to Salome and said, "Remember, the lion can roar Salome, but his bite has already been destroyed! Fear not, for the Lord your God goes before you and prepares the way! Always take into account that angels stand behind you prepared to fight the battle. It is not yours to fight because the battle belongs to the Lord. All you need to do is to stand, and listen for His direction. Be still and rest in who you are in Christ. Then, you will see victory take place. Don't weary in well doing for in due season, you will reap a harvest if you don't give up! We are all cheering you on Salome. Are you ready to fight?" (See 2 Chronicles 20, Psalms 46:10, Galatians 6:9)

As quickly as the vision came, it was gone. Salome stayed still, allowing everything she had been taught to soak into her spirit. With that she prayed.

Lord, I am ready to walk out onto the battlefield and take back what the enemy has stolen from me. I know I cannot do it in my strength, but I do realize that I can do ALL things through Christ who strengthens me. I know this battle is already won because You defeated Satan on the cross! Father, thank You for training my hands for war so that I can help train others, in Jesus' name!

As she headed toward her office, she heard a tremendous shout go out in the spirit realm! In that moment she knew, this enemy is defeated!!!! "There are more for me than there are against me," Salome replied. "With the weapons the Lord has given me and obedience to Him, I will prevail!"

*Faith is the confidence
that what we hope for
will actually happen;
It gives us assurance
about things we cannot see.
Through their faith,
the people in days of old
earned a good reputation.
Hebrews 11:1-2 NLT*

CHAPTER **19**

WAKING UP FEELING fresh seemed like a completely new experience and one Salome thanked God for. As she stretched, visions of all the Lord was teaching her began to play through her head. "Thank You Lord, for the power and authority over the enemy. He is under my feet and You have already defeated him at the cross. I loose angels to take back the people, things, position, property and money he has stolen from me and my family. I know Jeremiah 29:11 is true and I am fully prepared to move forward and walk in the anointing you have given me for this day. Thank you Jesus, it is going to be an amazing day!"

Slowly getting up, Salome placed her feet on the floor and chuckled to herself. Praying she thought, *Father, make me such a prayer warrior that when my feet hit the floor demons tremble. Let the power and anointing You have provided for me defeat Satan, not only in my own life, but the lives of all the people You place in my path. This is a new day—thank you Lord!*

As she glanced at the clock she realized she had to hurry to get ready for her appointment. Chuckling she stated, "One day, there will be no more appointments with doctors, therapist, anything physical! I know healing is coming and I will trust in You Jesus." Heading for the bathroom, Salome made ready for the day.

━━⬛❨❩⬛━━

"Such a beautiful day," Salome stated as she drove down Old River Road heading for physical therapy. She could not help but bask in the wonder of it all. For the first time in her life, overflowing confidence and joy filled her. Everything in life seemed to develop a fresh heartbeat! *The Lord's love and grace is all around me,* she thought. *His grace is sufficient.*

It dawned on her as she drove that since she had been saved, God had allowed her to live in some beautiful places. Sighing, she smiled and asked, "Lord, how many people drive through this gorgeous scenery every day and never notice it? People are focused on the cares of this world instead of observing the splendor surrounding them. This is how the enemy is distracting believers, isn't it Jesus? By the time people fight the traffic, get home from work, take care of dinner, children, bathing, etc, they are pooped! They take no time for serious prayer. All they have time for is surface prayer. They're just too tired to seriously pray and do warfare on behalf of others. Their relationship with You consist of prayer time on the way to work and on the way back home. How sad, Lord! I know only because I used to be one of those people. Thank You for this thorn embedded in my flesh. It is making me be still and know You are GOD."

Glancing around, Salome realized she was already on Essen Lane close to the Lady of the Lake Hospital. *Won't be long before I arrive at therapy,* she thought. She dreaded this session! Her back was more swollen than it had been and she was not looking forward to moving her body in any way, shape or form. Yet, she knew these treatments were supposed to help! Driving down alongside the hospital, she slowed down as she prepared to turn into the clinic parking lot. Salome loved the therapist and the sessions gave her a chance to be with people again. It was a lifeline to normalcy.

Parking her car, she got out and pressed the key to lock the door. Heading into the clinic, she heard a little bird that was perched on a lamp pole, just singing away! She stopped and listened to it for a moment as the happy little tune filled her heart with joy. *Thank you, Jesus! In my heart I know You placed that little bird there just for me!* Turning into the clinic, she headed to the physical therapy section. She walked in and wrote her name on the signin sheet at the receptionist desk. Just as she was about to sit down, the door opened and Adam, Salome's PT appeared with a big smile!

Adam called, "Salome, ready to come back? How are you today?"

Salome looked Adam in the eyes and asked, "Do you want the truth?"

Giving Salome a firm look, he stated, "Yes, indeed! I want to know exactly how you feel!"

"OK, you asked for it! My back really hurts from my waist on down. It is swollen and feels like it could pop." Smiling, Salome confided, "Maybe that's what needs to happen, pop the thing. I'm afraid it's not better, Adam. It feels like it's worse than before surgery."

Adam addressed her as he lead her into a room, "Salome, wait right here, I'll get Maggie to come and work with you before we begin to do the manual exercises. We need to see what's happening."

Salome climbed up on the table and lay on her stomach. For some reason, the padded table felt so much better than anything she had at home. Lying there, she was almost asleep when Maggie came in. "Good morning, Salome! So good to see you today! Adam explained that you feel like your back is swollen. Let me take a look and I'll see if we can help." Slowly, Maggie raised Salome's shirt, glanced at her back then quickly put the shirt down again. "I'll be right back!" With that, she walked out the door!

Staring at the door, Salome wondered, well, that was strange! Suddenly, the door opened and Maggie and Adam walked in together. Maggie began, "I'm not going to touch her, this protrusion is so swollen that it's causing her whole back to swell. It's actually moving things out of proportion. I suggest we send her straight upstairs to the doctor. Can you call and get them to see her as soon as possible."

The look of concern on Adam's face made Salome wonder what in the world was going on! Adam asked, "Salome, how long has your back been swollen like this?"

"Oh, about four days now," confessed Salome.

"Why didn't you call someone, my dear? You have to be in severe pain," Adam chided. "I'm calling upstairs, stay here until I get back."

Just like that, Maggie and Adam walked out the door, closing it behind them. Salome prayed, "Lord, what is going on? This is getting plain crazy. Actually, this is the least amount of pain I've had for a long time."

Fear began to grip Salome as she lay alone in the room. Just as quickly as it gripped her, she shook herself and said out loud, *No, the Lord says*, "Fear not for I have redeemed you and called you by name, child, you are Mine. When you pass through the waters I will be with you, and when you pass through the rivers they will not sweep over you. When you walk through the fire you will not be burned, the flames will not set you ablaze. For I AM the Lord your God the Holy One of Israel!" (Isaiah 43:1-3a NIV)

Adam opened the door and said, "Salome, go up stairs to the second floor. Doc has scheduled an MRI so they can see what's going on. We believe the protrusion is causing these issues. You have an appointment scheduled with Sammy, the Physician Assistant at 11:30 a.m. And, Salome, I'm praying for you, sweet lady! You are a true testimony of the Lord to everyone here."

Touched in her heart, Salome got up and made her way out the door to the elevator. *Oh Boy, Lord, what a day and we are just beginning!* Almost in a daze, Salome got on the elevator and rode up to the second floor. Checking in, she heard her name called. *That's a first*, she thought! *I never got to sit down.* Following the voice calling her name, Salome raised her hand signifying she was there.

The nurse said, "Hey, Mrs. Salome! We're going to do an MRI to see what's going on in your back. The test should take about thirty minutes if you do not move. Once the test starts, we cannot stop until it is over, any questions?"

Salome slowly shook her head, no. Everything was happening so fast and she didn't have time to panic or even think about the whole situation. *What did they say? Finally, they're going to deal with the protruding thing on my back. YEAH!!!!!! Thank you, Jesus,* she thought! *There is a bright side to this situation!!*

A nurse's aide led her to a little dressing room and instructed, "Remove your clothing, except for your socks and underwear, and put on this gown. We have a blanket if you are cold. I'll be right back to get you." With that, she closed the door and left.

Salome glanced at the gown and wondered who in the world had ever designed these drab things. She was rather small in frame and the very large gowns always seemed to almost fall off of her. Organizing her thoughts she mused, *There is no way I'm going anywhere without this thing tied up in the back really well! Where are the ties for the middle section? Don't tell me there are none? This thing must be size ginormous! I could fit four of me in it.*

Just then, there was a knock on the door and the nurse's aid asked, "Are you ready?"

"Yes, I'm coming," she affirmed. As Salome tried to wrap her mind around all that was happening, a thought assaulted her. *So this is how God takes care of His own! If he wanted to, all He has to do is touch you and you'd be healed. Must be all the sin in your life for this to happen, either that or God really does not love you! Or, maybe it's your bad marriage. Is this how God really loves HIS chosen?*

Grabbing that thought, Salome said out loud! "This is not pure, holy, true, worthy of praise or of a good report, so get behind me, devil! God works all things for my good and for His glory! You watch, because this is working for a bigger purpose than I can see. His promises are yes and amen and I trust in Him! Now go, in Jesus' name!" (See Philippians 4:8 Romans 8:28)

She grabbed the door knob and walked out of the room, holding the flappy gown closed behind her! Silently she stated, *Lord, when this is over, I never ever want to see a flappy gown again!*

―◦ⅧℓℲ℩ℿℿℓ◦―

"Thank God the MRI is finished! Hopefully they can find out what's going on," she said. *Sitting in the doctor's office waiting and waiting and waiting some more is beginning to drive me crazy.*

Normally, she would have taken a book to read, but since she had not brought one, she looked around for something to read. Nothing in the waiting room looked interesting. By this time she'd checked all her e-mails and Facebook page, played a few card games on her phone and still she waited! *Who picks these magazines? Golf, fishing and physical therapy magazines were scattered throughout the waiting area. Nothing like a Romantic Country Homes, Better Homes and Garden, House Beautiful or Writer's Digest,* she brooded. Sitting just plain hurt and walking was not much better. Staring at the floor, Salome was seriously considering lying on her tummy just to take the pressure off her spine. Rolling that thought over in her mind, she suddenly heard her name, "Salome!"

"Oh, thank you, Jesus!" Suddenly, Salome realized she spoke out loud! Smiling shyly, she looked over at the nurse and said, "Sorry!"

"Understandable, you've been waiting for quite some time. We're working you in," the nurse stated.

"Thanks," Salome stated.

"The doctor's PA will be in with you shortly. There are only four people before you. Just have a seat."

Laying her purse on the chair, Salome walked over to the spine chart that was hanging on the wall. It listed the location of each disc. Studying the chart carefully, it suddenly dawned on her how delicate our bodies are. Who could ever look at this and question the existence of a Creator? Running her finger down the chart, Salome stopped at the L4 and L5 disc. As she stared at the two discs she thought, *Crazy that such a small thing on my back could cause such great trauma all the way down to my feet!*

Just then, the door opened and Sammy walked in. "Hello, Salome, we just looked at your MRI report and the doctor believes the protrusion is scar tissue. He'll be in soon because he wants to take a look at your back and see what all the fuss is about." At that moment, 'his majesty', the doctor, walked in.

See what all the fuss is about, she fumed! *How dare him*! She turned her back to Sammy and the doctor and raised her shirt so they could see "what the fuss" was about. Then she heard a loud gasp!

"It's severely irritating your back and causing the whole back to swell," the doctor said!

Salome controlled herself because everything within her dearly wanted to say, "Dugh!" The nerve of him, irritated—she took a deep breath and said "I do hope you see what I've been talking about! The Flextor Patch is the only thing that helped. However, I've developed an allergic reaction from the adhesive used on the patch and can't wear it anymore."

"Well, here are your options," he began. "I can give you an injection to see if it would help or would you rather we go in and cut it away?"

"No more playing around. Please, take it out whatever it is," Salome replied.

"Alright, we can do it here in our facility downstairs. Come out here to the appointment desk and set it up. This should do it. Ok,

I'll see you next week," and with that he walked to the appointment desk and said, "Set her up for next week."

While sitting at the desk, Salome wondered, *If he had paid attention to my symptoms earlier, would I be better by now?* Settling in the chair, she remembered, above all **God** is in control of all things. *Therefore, there is a reason even if I cannot understand it now.* She realized the anger she had toward the doctor had to be given to God or it would quickly turn to bitterness. No way around this, she had to forgive him and trust God. There will always be human error. The doctor was not perfect. Through Salome's situation, it seemed as though God was determined to prove that fact to this doctor.

The lady across the desk said, "Mrs. Salome, are you ok?"

"I'm sorry," she stated, "I was just thinking."

"OK, we have Tuesday, at 7:30 A.M. open for the surgery. Here is the sheet instructing you about the meds you must stop taking today and your prep the night before. Do you have any questions?"

"No, I believe I'm getting used to this," Salome said. Smiling she got up and headed toward the elevators. As she waited, she prayed! *Lord, I do not understand why this crazy thing is continuing. However, I will trust You! Your will be done, in Jesus' name.*

Stopping by the Physical Therapy office, Salome asked if she could see Adam or Maggie. Adam came out and said, "Ok, what did they decide?"

"I'm going in Tuesday to have the scar tissue removed," Salome informed him.

"Scar tissue?" Adam was astounded! "No way, that cannot be scar tissue? Salome, you are one of the strongest people I have ever seen! You've always walked in here with a big smile on your face even though we all know you are in pain. In the beginning the diagnosis was that the screws they implanted in you were too big. Now you're being told the issue is scar tissue. Surely, once whatever it is, is removed you'll feel like your old self again. I'll pray for you, friend."

"Thanks, Adam," Salome sadly stated, "I needed to hear that. I'm excited it's going to be over soon. Then I can begin to heal."

━━◦៣៣∩ᢳ∩៣៣◦━━

Tuesday AM, Surgery is over.

Salome asked, "What was the protrusion on my back?"

"Bone," the doctor said then turned and left.

"This whole thing is crazy," Suzy, Salome's friend, said!

Salome was so thankful that Suzy was able to take her for surgery. "Suzy, want to hear something crazier? I woke up before surgery was over. First thing I remember is seeing my head under a tent like contraption, then I heard instruments clinking together and feeling a pulling sensation on my back. That's when I realized I was awake and they were still doing surgery."

"I said, 'Hello, I'm awake!' There was suddenly complete and utter silence then I said, 'I'm sure glad you put some of that nummy stuff on my back because I cannot imagine how I would feel while you are stitching me up.' A nurse appeared under the tent that was draped over my head and said, 'Ugh, we are almost finished. I'll pull this tube out of your nose. Sorry, it's bleeding." Wiping the blood oozing from Salome's nose the nurse added, 'It'll be all right.' The nurse seemed very nervous and confused. Imagine that, she was confused!"

Suzie's mouth dropped, she roared with laughter and said, "Girl, I wish I was a fly on the wall when you started talking to them. I can almost imagine their faces! You're so calm! I'd be screaming by now. Just ask my honey, those doctors and nurses would have dealt with a major fit from me!"

Just then, Lewis came in and Salome relayed the story to him. Lewis asked, "Did the doctor come in yet?"

Suzie said, "Yes he did. We asked him what the protrusion was and all he said was, 'Bone' then walked out."

"Bone! Can you believe all this time, bone?" Lewis was stunned. Still under the effects of the "happy drug" Salome said, "It is ok, at least the thing is out and I can go on with life! Wow, I haven't been able to even think about a future for the last six months! I'm so excited to finally turn the corner!"

Suzie and Lewis stared at her as if she had lost her mind. *Didn't they get it? I can finally start planning again. Not sure what I'll plan yet, however, at least I have options now!* Thoughts of the future began float in her head as she embraced hope to its fullness! Things were going to be ok, she could feel it! Oh she wanted to get up and dance in the rain, singing praises to the Lord and bask in His faithfulness and goodness!

A nurse came in, took out the IV and gave Salome some grape juice. After fifteen minutes, Salome was on her way home with more hope than she had had in months! *It does come to pass, doesn't it, Lord? I'm going to trust in You! I promise, in Jesus' name!*

The early church got together,
shared a meal, encouraged each other
and had fellowship together.
(See Acts 2:24)

CHAPTER **20**

A FEW WEEKS later Salome relished in the feeling that everything was going to turn around. "It has been nine months since the big surgery. Lord, I feel like something is about to be birthed! Finally, I'm beginning to see an end to this very long leg in the journey," she whispered. As she gazed through the dining room windows, the scripture she read that morning in Acts 2:43-47, continued to marinate within her spirit. *The early church got together, shared a meal, encouraged each other and had fellowship together.* Rolling the words around in her head, she realized that it was the very thing which promoted love and unity in the body of Christ.

As she continued to muddle it around in her thoughts, she heard the sweet gentle voice of the Lord speak to her heart. *Salome, open your heart and home to women I will show you. I've given you various gifts and talents to make them feel special, at home and part of the family of God. In order to receive love, you first needed to embrace Me, because I Am Love. Now, as you pour love out to others, you will see that it shall come back to you. Open your heart, daughter, and learn to receive love and caring from people without fear.*

Excitement filled her heart! She turned and began to inspect her home. Tears of joy filled her eyes and slowly trickled down her checks as she saw her home through new eyes! God had truly blessed her and Lewis with so much, most of which they did not purchase. Many of the things were gifts others had given her throughout the years. Suddenly, ideas began to spring up in her head and an anticipation to welcome guests sparked within her heart. As she pondered who she would invite, faces of beautiful women began to cross her mind. All she had to do was set the day.

Walking into the utility room, Salome picked up the calendar hanging on the wall and headed back to her kitchen table. Studying the calendar with the various therapy and doctor's appointments, she landed on the perfect day! "That's it," she smiled proclaiming, "Monday, September 24, 2012 at 10:00 a.m., the perfect time for a brunch!"

Salome began planning the menu and a theme for the dining room table. Fall blessings, that's what she would label the theme! Her gaze landed on the beautiful dinner service that had once belonged to Lewis's grandmother. She knew it would make the perfect place setting. Just recently, Salome purchased some beautiful plaid-napkins to compliment the dinnerware. Already, in her mind's eye, she could see the table set.

A few years ago, she had bought some outdoor fabric to make tablecloths. With grandchildren in the mix, the waterproof material was just the trick needed for the table. The prints were beautiful and the orange, beige and white tablecloth would create a beautiful backdrop for the china.

As she allowed her imagination to go wild, she envisioned little bookmarks made out of orange plaid ribbon with a large flower sewn at the end. The ladies are special and God placed it within her heart to treat them like royalty! Most people have chosen to use paper for everything. Salome loved using some decorative paper goods for her table but, it was a shame to have such beautiful dinnerware and not share them with her old and new friends!

She was in her element, decorating and hosting all at the same time! With a smile that stretched from ear to ear she shouted out, "What could be more fun than this? Thank you, Jesus, it is a joy to once again have the privilege to serve."

Salome mind went back in time to a sweet, intimate dinner party she had held for a few friends who were walking through some pretty rough waters. As she guided her guests through her living room and kitchen into the screened-in-porch, they stood amazed by the scene displayed before them. Salome had set a dazzling table. In the center of the table sat a large, single, crystal candle-holder. Ivory brocade chair covers dressed-up the folding chairs and soothing, neutral tones covered the table. Candles were situated in various places around the porch while a beautiful, cherub fountain gurgled as water flowed down in a sweet melody, filling the place with an ambiance of peace.

Katie, Salome's friend, said, "Salome, you need to write a book, *How to Have an Elegant Dinner Party on a Shoe String Budget!*"

All the ladies broke out in laughter over the remark. However, suddenly, her friend, Barbara, became very serious. "Salome, do you understand that hospitality and the creativity to assemble these marvelous atmospheres, is a gift from God? You have the most remarkable way of making anyone feel at home, like they are part of your family. As you well know, from your own experiences, there are many people who would love to become part of anything. God has given you the talent to bring people together, making them feel safe and at home. Slowly, Salome, they will open their hearts to you. Then you can you point them to the Healer and fill them with wisdom from His Word."

Staring at Barbara, Salome comprehended exactly what Barbara was talking about. She knew, firsthand, what it felt like to be alone in this world. It had been her heart's desire to hold her arms open to everyone with whom she came in contact. That is what Jesus had done for her all those years ago.

As she mused over that long ago little dinner party, she embraced her gift with gusto! Sitting in the kitchen chair, she began to focus on a plan. Now, the fellowships would only include women.

But prayerfully, whenever Lewis allows the Lord to heal him, she prayed that God would send couples their way so they could help them create a strong marriage with God in the center.

"Ok," she stated, "I'm getting way ahead of myself! God has to break down that wall surrounding Lewis' heart. Finally, I accept the fact that I cannot help him. It will be something that happens between Lewis and our heavenly Father."

With that, Salome once again began planning! The menu would be easy. Ginger Pumpkin Bread, Apple Bread with some of my Cinnamon Honey butter, a spinach and cheese mini-quiche and fruit sounded wonderful. I'll also pull out my server that has four tiers so everything can be on the table. We'll have some wonderful French-Vanilla Coffee with Crème Brulee or Italian Sweet Cream creamer along with orange juice and milk. Yummy, sounds great! Within the hour, she constructed the table-scape, menu and invitation list.

Heading to her office, she created place-cards for each guest and remembered she had some tiny buckets that could hold mints at the place settings. Opening the drawer, she found them! "Perfect," she proclaimed.

"That day will not come fast enough! How exciting! Thank you, Jesus. You knew exactly what I needed. It is time to take my mind off my issues and simply love others. I do not have any idea about my future. Truly, it's all fuzzy at the moment. However, I've decided to enjoy every step and each person on the path along the way."

—◦◖◗◦—

"Yew!" Waking with a start, just a few days before the brunch, pain shot through Salome's left leg and foot. "Not again! The bone is gone, now what?" She rose slowly to a sitting position and tried to stretch-out her back. A searing pain shot from her back to her left hip then down her leg to her foot. "Please, not again!" Electric shocks began to shoot from her big toe down into her foot. *Lord, she prayed silently, please don't let this happen again! I'm so tired of this.*

"Be still and know that I Am God, Salome. I will be exalted in the earth, I will be exalted in the nations," she heard whispered in her heart.

"I'm trusting in You, Jesus! But, do I have to go through this again? When does healing begin," she asked?

"Salome, healing is a process. Deep healing of your heart began taking place over a year ago. Daughter, Lewis must walk through healing as well. He needs to learn to depend on Me, not you. Trust Me, I have your best interests in mind," she heard the still small voice of the Lord.

Walking into the bathroom, a cramp in her foot and calf caught her as she cried out in pain! "Oh, Lord, what now," she screamed? Once the cramp finally subsided, she pulled out the drawer, got the bottle of mild muscle relaxers and took a pill. Salome hated taking medicine but, it seemed the only way to survive was by taking the mild muscle relaxers and Aleve. The meds were playing havoc with her stomach.

Going to her closet, she pulled out her gym pants and a t-shirt then sat down on the chair in her office. She had a physical therapy appointment this morning. However, she would go nowhere until she read her Bible. Turning to Psalm 91 she began to drink in His Words of life. *Those who live in the shelter of the Most High will find rest in the shadow of the Almighty. I will declare about the Lord; He alone is my Refuge, my place of Safety; He is my God, and I trust Him. For He will rescue me from every trap and protect me from deadly disease. He will cover me with His feathers He will shelter me with His wings, His faithful promises are my armor and protection.*

As Salome read the Psalm, she made it personal. *These are promises for me,* she thought. As she meditated on the words, gentle tears of joy flowed from her eyes. She proclaimed aloud, "He is my Refuge and my Safe Haven, My God and I do trust in Him. He will protect me and cover me with His feathers, sheltering me under His wings. His promises are another piece of armor to protect me! I will believe in Your promises, I will trust in You, I will rest safely under Your wings and abide in Your presence, in Jesus Name!"

In the days that followed the second surgery, the swelling disappeared and her back felt so much better. If this is happening again, there is a purpose. I cannot understand it yet, how can any of us comprehend what God is doing. His perspective is one that we cannot begin to fathom and honestly, I'm not going to try. I've made a decision! I'm just going to continue to praise you, Jesus! Praise You through the pain, praise You through the joys and sorrows. Praise You in the morning. Praise You in the darkest night! In just a few days, we will have our first brunch and I cannot wait! There is so much more that is good than there is that disappoints me. Therefore, I'm going to look forward to the good!

❧━━✦❧❧✦━━

The next day as Salome opened her eyes, an excitement she could barely contain overwhelmed her. In just a few hours the ladies would be here. She slowly stretched, sporting a smile that made her whole face shine with joy. She set the table, picked out the soothing music that would play in the background and prepared the breads and fruits, the night before. Softly, Salome prayed, "Thank You, Jesus for this grand opportunity to use our home once again. You have opened my heart and I haven't the words to say how grateful I am. How fulfilled a person feels to be a part of fellowship, part of a family!

Father, I am obedient to Your Word as *I put on the full armor of God so that I am able to stand against the wiles of the devil and, having done all to stand.* (See Ephesians 6:10-18) Lord, I'm praying for each lady coming this morning. Be with them and fill them with as much excitement and love as You have poured inside me. Let us sense Your presence sitting at the table with us as we share the meal. Be with us as we fellowship and praise You, enjoying goodwill for each other and for all You have done and are doing within our lives.

If there is a heart among the ladies that is hurting, show me how to minister to them and reveal the lie that is holding them bound. Lord, thank You for this opportunity! Thank You that Your promises are true. You are holding every member of my family, my friends and neighbors in the palm of Your hands, and You promise to teach them and great shall be their peace. (See Isaiah 54:13) I plead the Blood of Jesus over, around, on top and on the ground beneath my home and on my family, friends and possessions. I loose a wall of angels to stand guard over us and our property and around my friends and family. Father, let the Holy Ghost have a tangible presence in our home today and fill Lewis with Your love and peace, in Jesus' Name, I pray.

Salome put a praise CD in her player while she dressed. Once she finished, she placed the food on the table. Just as she completed her task, the door bell rang.

Glancing one more time to make sure everything was just so, Salome turned and went to answer the door. All the ladies arrived at the same time! Opening the door, she smiled and said, "Welcome! I'm so excited to see all of you!"

Each lady came in embracing Salome with a big hug and smile. She immediately walked them into the kitchen/dining room! "Oh, my," Lucy said! "Everything is beautiful! What a treat!"

Chatting and hugging each other, the ladies began making their way to the kitchen. Just then Sam spoke, "We want a tour, Salome."

As she walked her friends through her home, a sense of humility came over her. Suddenly, she realized what the Lord was doing within her heart. She had many talents; however, she had lacked the confidence to use them.

Recalling the time when they had built their home, she chuckled as she thought about the walls in the house. She had been so afraid to mess something up that she painted everything white. Color was a fearful thing to behold as far as she was concerned. Some of her children's friends used to call it the "white house".

God definitely healed her from the fear of expressing herself with color! There was not a room in the house lacking in color. Her living room was painted with a bright Tuscan yellow and the ceiling a lighter shade of yellow. When they found the plans for their house, Salome designed a set of shelves and cabinets to go on either side of the fireplace in the living room. Today, they were the only things painted white. Chuckling to herself Salome proudly began to show her friends her daughter Addie's paintings.

Pictures displayed on the walls portrayed beautiful trees which always reminded her of the Father's creation. Addie had painted a beautiful canvas of a forest. Shadowed within the trees of the forest were three crosses. When Salome noticed the crosses she pointed them out to Addie. Staring at the canvas, Addie told her she did not purposely place the crosses there, they just happened. For Salome's birthday that year, Addie had surprised her with the canvas. Since the frame was removed, it became a challenge to see how she would hang it. Staring at the painting, the idea came to hang it like a tapestry. It worked out beautifully.

Sitting in the center of the living room was a large, shaggy rug. It created balance for the two deep-brown couches and two printed large chairs and footstools. Addie found the identical fabric of the chairs and told Salome where she saw it. Promptly, Salome made a trip to Hancock Fabrics and purchased enough material to construct and cover the two footstools. Lizzy, her granddaughter believed that they were built just for her and Andy, Salome's grandson because they were just their size.

The end tables were special because each one was an answer

to prayer. Salome knew what she wanted, but had only a limited budget. She spotted a beautiful end table in a magazine and fell in love with it. However, when she priced it, the little table was $450.00. She gasped and said, "Oh, well!" That week she went to one of her favorite antique shops. There, sitting in a corner, was a table almost exactly like the one in the magazine. It had a glass top with a metal base that was designed to resemble a tree branch with a little bird sitting on one of the branches. The table was very much like the one in the magazine. She stooped down to check the price and almost laughed out loud, $25.00!!! Thank you, Lord! He gives us the desires of our heart, such a sweet Father!

Considering what she wanted for a coffee table, Salome called a friend who had an antique store and asked, "Hey, Becky, could you keep your eyes out for a low round coffee table? It needs to be low enough for Lizzy to have her tea parties and for Andy and me to do art projects."

Becky replied, "Someone brought one to the shop today. They gave it to me, just trying to get rid of it because they are moving. It's on the porch if you want to have a look. If you like it, take it home and we'll settle-up later."

Excitement filled Salome's heart and she headed straight to the shop. When she pulled up, she saw it on the porch. It was perfect! Picking up her phone, she called Becky. "Hey, Becky, I love it! How much?"

"Hum, how about $35.00," Becky responded?

"I'll take it," Salome cheered! "Is it alright if I put the check in your mailbox?"

"Sounds great to me," Becky said.

"Thanks Becky. This is answered prayer, God is soooo good," Salome said.

When Lewis and Salome were coming back from a trip to Tennessee they decided to stop in Memphis to rest a bit. Glancing up, Salome saw an **Old Time Pottery** store! "Lewis, look, let's go in please!"

Smiling, Lewis said, "I thought you'd like it here."

Walking into the store, Salome went straight to the furniture department. There sat an old fashioned two-tiered round end table. When she inspected it, she found a scratch on the side of the table. Just then, one of the employees came by and she asked, "Excuse me; I see that this table has a scratch, how much will you sell it for, as is?"

"Give me a minute," he said. He headed back the way he came. Salome prayed that God would give her favor. Ten minutes later, he came back to her with a smile on his face. "The manager told me to offer $40.00. How does that sound?"

"Sold," Salome exclaimed! With a smile on her face, she knew God had indeed blessed her. Lewis picked it up and hauled it to the front register.

The employee followed them to the register and told the clerk "$40.00." The clerk's mouth dropped open, the employee smiled and said, "Somebody must have prayed, is all I can say!"

Salome beamed with excitement! God is good!

A few weeks earlier, Lewis had been sitting on "his" couch and said, "Salome, I need a table for this side of the couch. Can you find one for me?"

"No problem," Salome said, "I'll head out now."

Traveling to the antique shops around town, she walked in and fell in love with a beautiful table with rounded corners and two little doors. The inside of the table was lined with copper. As she studied it, a friend stepped over and said, "This is a tobacco table. Gentlemen stored cigars, tobacco, or cigarettes in here. These tables normally stand in the "Gentlemen's room". After meals, the men got up and went to the room for a smoke and talked over the events of the day."

Looking it over, Salome asked, "How much is it? I don't see a tag."

Leaning over, the friend said, "Salome, I'll give it to you for $35.00."

"I am so blessed," Salome exclaimed! She reached up and gave her friend a big hug! Lewis is going to love this table.

Salome shared the stories with her friends and once again, she was humbled by the goodness and faithfulness of God. God proved that He does answer prayers, even prayers like these! How could she ever doubt what He was doing now? All she had to do was walk into her living room and see that not only does God hear He answers as well.

As her friends oohed and awed over the blessings of the Lord, Salome felt tears in her eyes. Her heart was overwhelmed with the Lord's faithfulness and goodness. Finally, she came to the place of embracing all that God will do and was doing in her life. It doesn't matter how things may appear, He is God and He had proved His faithfulness to her. She would trust Him even in the fiery trials of life.

Once the tour was finished, Salome sat with her friends at the table and simply smiled. These precious, beautiful ladies are my sisters in Christ. A deep love and respect for each one seemed to burn brighter with each passing moment. They laughed, cried, shared and prayed together through the meal as they walked out what was described in the Book of Acts.

When their time together had come to a close, Barbara suggested, "Hey, let's do this every month! We could do pot luck! I've had so much fun and have enjoyed getting to know everyone. What do you say, Salome?"

Smiling at her friends, Salome simply stated, "I believe it's a wonderful idea! Also, feel free to invite anyone, everyone needs fellowship."

"Here, here," Sam answered.

The ladies all began speaking at once. They were so excited! Salome beamed when she realized what God was beginning.

Right before her eyes, He was answering the prayer she and Lewis prayed seventeen years ago when they first bought the property. They had joined hands and prayed over it, asking the Lord to use the land for His glory and to draw people to a closer walk with Him.

After everyone left, Salome prayed a simple prayer, *Thank you, Father. How do I express just how much this meant to me? I love You with all my heart, soul and mind! You are worthy of all praise and You have proved Your faithfulness time and again. I trust You, Lord, no matter what! I will trust You, Abba!*

Stay Alert!
Watch out for your great enemy the devil.
He prowls around like a roaring lion,
looking for someone to devour.
Stand firm against him,
and be strong in your faith.
1Peter 5:8-9a NIV

CHAPTER **21**

FOUR WEEKS LATER Salome's issues with her left foot became worse. There seemed to be something pulling her toes downward and she began to notice, that if she walked outside, she would lose her balance and come close to falling. For the past few days, more of the electric shocks had flowed through her big toe, bringing searing pain from the top of the toe to the bone in her foot. Her follow-up from surgery was in just a few days so she prayed that she could handle the pain until then. She had just finished putting the dishes into wash when Lewis walked in the door.

"Hey, Lewis, how was your--" Salome stopped in mid sentence. One look at his face told her he was furious! "What's wrong?"

"What's wrong? What's right? The plant manager is cutting everyone's hours because he says we are making too much money," Lewis fumed! "He's making his own rules and breaking every rule that has been in place. That man is demoting everyone. He demoted me, Salome. Don't tell me God is going to work this out! I don't want to hear it! All the years I've given to that company and what did it mean? I'm reduced to nothing more than a slave!"

Lewis went on ranting and railing for awhile. Salome knew there was nothing she could say, or do, but listen! Honestly, this is one time Lewis had to trust in God or he would become even more bitter and angry than he already was. There was no reasoning with him—only God could help him now. When he finally finished spouting off, Salome simply stated, "Lewis, I'm praying for you. God will give you the wisdom you need as you seek Him."

Little did Salome realize that Lewis was now working a swing shift. Three days one week and four days the next. All she knew was that he was driving her crazy, sinking deeper into the dark pit of depression each and every day.

Try as she may, there was no encouraging Lewis. The depression Salome fought and his pity-party of poor- pitiful-me was just too much. He never seemed to see the trials Salome was walking through. Suddenly catching her thoughts, Salome chided herself, *You're being selfish, he needs you right now. This is not the time to think about me. Lewis has never had to lean on God. I can see that now. Either his own reasoning or his family's money had always been there to help him out of tight circumstances. It was now time for Lewis to come face-to-face with God alone. This was my time to simply pray for him and try to stay out of his way.*

His emotions were all over the place. One minute he was depressed, the next he was angry. Salome began approaching him cautiously because she never knew what he was going to do. After weeks of his behavior, she dreaded him being home. She was so sick of hearing him complain that she finally said, "Have you ever thought about looking for another job? Don't tell me you will, do it! Do it! Otherwise, don't complain to me anymore!"

As soon as it was out of her mouth, she was sorry. *There is no winning this battle,* Salome thought. When Lewis was home, she faded into the background or she found something to do away from home.

Salome could no longer deal with his issues. Fighting defeat, she turned to the Lord, crying out, "You make all things beautiful in Your timing! This is Your problem, Lord, I cannot handle it. You are the only One who can change a heart, therefore; I'm giving you Lewis' and mine, in Jesus' Name. I give up!"

———◦⟋⟍⟋⟍◦———

When Salome went for her check-up, she knew that her calf and foot were going numb. A new PA examined her and found that she had lost most of the strength in her big toe on her left foot. Her foot was weakening as well. Now face to face with the PA, Salome began to realize her condition was worse than before the first surgery. *Oh, my, this is why I lose balance on uneven ground,* she assumed. The PA pulled up her last MRI report and saw that the L5 and now S1 discs were bulging. Salome could not believe what she was reading or the things she was hearing!

NO!!! Not again, please, Lord! You said You would not tempt me beyond that which I could handle! With the temptation You would make a way of escape! What is my escape, Lord? This is beyond anything I can handle, she screamed inside her mind! (See 1 Corinthians 10:12-13)

Stunned and almost numb, she shook herself so she could hear what the PA suggested. "It looks like we need to work on those discs. We can try a steroid injection to see if that will reduce the swelling, then use physical therapy to try and get it back in place. Salome, did you hear me? Do you want to set up a date and time for the injection?"

Salome stared in disbelief! Almost like a robot she replied, "Yes, that's fine."

The PA asked, "Do you have any questions?"

Softly, Salome answered, "No, I've been this way before, more than once, remember?" On the outside you would think she had everything together, however, inside she was imploding, silently shaken with all the issues confronting her.

Standing up, the PA walked over, opened the door and signaled for Salome to follow. Dutifully, she got up slowly and followed the

PA to the appointment desk.

Salome heard herself say all the right things, sign all the necessary papers, take the packet and leave in a daze. Glancing at the paperwork in her hand, she wondered who would be able to take her to the clinic to get the injection. She honestly did not want to ask Lewis and after all he would have to work that day. A good friend came to mind and once she made it to her car she would call her. She felt like she was walking in a very bad dream and wished someone would wake her up.

Arriving at the parking lot, she walked to her car, opened the door and climbed in, shutting the door behind her. She turned the key in the ignition and started it up. Placing her head on the steering wheel she prayed. *Lord, what is going on? I'm coming boldly to Your throne of grace and pray to receive mercy in my time of need. No one could possibly understand all that I am feeling right now except for You! Father, I know that in the middle of this hurricane, You have a plan. Oh, my Lord, it has been a year and eight months since this nightmare began, and it continues to get crazier and crazier. **Faith** is the substance of things hoped for and the evidence of things not seen. Right now, Lord, I can see **nothing**—nothing but trials, testings and the stretching of my faith to see just Who I believe and what I believe. Give me the strength to go through this, Jesus. I cannot count on Lewis to help me stand. However, I know people are praying for us right now and, my God, how desperately I need those prayers. As Jehoshaphat prayed in 2 Chronicles 20, 'I have no power over this vast army surrounding me, but my eyes are upon You.' No man can do anything for me here, only You! Lord, I'm choosing to cast these cares on You because I BELIEVE and KNOW YOU LOVE ME, in the Name of Jesus, I pray!*

Suddenly, God reminded Salome of that early morning in October last year when He dropped that blanket of peace over her. Like a bright flash, a scripture written in John came to her,

Peace I leave with you, My peace I give to you. I do not give to you as the world gives. Do not let your heart be troubled and do not be afraid!

Just like that October morning, a blanket of peace fell upon her once again. A long ago song rang in her ears,

In the eye of the hurricane in the center of the storm.
In the chaos there's a comforter, a harbor safe and warm.
The strong winds may blow, but they can't take what I know,
when I hold to the Rock the winds won't prevail!

This was just like the hurricanes that racked Louisiana. It was something she would just have to endure. As she thought about the whole situation, she felt like the eye had just passed over and she and Lewis were heading into the second brunt of the storm. In this spiritual storm God would remain her shelter. If only Lewis would come under His protection, it would be all right.

———◄◖◗►———

Lewis' job suddenly changed again, switching him to the rotating shifts. This month he started the shift from 3pm to 11pm. That came as a great relief to Salome. Now her nights were free to seek God and rest. Her friend, Cindy, agreed to take her for the steroid injection. Salome was so thankful for her friends and church family. She could not imagine what she might have done without them.

As much as she hated having to get the injection again, she was thankful for the relief it would surely give her. "One more day! Lord, thank You for these injections and thank You that Lewis is not going to be there. He is so negative and I cannot deal with his issues and mine together.

Why can't he be the strong one just this once, Lord? Why do I have to always stand up and take that role? Honestly, I'm tired!

Help me to rest tonight, Lord, and please fill me with Your peace, in Jesus' Name." With that, Salome placed her head on her pillow and fell into a deep sleep.

⌇⫘⫘⫘⌇

Cindy picked her up early the next morning and they were on their way! Salome turned to Cindy and said, "I don't know how to thank you. You have no idea how much this means to me,."

Cindy smiled and replied, "Not a problem, I'm happy to do it. Are you ready for the injection?"

"Yes, I know the drill by now! Been through this five times now, I'm ready for the relief the shot brings," Salome chided.

They chatted back and forth and, before they knew it, they were at the clinic. A Tens Unit salesman was scheduled to meet them before surgery to deliver a unit to Salome.

Nothing was going right! The doctor was running almost an hour behind and the Tens Unit salesman was forty-five minutes late. Finally, he rushed in with an apology, "The traffic was horrible this morning. I thought I'd never get here. Please forgive me for being late."

He opened the Tens Unit case and showed Salome how to operate it. The Tens was a machine that helped to stimulate the muscles and nerves to relax. It felt like Christmas morning, she could not wait to get home to try it out. Since the physical therapist used one as part of her therapy, having the unit at home was a super treat.

Just after the salesman left, the nurse called Salome back in order to prep her for the injection. As soon as that was done, they allowed Cindy to come back to her cubical to wait with her, and then the parade began!

First, the nursing assistant led Salome to the scale, weighed her then escorted her to the stall. After taking her blood pressure, temp and asking Salome to verify her name, address and insurance information. In came the RN to ask the same questions the other nurse had and to start the dreaded IV.

Salome's veins rolled so starting an IV was always a problem. Suddenly, Salome asked the nurse, "Could we pray for the IV stick?"

"Sure," the RN stated.

After Salome prayed the nurse tied the rubber band around her arm and asked Salome to pump her hand. Closing her eyes, Salome prepared herself for the stick. She suddenly felt the RN releasing the band and glancing down realized the IV was in! "Praise God," Salome cheered! "I didn't even feel it!"

"Looks like the Lord answered our prayer," the RN replied with a big smile.

Next, the anesthesiologist came in giving his spiel and asking the same questions. The orthopedic surgeon was next. He casually walked in said, "Raise up please," then marked Salome's back, indicating that he had seen her.

The nurse checked her vitals once more. Everything was set, ready to go. Salome could not wait to get it all over!

Two cheery nurses came in with crazy colored caps on their heads, saying, "Ready! Wait a minute, where's your hat? What, you don't want to wear our lovely hat?"

"Oh joy," Salome countered. "Ok, I'll put your hat on."

They moved into position and pushed the bed to the operating room. Once there, they instructed, "When we stop, roll onto the table very slowly. We'll help you."

Carefully, she did as she was told. As soon as she was position, they begin to work. "You'll feel something cold on your back. I'm applying an antiseptic to sterilize it. Ready!"

Salome responded, "I bet you like your job, torturing people all day long as you plop super cold liquid on their back."

The guy chuckled and said, "This is what I live for! Ready?"

"No, ok, go," Salome said as she tensed for the cold fluid to hit her back.

Glancing up, Salome asked the anesthesiologist, "Are you ready to give me that happy juice yet?"

The anesthesiologist chuckled and said, "Yes, I am. You'll feel a little burn at first then everything will be all right."

Slowly, they started injecting the medicine into the IV. It burned more than Salome remembered. Opening her mouth to say so was the last thing she remembered.

———❦———

The nurse and Cindy keep calling Salome. "Hey, sleepy head wake up! It's all over; time to get ready to go home.

Salome managed to open her eyes and saw Cindy's beautiful, smiling face. She said, "Hey, Cindy, can I have some grape juice?"

The nurse said, "Grape juice coming right up and how about some graham crackers to go along with the juice?"

"Sure," Salome answered. She tried to move her left leg and realized she couldn't. Touching her leg, it dawned on her that she had no feeling in it either. Suddenly wide awake, she tried again, nothing. Her left leg and foot were tingling something awful and she could not make the limb move. "Nurse, I can't feel my left foot and leg and I cannot move it. What's wrong?"

The nurse smiled and replied, "Some people have that reaction for a little while. It will be fine in just a minute."

"But you don't understand, this is the sixth time I've had this procedure done and I've never experienced this. Normally, I have immediate relief. This is horrible," Salome fearfully said. *Now what?* Fear begins to take hold in Salome's heart as she searched the nurse's face for comfort.

"Just give it some time, honey, it'll be all right," the nurse reassured her. Another nurse walked in with her grape juice and crackers. "Drink this slowly and eat your crackers. By the time you finish eating, your leg will be fine."

A few minutes later, Salome needed to go to the bathroom. She and Cindy managed to get her dressed and even put her shoes on; however, her leg was still completely numb.

Sliding to the edge of the right side of the bed, Salome lowered her feet to the floor. As she tried to stand up, her left leg gave way, it had no strength. Cindy grabbed Salome and helped her lean back on the bed. Fear seemed to grip both of them as they faced this new development together. The nurse kept assuring them that feeling and strength would come back soon. Finally, after a heart-wrenching length of time, Salome was able to use her leg a little and hope began to flood her heart once again.

Forty-five minutes later, the nurse helped Salome get seated in the wheelchair while Cindy left to get the car. The nurse continued to encourage her that this leg episode was a passing thing and her leg would return to full strength by the end of the day. Just then Cindy drove up and the nurse helped Salome to get into the car. They headed for home.

All the way to the house, Cindy tried to make light conversation, sensing the fear Salome was struggling with. However, the tingling continued and when they finally arrived home, Salome had to lean on Cindy in order to make it into her house.

Sitting on the couch, Cindy looked at Salome and asked, "Do you want me to stay with you? I don't mind."

"No, I'll be all right," Salome answered. "It will work out just as the nurse assured us. By the end of the day, the shot will begin to work and my leg will be fine."

"Ok, I'll go on home, however, if you need me, call! Promise me, Salome?" Cindy waited for an answer as she studied her friend.

"I promise!" With a hug, Cindy headed to the door and told her she'd talk with her later. Since Lewis had to work a 6:00 P.M. shift tonight, Salome did not want to chance waking him up, so she lay down on the couch to sleep. Softly, she whispered, "By the time I wake up, it will all be OK!" Closing her eyes, sleep finally overtook her.

Lewis woke up and began preparing for work and wondered, Where *is Salome? I hadn't heard from her at all today,* he fumed. *It's almost time for me to go to work and she still isn't back. I'm always the last to know what's going on around here.* Walking into the living room he saw her sleeping on the couch. *Surely, she hasn't been here the whole time?* Just as he looked at her she grimaced, he presumed from the pain the shot caused. She turned. He got a glimpse of her back! His mouth gaped open. He stood, stunned at the swelling and purplish undertone of her skin as if she were bruised from the inside.

Salome began to feel the pain once again and groaned as her eyes fluttered open. Lewis stood there staring down at her. Immediately, she was on the defense. "Hello, Lewis," she stated stiffly.

"Hey, Salome, how'd it go?" Smiling, Lewis looked down at his wife. If he was honest with himself, he was jealous of her. Jealous of the relationship she had with people and of the relationship she had with the Lord. It seemed that she had a direct line to the Creator and he had trouble getting anywhere close to the throne room of God.

Speaking softly, she said, "Not good. For a while after I came to, from the anesthesia, I lost the use of my left leg and foot completely. It's still numb and tingling something awful."

"Well, isn't that great!" Lewis roared. "Just what we need, what else will go wrong with you?"

Suddenly tears appeared in Salome's eyes and a hurt deep inside showed on her face. Watching her, Lewis knew those words pierced her heart but he could not bring himself to apologize. "I'm going to work. Good night," Lewis shouted as he stormed out of the house.

Salome stayed silent as she watched him go. She prayed, *What can I say, Lord? I feel so bad about this. There is nothing I can do to make it better. He's so bitter and resentful, Lord. Please, do something!* Guilt over the whole situation began to engulf her. It seemed to her that their financial situation and the inability to do anything about it was all her fault. The old tapes from her mom began to play in her head once again trying to take her down into the pit of despair. *Lord, help me, please! I hate feeling like I'm an intruder in my own home. But, maybe that's the way he feels, as well. I have no idea but, I desperately need You to do something Lord!*

The sweet, soft voice of the Lord spoke to her spirit. *Salome, his fight is not with you, it's with Me. When he bellows like this, it is because I'm convicting him of the pride and jealousy he harbors. It's a form of manipulation; he's trying to put the blame on you. Lewis will have his own Damascus road and rooster-crowing experience. You, be still and trust Me.*

Slowly, Salome tried to stand. She placed all her weight on her right foot and tested her left leg for strength. It was a little better. However, it still had a long way to go. Her back felt worse than it did before the shot. *Lord, I don't understand this, why Father?*

Closing her eyes, she focused on the Lord. She cautiously took a step, then another and carefully continued down the hall, watching for any sign of weakness in her leg. Walking to her bathroom, she prepared to take a hot shower, put the Tens Unit on and then fall into bed and read.

See, it is I who created the blacksmith
who fans the coals into flame
and forges a weapon fit for its work.
And it is I who have created the destroyer to work havoc;
No weapon forged against you will prevail
and you will refute every tongue that accuses you.
This is the heritage of the servants of the Lord,
and this is their vindication from me,
declares the Lord.
Isaiah 54:16-17NIV

CHAPTER **22**

A WEEK LATER, Salome sat on the back porch gazing at the beautiful landscape that was her backyard. *Creation itself declares there
is a God!* As she looked over at the long tall pines, sycamores
and oak trees, a chill fall breeze began to blow, causing a shower
of cascading leaves to fall across the yard. *Lord, it's like a mysti-
cal fairy land! So beautiful, Father—I love fall!* As she drank in
the sights and sounds around her, her heart rested in the fact that
God is in control. The seasons proved that to her. *Governments
and craziness may seem to overwhelm me at times; however, it is
moments like this that I remember that You are ultimately in control.* Salome smiled at the witness of His presence all around her.
You're here thank You for these subtle reminders, she whispered
softly under her breath.

After a long day of therapy, baking and studying, Salome show-
ered and prepared for a quiet time to read a good book. Lying
down, she sighed. Turning on her Kindle she prepared to continue
reading a story she had begun the day before. Just as she got com-
fortable, she heard something. Straining her ear, she listened intently. The voices stopped, silence! Shaking her head, she smiled
and said, "Great, now I'm hearing things."

Fixing her eyes on her Kindle, she heard it once again clear soft
raspy whispers. Her ears tuned in to the sound. Low harsh voices
speaking about an attack strategy. "What on earth," she whispered?

"This is the assignment handed down from the Prince. Kill her! If she lives, she will be a deterrent to the Prince of Darkness and his kingdom. Infirmity! Strike her body with inflammation to cause deep pain. Surely this will stop her in her tracks. Fear, whisper in her ears words of destruction about her life, marriage and family. Torment and offense, you hit her family, stirring up strife, division, unforgivness and bitterness. Use her husband against her. He is putty in our hands because pride and shame have him locked up tight. She will not win this battle because our Prince plans to strike her family, finances and ministry, along with her health. We have many soldiers battle-ready to defeat her and take her as our captive."

As soon as the last words were out, Salome began to hear a deep, dark, sinister voice speaking. "Move out of my way! You had the chance to strike her and still she defeated you. I'll do this myself. This one has become too dangerous. She is starting to walk in the power and authority God has given her.

Look at her! She is even wearing that dismal mantel of meekness her Lord has given her which protects her from pride. If she continues on in this way, she will destroy the workings of my kingdom in her marriage, family, neighbors and those within her church. She challenges others everywhere she goes because of her walk of faith in Jesus. She must be taken out of the picture! We will stop at nothing. I plan to broadside Salome with every form of evil I can. We'll use them all—division, strife, pride, jealousy, resentment and bitterness. We'll build walls between her and her husband, because as long as we have him, it will be easy to attack her."

Outraged, Salome could stand it no longer. *What on earth is going on,* she thought? She slid her feet into her slippers, prepared to head to the living-room. Just then, Jesus stopped her and said, "Salome, you will not defeat them this way. Remember first keep your armor in place. Then allow your army of angels to fight this battle for you. Faith, Hope and Love are there on either side of you and behind you.

Daughter, it's time to begin those warfare prayers, allowing your angels to go before you and prepare the way. Don't forget! *Whatever you bind on earth is bound in heaven and whatever you loose on earth is loosed in heaven.* (See Matthew 16:19) What you hear and are preparing to defeat, are evil rulers and authorities of the unseen world and demon powers in this dark world, and evil spirits in the heavenly places. Your fight is not earthly, this is spiritual."

Just then, Jesus appeared to her. He touched her eyes and ears. Gazing into her eyes He said, I've opened your spiritual eyes and ears to see the intensity of the warfare around you. Remember, fear not daughter, for I have redeemed you and I have called you by name. Salome, you are Mine! Greater is He that is in you than he that is in this world. No weapon forged against you shall prosper. When the enemy comes in like a flood, it is the Spirit of the Lord that will raise a standard against him. (See Isaiah 43:1, 54:16-17) Now, Salome, fear not and do not be discouraged because of this vast army before you. Send out praise first in My Name and loose confusion in the enemy's camp. (See 2 Chronicles 20) When My people begin to praise My name, the enemy becomes confused and defeat themselves. Listen to the Holy Spirit's direction and obey immediately.

Salome caught a glimpse of her reflection in her dresser mirror. It was easy to see that her spiritual eyes had truly been open. As she stared at Jesus, she saw the love and confidence He had in her and **that knowledge** drove her forward. She was not afraid. Jesus stood at the right hand of the Father. His light, reflecting on her armor would cause a brilliance that would blind the enemy. Jesus then touched her mouth and beautiful praise and worship began to flow from her lips to heaven. "Give thanks to the Lord for His love endures forever,"—over and over she repeated the chant.

MY JOURNEY HOME ❧

Then she sang, "The Blood of Jesus cleansing us from sin, sets the captive free and restores life once again." She continued singing over and over the words the Lord gave her. As she sang, she caught movement on her side. Glancing over, she suddenly saw a troop of armed angel running out from behind her, engaging the enemy before her.

The veil, which separated the natural world from the spiritual world, was suddenly pulled aside and Salome saw her first glimpse of the hand-to-hand combat taking place against her and her family. Down the hallway and into the living room Salome moved, singing all the way. When she moved to the end of the hall, she caught sight of the ceiling in the living room. The appearance was as though the ceiling had been blown away and in its place were deep, dark, sinister clouds turning in the shape of a tornado. In the midst of the clouds were bald naked deformed creatures with twisted hands and feet. They were standing in a circle holding hands and chanting curses, vexes and hexes.

Somehow, Salome knew that each demon represented a cult of witches praying against her and her family. The chants drifted into their own menacing dark army. As Salome continued to praise the Lord, the angels slammed into the large beings that were filled with all sorts of evil. She noticed, as she continued to praise and pray in the Spirit that Satan's army became weaker and began fighting amongst themselves.

Suddenly, the Holy Spirit prompted her to plead the Blood of Jesus over herself, her family, their home and all their possessions. As she did, loud horrendous cries of searing pain came from the demon forces sent to attack. Just then, she began to wield her sword and held up her shield. Fiery bombs coming from the demon's mouths began flying through the air, hitting her shield. Not one bomb touched her. The shield's covering put out every fiery bomb. Glancing upward, she spotted Love standing just behind her helping her hold up the shield. It was then she caught sight again of Faith and Hope as they formed a fortress around her.

She remembered the scripture in1 Peter 5:8 NLT "Stay alert! Watch out! For your great enemy, the devil, prowls around like a roaring lion, looking for someone to devour. Stand firm against him and be strong in your faith."

Salome firmly planted her feet that were shod with the six-inch-spikes to hold her position. Just then, an army of demons headed straight for her. She opened her mouth and spoke, I will be strong in the Lord and the power of His might! I will put on the full armor of God so that I can stand firm against all the strategies of the devil." (See Ephesians 6:10-12) Praying in the Spirit, Salome suddenly witnessed another dispatch of her angels colliding with the demons heading toward her.

Just then, Salome turned as she heard the demon Pride behind her saying, "You're going down!"

Salome shouted "I submit to God, I resist the devil and he must flee! I bind you in the Name of Jesus Christ! The Name above all names!"

Several angels came from the side carrying golden chords covered with the glory of the Lord. As she continued to pray, the angels began to bind the demons who accompanied Pride. Suddenly another angel, bigger than the others, headed straight for the spirit of Pride. This angel's name was Meekness. He took the cords and began binding Pride. However; Pride continued to shout threats, twisting God's Word with lies.

Meekness looked over at Salome and she knew immediately what to do. "I command you, Pride, to be quiet, in Jesus' Name. I forbid you to speak or manifest in Jesus' Name. In that moment, gags suddenly appeared in the angel's hands. They shoved the gags in the mouths of the demons, hindering their speech.

Salome studied the creatures of Satan's horrific army and began to realize that they were exactly like their names. Fear was fearful of everything. Infirmity was sickly and weak. Depression was oppressive. Somehow that knowledge gave her more under-standing and power against the attacks of the enemy.

Just when she thought the battle was over, a huge, dark demon gave the order, "Hit her family and finances." Salome pleaded the Blood once more over her family and loosed angels to protect them. She again began to quote scripture and with each scripture, a band of angels was sent out.

Suddenly, she felt like a director over a battle scene in a movie. Scripture began to pour out of her mouth! Each time she spoke it, a demon would cry out in fear and terror. "If you shall call on the Name of the Lord, you shall be saved, you and your household. If God is for us, who can be against us, what can man do to me? God works all things for the good of those who love Him who have been called according to His purpose. You shall teach my children, Lord, and great shall be their peace. God provides all my needs according to His riches and glories in Christ Jesus. He will never leave me nor forsake me—we've never seen the righteous forsaken or their seed begging for bread."

She then shouted, "I bind every assignment against me and my family up until the time the Lord comes back. Loose our health, finances, minds, wills and emotions. Father, I loose a Spirit of Wisdom and Revelation in the knowledge of the Lord Jesus Christ! This is our heritage passed down by the Blood of the Lamb—The Spirit of the Sovereign Lord is upon us, for the Lord has anointed us to bring Good News to the poor. He sent us to bind the broken-hearted and to proclaim the captives free and prisoners released through Jesus' death, burial and resurrection on the cross! He sent us to tell those who mourn, that the time of the Lord's favor has come through the One, Christ Jesus! He gives us a crown of beauty instead of ashes, the oil of gladness instead of mourning and fes-tive praise instead of despair—

Each time she quoted scripture; demons would scream out in pain and begin to retreat! She continued on—His righteousness in us will be like great oaks planted by the Lord Jesus for His own glory! (See Isaiah 61)

Suddenly, Salome realized just how quiet the house had become. The demons were fleeing. In their place, a thick fluffy brilliant white cloud of peace began to fill every nook and cranny in the house. As she continued to quote scripture, the angels stood at attention as a reverent silence began to fill the air. Continuing on in Isaiah 61 she stated His promise, *"We will rebuild the ancient ruins of our family-line that were destroyed long ago. We will revive them through they were deserted many generations ago. We shall be called a priest of the Lord, ministers of our God and we will feed on the treasures of the nations and in their riches, we will boast. Instead of shame and dishonor, we will enjoy a double share of honor! We will possess a double-portion of prosperity in our land and everlasting joy is ours! My descendants will be recognized and honored among the nations. All who see us will KNOW that we are a people the Lord our God has blessed!* (See Isaiah 61)

When Salome finished, a shout of victory rang through the army of the angels while joy, peace and confidence in who she was in Christ Jesus began to flow and fill up every part of her heart and home.

Jesus then stood in front of her. Lifting her face with His beautiful nail-scarred hands, He smiled and said, "Well done, My good and faithful servant! It is always darkest before the dawn. Weeping endures for the night, but behold, joy comes in the morning." (See Psalm 30:5)

Somehow in that moment Salome knew dawn was about to break forth. Breakthrough was coming no matter how it may appear in the natural.

With that thought, Shalom filled every part of her being, what a beautiful word, Shalom! In Hebrew, it means simply, wholeness, fulfillment, rest, health, happiness and blessing in all areas of life. Peace with God through Jesus means not only being freed of conflict between us and God; it also means that we will enjoy the fulfillment of life together in heaven with the Father forever.

Softly she spoke, "I know Whom I have believed and that He is able to keep that which I have committed to Him until the day of our Lord!" (See 2 Timothy 1:12) Glancing around her home, she could not remember sensing so much peace. "The battle truly is the Lord's," she whispered. She headed toward her bedroom and enjoyed a night of rest, with no pain, for the first time in months!

Lying down, a little song ran through her mind, *Peace I leave with you My peace I give to you, I do not give to you as the world gives. Do not let your heart be troubled and do not be afraid! Good night, Lord, how I love You!*

So now, I am giving
You a new commandment;
Love each other, just as I have loved you,
You should love each other.
Your love for one another will
Prove to the world that you are my disciples.
John 14:34-35NLT

CHAPTER **23**

IN REFLECTION, SALOME stopped for a moment to consider all that Jesus was becoming in her life. She did not want to imagine where she would be without her relationship to the One and only God? A smile spread across her face as freedom and assurance of Whose she was, began to overflow her heart.

Just then she heard their front door close. "Hello, Lewis?"

"Yes, it's me, how was your day?" Lewis commented.

"Just fantastic, and yours," Salome inquired?

"Another day at the funny farm, what can I say? The plant manager hates me and now he has decided to cut our hours again. It may get really tight, Salome, we might have to get rid of our internet service," Lewis stated, almost testing her reaction.

Staring in disbelief, Salome simply stated, "There's no way, television should go first, internet is very important. It's how I stay connected to my website and people. Television is not a necessity; honestly, I rarely ever watch the thing."

"I watch television! We can't get rid of that! It has to be internet!" Lewis bellowed.

As he turned to leave, Salome bit her tongue so she would not speak. Closing her eyes, she took a deep breath and prayed silently. *Lord, this is your problem! I do not wrestle with flesh and blood, I will not look at Lewis, help me to see the spirit behind this, in Jesus Name.*

Father, help Lewis, he seems like a drowning man who is about to take his last breath. The sad thing is I have no clue who he really is on the inside. He keeps himself so closed to everyone. Father, he desperately needs your help reach out Your hand to Him, Lord. Let Lewis hear your voice.

As she lay down, she thought, *I think it might be best if I just go to sleep. Honestly, I don't know what to say and anything I do say is taken the wrong way. This battle will only be won as I pray.* With that Salome prayed for Lewis and began to fight the battle surrounding their relationship. Before she knew it, peace overcame her and she fell asleep.

———

Softly, Salome began to hear the sound of singing, a sweet melody that made her smile. A soft, sweet voice calling, "Come, come and see the things I have to show you!"

Slowly opening her eyes, she glanced at her clock and saw it was only 4:00 A.M. Lying quietly, she listened and heard nothing, so she closed her eyes and fell back to sleep.

At 4:30 A.M. the lovely voice called again, "Come, come and see what I will show you!" Opening her eyes, Salome knew God was calling her, even at this early morning hour. Rising slowly she sat on the side of the bed, wondering, *Why is it necessary for You to wake me at such an early-morning hour.* Picking up her robe and glasses, she ambled to the dining room.

Walking down the hallway she almost groaned out loud. *Boy, Lord, a few extra hours of sleep would surely feel great! Is this the only time you can get my full attention?* Turning the light on in the kitchen, she went to the counter and began fixing a cup of cappuccino. The rich smell of the sweet brew did its magic as Salome inhaled the sugary flavor. Taking a sip, she smiled, and sat down at the dining room table to begin her study.

Carefully placing her cup on the table, Salome lowered her

head and silently prayed. *Father, please forgive me for my attitude. I know You must have something astonishing to show me and I really cannot wait to embrace it. As I read Your love letters and gather wisdom and understanding, help me to know how to apply it in my daily walk in life. Change my heart and my mind and enable me to emulate Your example here, right where I live, in Jesus Name.*

Opening her *Daily Walk Bible*, she turned to *Walk Number 304*, Ministry to the Disciples by God's Son. Reading the passages in John 13-17, Salome saw how Jesus loved and served the twelve disciples, even Judas. All twelve were there for the final supper although Judas left in the middle of Jesus' last supper. Even knowing what was to come; Jesus loved Judas to the end. The Lord instructed His beloved apostles by example in those last hours before His horrific walk from Gethsemane to the cross.

Jesus served them this last Passover meal Himself. Taking off His robe, He then washed their feet. As the good Shepherd, He instructed the eleven about staying in the vine in order to bear fruit and tried to prepare their heart for the events about to take place. Here, in His final few hours, Jesus prays for His bride.

Throughout His prayer, two thoughts continued to repeat themselves as they flowed through Salome's mind. Just like a broken record they resonated in her heart, unity and love. Hidden within the beautiful words of the Upper Room discourse was a deep message, become a servant. "Serve one another as I have served you," Jesus stated.

All of us are on equal ground, no big "I's" or little "you's". Jesus gave them a new commandment in John 14:34-35 NIV. *So now, I am giving you a new commandment; Love each other. Just as I have loved you, you should love each other. Your love for one another will prove to the world that you are my disciples.*

The attitude of the world is selfishness. It acts as a rudder on a very large ship, steering us to the final years of life this side of eternity. Thoughtfully, Salome wondered, "Imagine if we Christians would stop and consider everyone in the church body and beyond, more important than ourselves or our agendas. Unity would explode and this planet would catch a sudden glimpse of His deep abiding love. The kind of love it is looking for. The love of our Savior/King, Jesus!

Salome solemnly asked, "Lord, how did we get so self-centered?" As she pondered this question, a thought began to take shape in her mind. With both parents working, the husband and wife carried more weight and responsibilities on their shoulders than God ever designed for them to bear. Feeling guilty for spending so much time away from their children, love and parental time were replaced with things like social media, cell phones, television and the like. Satan has everyone looking for love in all the wrong places. Actually, I doubt if anyone understands what and Who Love really is. By the time Mom and Dad got home, both of them are exhausted, having given all they have, at work. People, in general, are really looking for unconditional love, understanding and compassion. They don't even realize it. Because of the cares of this world, the devil cleverly drives a wedge between husband and wife and before long, the family falls apart. A house divided will not stand! (See Matthew 12:25)

Just then an idea struck her. Picking up a sheet of paper, she created two columns, naming them simply Unity—Division. She began to write what came to mind:

Unity	Division
Love one for the other	Selfishness or self-love
Builds up others and encourages	Gossip, slander, tears down
Forgiveness	Unforgivness, bitterness, hate
Thankful heart	Ungrateful, always wanting more
Obedient	Disobedient, self-willed
Humble, Meek	Pride, Arrogance
Love of God	Love of money

Satisfied, joyful	Covetousness and jealous
Pure—Holy	Lust of the flesh, eyes and pride-of-life
Embracing trials and tribulations with joy	Murmur and complain
Strong in the Lord	Greedy, unstable in all their ways

As Salome stared at the list, conviction fell upon her as she realized how many things she did that brought division and strife into her marriage. With the verdict in, she embraced the conviction! Scenes flashed before her eyes of all the times she allowed the enemy to cause division. Tears of sorrow trickled down her cheeks. Not only had she sinned against God, she had become a partaker in the very thing that would destroy their marriage. Gazing up, with a hushed cry, Salome repented and asked the Lord to forgive her for every time she opened the door to allow division or strife in their household. Then she took authority over the enemy she had allowed to come into her family and fought him, using the Word of God and the Blood of Jesus. She had to repent of one more thing. Not loving Lewis as Jesus would have her love him.

Reflecting back to her great-grandmother's journal, Salome remembered the story of Sarah. Although Abraham had some crazy demands, Sarah remained meek as she loved and respected Abraham. At the tail-end of her musing, Salome heard the Lord's beautiful voice.

"Salome, come outside, I have something to show you."

Immediately she got up and headed for the back door. Glancing at the clock, she saw it was already 6:30 a.m. The air was crisp with only a slight bit of humidity. As Salome stepped outside, she lifted her head and gazed at the dark blanket of the heavens stretched out before her. Numerous tiny, blinking stars splashed across the sky as dawn slowly began to make its appearance. Staring at the twinkling lights, Salome contemplated the fact that the same God that breathed them into existence, lived on the inside of her heart. That fact seemed completely incomprehensible and amazing to her all at the same time.

Allowing these thoughts to simmer, she suddenly heard a rooster crow. Within a split second, God seemed to pour every feeling Peter experienced when his rooster crowed, into her heart. It was as though she were seeing and feeling the things Peter suffered in that early morning hour over 2000 years ago. Turning her eyes, she suddenly gasps as she sees Jesus. His eyes looked deep into Peter's eyes just after the rooster crowed. The scene sent a sense of electricity, panic and fear that seem to radiate through her veins. It was very hard to comprehend all that was taking place within her heart. (See Luke 22)

Three other roosters began to crow, one at a time, as if they were being directed by a symphony conductor. Once again, she could feel the deep, heart-wrenching pain flowing from her heart out to every fiber of her being. Closing her eyes she whispered, "It's like seeing yourself as you really are, nothing more than a total, complete failure. Like gazing in a mirror and finally seeing the truth!"

That day so long ago, Peter came face-to-face with the pride, arrogance, self-assurance, human reasoning and understanding, along with the childish behavior, which had resided in his heart. However, when Jesus met Peter on the beach that first day of their relationship, Jesus said, "Upon this rock (Peter), I shall build my church.

In that one instant, Salome knew she was no different from Peter. As she meditated on the events for a time, she realized that every one of us has a Peter mentality. In spite of everything, Jesus didn't throw Peter back. Instead, He loved, molded, corrected, spoke to and enjoyed Peter as the person he was created to be. Jesus knew that, inside of Simon there was a Peter. Funny thing about the account is that, Simon is not called Peter until after Jesus ascends to the Father, on a cloud.

Peter's name is mentioned in the Gospels more than any other name except for Jesus. No one speaks as often as Peter. No one is spoken to by the Lord as often as he was. None of the twelve ever rebuked Jesus except for Peter. None of the others confessed Christ as the Messiah. Peter is praised and blessed by Christ and yet, he was also the only one Jesus ever addressed as Satan. He was spoken to in a harsher manner by Jesus because that piece of clay named Peter, had to be made malleable in order to become a leader.

"But go tell My disciples and Peter." (See Mark 16:7) Jesus began reinstating Peter from the moment the women found the resurrected Lord. Once again, at the end of the Gospel of John, Jesus and Peter meet on a beach. Three times Jesus asks Peter, "Do you love me more than these? Then Jesus stated, "Tend My lambs", "Shepherd My sheep" and finally, "Tend My sheep." (See John 21) After such a devastating failure in denying the Lord three times, Jesus reinstates him publically, three times, before the other ten. By this, He was telling the other disciples that, "He's still My choice."

Reverently, Salome turned and stepped onto the porch on the way to her office. As she reached the room, she headed straight to her Bible and began reading Peter's two Epistles written in the Bible.

Did that dear disciple ever learn to love, yes indeed! It is the hallmark of his teachings. 1 Peter 4:8 NIV states, "Above all things have *fervent* love for one another, for "love will cover a multitude of sins." Fervent stood out in Salome's mind. Pulling her concordance off the shelf, she turned to the word. In the Greek translation it simply means, *stretched to the limit*. The love Peter spoke of is not a feeling. It is a choice. It compensates for others' failures and weaknesses. It's a love that washes a brother or sister's dirty feet and serves them food; spiritual and physical food.

Standing there lost in her thoughts, Jesus whispered to her spirit, "Lewis is a Peter as well. He has a desperate need of a loving advocate here on earth. Salome, this is the next step in your journey on the narrow path. Peter walked with me for three years on this earth and in that time, I loved and coaxed him in the way he should go. All you have to do for Lewis is love him as I have loved you. It's your choice to see him through the eyes of Love Himself."

In an instant, Salome realized that she did not feel guilt or shame. She was experiencing the difference between punishment and correction. Punishment is harsh, like the religious leaders in Jesus' day. However, correction loves and it makes something that is wrong, right.

There was no question about it. She was convicted. Slowly, she smiled and said, "What a difference love makes! What a difference You make, Jesus! Thank You for loving me so completely. You love me enough to convict me of sin so I can repent and shut the door to the devil in our lives. Scripture came to mind, *Do not return evil for evil or reveling for reviling, but bless so that you may receive a blessing!* (See Romans 12:17)

Lowering her head, she prayed. *Lord, You showed me earlier that You reside inside my heart. Because You are there, I can love as You do if I allow You to love Lewis through me. Open my eyes, ears and heart toward him and help me see him through Your eyes. Forgive me, Lord, for my own stubbornness and create in me a clean heart O God. I love you, Lord, and I cannot imagine where I might be if You had not called me when You did. Help me remember Your amazing grace and mercy toward me. Show me how to shower it on Lewis. Thank You, Lord, I pray all of this in Jesus' Name.*

While she meditated on all Jesus accomplished in her life she thought, *He has done so much for me I cannot refuse what He asks me to do.* Being still and knowing He is God, Salome closed her eyes and suddenly began to see in the spirit. She saw the Lord standing in front of her. He reached down through her earth suit and picked up her heart, holding it within His hands. Tenderly and lovingly He cradled it. Then an aura began to pour out of her heart like a rushing living river. Within the waters resided true love, peace and joy. Anyone who dared to walk into the river couldn't help but experience a bit of those healing waters. Smiling, He looked straight into her eyes and said, "Your heart is now completely Mine. Don't expect to be perfect Salome, just walk like My bride who is forgiven and deeply adored by her Savior/King! You are My ambassador to show others, including Lewis, My deep abiding love."

Standing there, eyes still closed, with a smile spreading across her face, Salome felt as though she had finally come home! Healing had finally come and it was not in a person, place or a thing! Jesus held healing in His hands the whole time. Now was the time for her to bring the same healing waters to the world around her. This is her destiny. It's what God designed her for since the beginning of time! She was finally, almost home!

If you hold to My teaching,
You are really My disciples.
Then you will know the truth
And the truth will set you free!
John 8: 31b-32 NIV

CHAPTER **24**

SALOME STOOD ON the porch staring rapturously at the beautiful day the Lord placed before her. The woods behind her house echoed with the sound of wildlife all around her. Birds were excitedly chirping as they searched the ground and flew amidst the many trees seeking their breakfast on this glorious morning. *Woe be to the poor worm that poked its head up out of the ground on this fair day,* she mused.

Squirrels raced up and down tree trunks looking for tasty tidbits in competition with each other over acorns and pine nuts scattered throughout the branches of the trees. She saw a few squirrels scrounging for nuts among the fallen leaves. She delighted in watching to see what they would do next, always a bundle of laughs.

Casually sipping her cup of cappuccino, Salome was caught up in the grandeur of this promising day. Thanking God that His mercy is renewed daily, she wondered what was in store for her today. So many Bible promises began flitting through her mind that she didn't notice her fat cat, Minx, winding back and forth between her legs, until one of that rascal's claws got caught on a leg of her pants.

Quickly setting that to rights by sending the 25 pound behemoth outside, Salome finished drinking her cappuccino and returned the cup to the kitchen. Grabbing a cookie that was still warm from the oven, she began praising the Lord for the beautiful house He chose for them. She acknowledged that this was His house and prayed that it would be a refuge for hurting people to come in and be ministered to.

Stepping into each room as she passed by on her way to the office, she marveled again and was filled with joy as she felt the peace of the Lord filling every room. How blessed she was! Her footprint was in the entire house, from the wall paint to the décor, every detail just seemed to fall in place for her as she decorated and furnished each room.

After much giving of praise and thanks to the Lord, she finally arrived at her office. Settling down in front of her desk, she was filled with satisfaction at her home and her life. Pondering those things she had, she began to realize that she was inordinately proud of her home.

That fact brought her up short! *But, Lord, pride is a sin. How can this be? What are You telling me Father? I know I'm pleased with what we have, and we've worked hard to achieve it, but I'm proud? Of my house? Oh, Lord, please forgive me. I'm so sorry. How did I allow this to happen?*

Father is that right? I'm proud of my home because I'm not pleased with myself? I love my beautiful home because I don't love who I am? I'm not beautiful but my home is? I can open my home to people because I can't open myself to them. In other words, I'm a performer. I smile and go through all the motions, but I don't allow them to see into the real me. As she pondered, this sudden realization came to her. *It's because I'm a disappointment; unwanted at birth and unsure of myself today. So I have allowed my house, my home, to be my refuge and a place where people will see it and not me. OK, Lord! Thank You for revealing this to me. Yes, I still revel in this home Lewis and I have built under Your guidance but no longer will I be beholden to it.*

Our hearts are truly deceitful, aren't they Lord! When Your Blood washed my sins away, I became a new creature. All those things that used to beset me no longer have power over me. I'm Yours and You are mine! Nothing and no one can change that fact! I will choose to love myself because You loved me and fashioned me in your image and likeness. You know all there is to know about me and You still love me. Neither this marriage nor anything else in my life will define who I am again. You are the One who defines my worth.

I am not worthless, useless, or unwanted. You search my heart and found it pleasing to You. So, Lord Jesus, since you love me, I will love me and I will lower the hedge I built around my heart and allow others to know and love the real me. I can do this because You are there to show me the way! I am after all, the King's kid, the Bride of Christ! This is the definition of who I really am.

Oh, wow! I feel as though a ton of weight has been lifted off my shoulders. I didn't realize I was carrying the lies people and circumstances had said about me. Thank You, Lord, for setting me free! I want to sing and dance for joy! Free to be the me YOU created me to become!

Tears of joy spilled from Salome's eyes as she stretched her hands to heaven and praised her Lord! Freedom—liberation from slavery, imprisonment or restraint! Yes, indeed, Jesus set her free with His truth!

Unexpectedly, she sensed the Spirit of the Lord descend upon her, spreading warmth down her back, legs and feet. Standing in silence, Salome began to realize that the pain in her back began to dissolve into a dull ache.

Healing is your portion Salome, Jesus simply stated.

Cautiously bending over, she knew this long chapter of her life was finally coming to an end! A new one was just around the corner as she continued on her journey home.

With overwhelming joy Salome said, "I think I'll grab some lemon water and meander out to the hammock and watch the birds and squirrels run and play! And if I can round up that fat cat, I might put her in the hammock, too."

Afterword

Early in the morning, Salome gazed out toward the trees in her back yard. The woods seemed dark and terrifying right before dawn. Smiling, she understood that was exactly how her journey home began. Nothing seemed clear. Confusion and fear filled her mind. Each time God had shown His light into a dark area of her heart, a new sense of freedom and understanding flowed over her like a wave of peace.

As dawn began to break, Salome's eye caught sight of the two chairs sitting in the midst of the trees. Slowly, she walked over to the chairs rubbing her hand along the back of one, and then sat down. Taking in a deep breath as she relaxed in her enchanted surroundings, a cloud of God's peace began to engulf her. Closing her eyes, she melted into His presence and embrace.

Softly His voice sounded within her heart. "Salome, are you ready to accept a deeper truth which you have been blinded to? Your struggle has never been with man. It has never been with Lewis. Your struggle has been with Me, Salome."

Suddenly, scenes began to play within her mind and she realized how blinded she had really been. His soft voice broke through her pondering, "Remember, it is hard to kick against the pricks. Saul wrestled with me until he was knocked off his horse. Jacob wrestled with me all night over his life, then asked me to bless him. Truth is that I AM ultimately in control of all things. I love and respect each of my children. I give them the freedom to make mistakes, to fall, to struggle and wrestle so that they may see the results of thinking without My wisdom. Each one must learn that they do indeed reap whatever they sow. How else will my children learn that it is only profitable to sow good seeds? Then they can reap good rewards. These struggles in life teach obedience and the futility of leaning on their own understanding and not trusting in Me."

Just then, Lewis stepped out onto the screened-in-porch. He looked out over the yard and turned to listen to the ranker of the neighborhood ducks as they welcomed in the new day. Stretching, he reached for the lights and turned them on. Grabbing his Bible, he sat in the nearby chair and prepared to read.

As Salome watched Him, a picture came to mind. She suddenly realized that Lewis was human, wounded and lonely. He was not a brute beast without feeling. Thinking about her feelings toward him, it was with a shock that she suddenly understood that in her attempts to protect herself from Lewis, she had dehumanized him. It became easy to disregard his feelings if she presumed him inhuman, a beast.

No! On the contrary, he was fashioned in God's image and deserving of understanding and love as much as she was. A miracle began that day inside Salome's heart as tears of repentance began to trickle down her cheeks. It seemed as though God removed her old hard heart and put in its place a heart of flesh, one that was soft, tender and compassionate toward the man.

For the first time, Salome saw Lewis through God's eyes. A fresh wave of love for her husband, swept over her. Suddenly the words the Lord had spoken, sliced her heart like a double edged sword, cutting and healing all at the same time. Lewis needed her encouragement, love and acceptance not her anger and judgment. No matter how the outside package appeared, God gave Lewis to Salome for her to influence him to grow into all God desired for him to become. She also had to grow and become everything God destined for her. Lewis was not her enemy nor was he her responsibility. God is his potter.

Silently the light of the sun became brighter. Before Salome realized it, beautiful rays of sunlight glistened through the trees right onto the two chairs in the woods. The otherworldly ambiance was so enchanting and as the heat from the sun, began to chase away the chill in the air Salome lifted her face toward the sun. Smiling, she basked in the Lord's sunlight of love.

Just then, Lewis glanced up and suddenly saw her. *She looks like an angel sitting there in the midst of the trees,* Lewis thought. *She's my angel, a gift from You, if she will ever allow me to get close enough. Lord, I've had no example of how a husband is supposed to treat his wife. I desperately need your help. Honestly, I'm afraid I'll continue to drive her away from me instead of toward me.* A smile spread across his face as he placed his Bible on the table next to his chair, got up and headed toward her.

Closing her eyes, Salome watched as the Lord opened her spiritual eyes to see Lewis in a new light. When she opened her eyes, she saw him heading toward her. In that instant, she realized how much she had failed. *All this time, it was You, Jesus, I'd been wrestling with. I've had Lewis on my "potter's wheel" trying to mold him into the man I thought he should be instead of allowing him to become the man You are creating him to be. Oh Lord, please forgive me. I am so sorry!* Tears pricked her eyes as he got closer.

Lewis stopped and stood in front of Salome, smiling. Reaching out his hand, she took it and stood. Gazing into his eyes it seemed she was meeting him for the first time. Lewis took both of her hands in his, looked down at their hands entwined, and then he fixed his eyes on hers. "No matter what you may think, I love you Salome and I'm very proud of you. It seemed I have trouble showing that. Please forgive me. Can we start fresh? Will you please give me another chance? I'm going to make mistakes, so I need lots of grace. God does have a plan for us. I've been noticing marked changes in you that only make me love you more. What do you say, will you give me, give us, another try?"

Looking into his eyes, Salome smiled and said, "Yes Lewis, I'll give us a try. I love you."

Lewis softly wrapped her in his arms and held her close. Salome closed her arms around Lewis as soft, healing tears trickled down both of their cheeks.

Lewis whispered, "I want to become your friend Salome. We are not enemies." Gazing into each other's eyes, they slowly moved closer and kissed. Held within Lewis' arms it seemed as though they were suddenly standing under God's healing waterfall flowing with His grace, mercy and love. As they stood in an embrace of love, the waters washed all the years of frustration, confusion, fear and pain away. Salome could not help but think of the verse in Ecclesiastes 3:11 NIV, *He has made everything beautiful in its time. He has also set eternity in the hearts of men; yet they cannot fathom what God has done from beginning to the end.*

Smiling, Salome realized how much she had doubted that she would ever see this day. However, God knew about it from before time began. There is no way to fathom what God is doing—but He does make everything beautiful in the right time. At that moment, Salome knew she was home!

Epilogue

By
Shirley Singer

Salome's long journey home was a difficult road to travel with snags, roadblocks and detours along the way. All of her life she struggled against the horrific effects of abuse, neglect, abandonment, rejection, insecurity, physical pain and divorce. She agonized that she was not good enough, or not worthy enough and that she never quite measured up to others.

In her quest to find herself, who she really was and where she belonged, Salome made many unwise decisions. She reached out in all the wrong places searching for love and acceptance, only to be hurt and rejected again and again. The pain and anguish she experienced within the confines of her marriage to Lewis only proved to her that she was an unloved creature. Until, the Lord Jesus Christ entered her life.

Through an arduous path, she learned that God's love superseded all others. In discovering that He really and truly loved her, she was finally able to accept, that in spite of all her blemishes, she was someone of value. When this truth settled deep within her spirit, she allowed herself the freedom of acceptance from Him, from others, and mostly, from herself. The freedom to love and be loved and to accept and be accepted, truly allowed Salome to be the woman the Lord intended her to be.

Every obstacle and hindrance that rose up in her path on the journey home, only served to strengthen Salome's faith and trust in her beloved Savior. She embraced the Word of the Lord through each trial she faced and learned to praise and worship Him when heartaches tried to devour her. Through her faith and belief, Salome emerged from the battle victoriously.

And, as the Lord was doing miraculous things in her spirit He, at the same time, was also working in her relationship with her husband. Salome is now able to look beyond the hurts of the past and focus on Lewis, now seeing him as our Lord Jesus sees him.

The end is in sight. The journey is finished. At long last, Salome triumphantly finishes her journey home with a shout of joy!

Other Novels by Catherine Mae Clifford

The Journey Begins—Follow in the footsteps of a blended family as they hike the breathtaking and awe-inspiring sights and trails of nature in the Smokey Mountains of Tennessee. Surrounded by the beautiful scenery, God deals with a young woman's heart through parables He shows her while on their journey. Experience the simple truths we all seem to forget that will bring this broken family unit together. Can they become a family they all so desperately want and need? Will they draw closer to God through the struggles, or could this be the very thing that will destroy their hopes and dreams?

Journey to Redemption—Rape, fear, rejection and deep-seated anxieties were only a part of the devastation that caused mental, emotional and physical trauma in a young woman's life. Each poignant story reveals her journey from the depths of despair to the heights of exhilaration, as she began experiencing the unconditional love and acceptance of her heavenly Father. As you read through the stories, you will laugh, cry and be challenged by the redemption that can be found, in the midst of what appears to be impossible odds. As you journey through each story, the convicting truth found within the Scriptures, will open the door of your heart for your own healing, deliverance and finally redemption.

About the Author

Catherine Mae Clifford understands the devastation of rape, emotional and physical abuse, anorexia and bulimia, rejection, divorce, depression and co-dependency, because she lived through it. When the Lord came into her life on April 18, 1990 her journey of healing began. It was a long and painful process. But later the Lord began to use the things she walked through to reach out and touch the lives of many women. Through God's unconditional love and acceptance, the Lord brought wholeness, healing and restoration to shattered and defeated lives.

Catherine is an encouraging and dynamic speaker, teacher, author, and song writer. She has a heart to encourage, inspire and see people made whole by the power of the Word of the Lord. God has shown her first hand that it is His desire to reach all peoples no matter what their past.

She met her husband, William Clifford, in 1994 and together they have 6 children and 6 grandchildren. Through the trials and testings that they have walked through as a blended family, they have seen the proof that God does make all things beautiful in His own time.

God has given Catherine the opportunity to minister in many women's groups as a worship leader, teacher and speaker. She has ministered through *Woman's Aglow* in the Baton Rouge, LA areas and in several women's meetings in local churches and groups. For twelve years Catherine served on a team with *Prison Fellow*

Ministries as a praise and worship leader and teacher in three state prisons. While serving in this capacity, the Lord opened the doors for her to minister cell to cell to prisoners on death row at Angola State Prison. Also, through the *Full Gospel Women's Ministries,* Catherine has served as worship leader and teacher at *Louisiana Correctional Institute for Women, (LCIW)* at Saint Gabriel, LA. She was also one of four teachers at *LCIW's Bible School.*

Today, Catherine continues to minister to women, teaching Bible studies and speaking. More recently after becoming acquainted with human trafficking, she has begun ministering to some of its victims. Human trafficking is the second largest criminal industry in the world. This industry is growing. It is not just in other countries. Catherine was shocked to learn that it was going on right in her own back yard. The magnitude of human trafficking is staggering. I suggest you read the book **Caged**, by Molly Venzke to understand the violence and slavery involved in this industry. For more info on human trafficking go to: **traffickinghope.org**

Two years ago Catherine published her first book, **The Journey Begins**. In 2009 she released her first CD, **Redeemed**. The song titles later became the chapters for her second book that was published in 2011, **Journey to Redemption. My Journey Home,** her newest book was published in 2013. Catherine currently resides in Walker, LA with her husband. You may contact Catherine via e-mail at **journeywithcatherine@gmail.com**, website www.journeywithcatherine.com **or her Facebook page: https://www.facebook.com/catherine.clifford.52**

CPSIA information can be obtained at www.ICGtesting.com
Printed in the USA
LVOW10s0408230715

447320LV00001B/99/P

9 781478 725572